"THE POST AS MY MISTRESS HAS BEEN VACATED. WOULD YOU BE INTERESTED IN APPLYING FOR THE POSITION?"

"Captain Scott!" She raised a hand to slap him, but he caught her wrist and held it fast.

"Miss Upshall, you are far too highly wrought," he said silkily. He brought her wrist to his lips and brushed them across her pulse point, never taking his gaze from hers.

She tried to pull away, but his grip was firm and persistent. Like a bird charmed by a snake, she lost the will to resist and allowed him to continue to hold her hand.

He stroked the back of it with his thumb. Tendrils of pleasure followed his touch, ebbing and flowing like a rising tide. She knew she shouldn't allow it, but it felt amazingly good.

"In my experience," he said softly, his voice a low rumble, like a lion's purr, "when a woman protests this much, it means she hasn't had the attention of a man recently and is in desperate need of it."

That broke the spell.

"You conceited swine! Perhaps if you consorted with women other than barmaids and trollops, you'd recognize a lady's revulsion when you see it."

His gaze dropped to her breasts, where the hard tips showed like a pair of raised buttons under the man's shirt she was wearing.

"Believe me, Miss Upshall. I can read the signals you're sending, and revulsion is not in evidence."

Other books by Connie Mason:

CONNIE MASON

Lord of Devil Isle

LEISURE BOOKS NEW YORK CITY

I'd like to acknowledge Emily Bryan for her invaluable help in writing this book. Without her assistance this book would not have been written.

A LEISURE BOOK®

May 2010

Published by

Dorchester Publishing Co., Inc.
200 Madison Avenue
New York, NY 10016

ISBN 10: 0-8439-6403-0
ISBN 13: 978-0-8439-6403-5
E-ISBN: 978-1-4285-0849-1

The name "Leisure Books" and the stylized "L" with design are trademarks of Dorchester Publishing Co., Inc.

Printed in the United States of America.

10 9 8 7 6 5 4 3 2 1

Visit us online at www.dorchesterpub.com.

Lord of
Devil Isle

Chapter One

1775, Bermuda
Formerly known as Devil's Isle

Nicholas Scott wondered how much longer she'd last. Judging from the helpless little sounds she was making, his mistress would be fit to burst if he didn't let her come soon. Her muscles began to tighten. Her back arched.

Magdalen's release always made her whole body whip in shivering waves, like a beautiful fish writhing on the hook. He loved playing her, letting the line run out before he drew her back to his net. Nick took a taut nipple into his mouth and bit down hard enough to make her breath hitch.

She lifted her hips, pressing her hot mound against his hand. She was well and truly caught this time. He smiled in satisfaction as his talented fingers drew her closer to her peak. Any man who could make his mistress dance on the edge of pleasure this long had a right to a certain smugness about his bed skills.

She rolled toward him and hooked a leg over his hip, running a smooth heel along the curve of his buttocks and down the back of his thigh.

His balls throbbed and drew into a tight bunch. The little minx had skills of her own.

He ached to bury himself in her softness, but Nick considered it a point of honor not to take pleasure before he gave it. Love was never part of the bargain with

Magdalen, but bliss was coin he traded freely. A man could afford to be generous with his cock. Only a fool trusted a woman with his heart.

A flash of lightning illuminated his bedchamber, revealing Magdalen's sweetly rounded, sweat-slick body in stark flickers. Outside the multipaned windows, the jalousie shutters rattled with the force of the storm rolling over the island. Rain lashed the lime-washed roof, sluiced down the gutters and emptied into the cistern beneath Nick's fine, stout home. The wind moaned in tandem with Magdalen.

On a wicked night like this, what else did he have to do but torment his mistress with unrelieved passion? She was already beyond pleading.

She came with the next crack of thunder, convulsing under his hand and crying his name.

"About time," he chided as he settled between her splayed legs.

"As if you didn't enjoy making me beg." She squirmed down, teasing against the tip of him.

"So much that I'll see you do it again before we're through, wench!" he promised.

Her throaty laugh carried a challenge he was more than ready to rise to, but before he could sheath himself in her slick wetness, someone pounded on his chamber door.

"Cap'n! Cap'n Sc-scott!"

"Go away, Higgs!" Nick bellowed at his first mate.

Peregrine Higgs was a fine sailor, and he never stuttered when a deck was surging beneath his feet, but dry land seemed to clamp his tongue to the roof of his mouth.

"B-but, Cap'n." The banging resumed with urgency.

"Keep it up and I'll have to gut you, lad. I'm thoroughly engaged at present," Nick growled. He plunged into Magdalen, determined to ignore his first mate. Magdalen's breath hissed over her teeth as she expanded to receive all of him.

Higgs beat on the door as if it were a drum.

With a curse, Nick pulled out of his mistress and stomped to the door, the musky scent of sex clinging to him. Heedless of his nakedness, he threw the door open.

"Unless the Second Coming is upon us, you're a dead man, Higgs."

"S-sorry, Lord Nick."

Even though England had sent Bermuda a governor, the island folk still called Nicholas Scott the "Lord of Devil Isle," looking to him for practical leadership. If they could see him now—naked, enraged and fully roused— they'd surely shorten the title to just the "Devil Himself." Broad-shouldered, lean-hipped and generously en- dowed, Nick was a sight to make any woman melt.

And any man doubt his own masculinity.

Nick's black scowl made Higgs stumble back a pace. The first mate studied his own boot tips with complete absorption.

Nick glowered at him. "Well?"

Higgs tugged at his forelock, but kept his gaze glued to the floor. "B-begging yer pardon—"

"Out with it, man."

"Sh-shh-ship on the reef."

Here was a matter more urgent than even Magda- len's soft wet secrets. "Why didn't you say so? Sound for the crew."

"Aye, Cap'n." Higgs was off at a run.

Nick loped to the window and cranked open the shutters. Rain streaked the panes in gusting sheets, but he could still see well enough. He'd picked this spot to build his home for its commanding view of the treacherous reefs that ringed Bermuda. The squall was letting up as the storm moved eastward. When the clouds parted, moonlight showed the dark blot of a ship in distress, caught on the island's jagged teeth. In concentric rings, the ship-killing reefs lurked barely beneath the surface of the waves, waiting to claim the unwary mariner.

"Oh, Nick, never say you're going out there. Not on a beastly night like this." Magdalen sat up, arms crossed beneath her plump breasts.

"There's no help for it. Ships tend not to founder in fair weather." He bent to fetch his discarded slop trousers, tugging them up over his hips without bothering to don his smallclothes. There wasn't time. "If we can beat that cursed Bostock and his lot to the wreck, it's as good as a pirate's prize to me and the crew."

The long arm of British civilization had reached even this distant Atlantic outpost. The island's appointed governor saw to it pirates danced a hempen jig in short order. Folk came all the way from the southernmost tip of the archipelago to St. Georges when there was a hanging to be seen on the dock. Piracy no longer paid, but a *salver* was hailed a hero and awarded the foundered vessel, not to mention its valuable cargo, for his trouble.

Nick's crew would divide the wreck's stores—fine woolens, crockery, foodstuffs and livestock, perhaps even some serious coin. Once he claimed the beleaguered vessel as his, Nick could wait for fair winds to winch the hull off the reef, repair the damage and sell it, if he wished.

Of course, he could always use another ship for his salt-raking runs to the Turks. Despite his threat to gut

Higgs earlier, Nick figured his first mate was almost ready to captain his own vessel, sailing under Nick's colors.

Sullenly, Magdalen rose from the bed and helped him pull his long shirt over his head.

"I might be gone when you return," she threatened and gave him her back.

He swatted her bare rump. "No, you won't."

She turned and molded herself against him, grazing the drop front of his trousers with her hand. His cock strained toward her of its own accord. She laughed, low and musical.

"No, I guess I won't be gone." She rocked against him, pressing kisses to his neck. "But it's so horrible out. Just this once, why don't you let Bostock have it?"

That bastard's already taken enough from me. The words almost escaped his lips, but he bit them back. Magdalen Frith might share his bed, but that didn't entitle her to a share of his private pain. The ledger of wrongs between him and Adam Bostock was woefully lopsided and the reckoning long overdue. Nick waited only for the opportune moment, when he was sure his final victory wouldn't taint anyone else. Perhaps on that day, the ghosts could finally be stilled.

But that didn't mean he wouldn't try to outsail the man at every opportunity in the meantime. Nick pulled out of Magdalen's grasp and shrugged on his jacket.

"Don't wait up." His gaze raked her wolfishly, and he flashed a wicked grin. "I'll wake you when I return."

Magdalen climbed back into the sumptuous bed and plumped a pair of pillows behind her head. She stretched like a cat, arms and legs spread wide, then sat up straight and hefted her own breasts, pinching the mulberry nipples taut, offering them to him.

"Sure you won't stay?"

"The wreck won't wait," he said over his shoulder. "Your lovely tits will."

He slammed the door behind him just in time to miss the crash of crockery on the other side. Nicholas shook his head. "Damn. Shouldn't have had that tea in bed. There goes the last of the Wedgewood."

Higg's signal bell clanged over the rush of wind through the palm trees. Nicholas slid off his horse's back and tossed the stallion's reins to a "wharf rat," one of the boys who haunted the docks. There were always a few around, lolling behind barrels of pitch or coils of rope, hoping for a berth as cabin boy on one of the bigger ships that put in to St. Georges. Nick sent tuppence sparkling in the air after the reins.

"Walk him back to his stable and tell my steward I said to give you another pence if the horse isn't lathered when you arrive. There's a good lad." Nick strode up the gangplank and onto the *Susan Bell*. "Belay that racket, Mr. Higgs. You'll wake the governor. Lord knows, the honorable Mr. Bruere needs his beauty sleep."

"Aye, Cap'n." Peregrine Higgs stopped tugging the cord on the ship's bell and ordered the remaining wharf rats to loose the mooring lines. "All hands present and accounted for, except Digory Bock. Tatem says Bock had a tooth drawn at the barber yesterday. He's been nursing it with a bottle of rum ever since."

"Very well. Make a note in the ship's log that Mr. Bock shall not receive his customary share of this night's gain."

"Aye-aye, Cap'n. I'll see to it immediately."

Nicholas was no longer surprised by the change in his first mate's speech once he was aboard ship. Perhaps Peregrine Higgs just needed to be where his world made sense for his tongue to work freely. Whatever the reason, Higgs never gave Nick cause to regret elevating him to first mate.

Nick's crew scrambled over the *Susan Bell*, shinnying up the rigging and making her ready to sail into the blustery night. A two-masted sloop, she was shallow on the draft, quick as a whore's trick, and answered to the helm like a lady, gently bred.

Nick set his face against the wind and rain and took the wheel himself. He piloted her out of St. Georges Harbor, muscling her through the narrow path between the little stepping stone islands that dotted the waterway. The *Susan B*'s running lamps were lit. Once she cleared the mouth of the inlet, the souls on board the wreck should be able to see that help was coming.

He hoped the captain of the wreck would heave to and surrender in time for him to save whatever crew and passengers were aboard. Sometimes, a ship's master refused help, knowing he forfeited his ship and all his goods by accepting aid. Nick hated to see lives needlessly lost.

Nicholas fingered the pistol he'd shoved into his belt at the last minute and decided he'd help the other ship's captain make a quick capitulation, if need be. This wasn't a forgiving night to be abroad.

The back side of the squall buffeted them. Nicholas shouted an order to lay on as much canvas as he thought the *Susan Bell* would bear. Her sails billowed out like a woman's breasts, and the ship quickened, running before the wind like a tart leading her lover a merry chase.

"Shall I relieve you, sir?" Peregrine Higgs was beside him now, ready to take the wheel.

"I stand relieved." Nicholas gave up the helm and strode to the heaving rail, pulling out his spyglass. He trained the lens on the wreck.

She was a brigantine. Not a slaver. They'd have caught

wind of her by now if she carried a hold full of human misery. She was a fine merchantman, no doubt full of goods bound for the Colonies. But now she canted on her side like a beached whale, her canvas spilling wind. The sea poured in through a breach near the waterline. Nicholas counted twelve guns along her port side. Well armed meant she was richly loaded. There seemed to be a small fire on the poop, but the steady rain kept it from taking hold.

"Praise be to God for small favors," Nicholas murmured. Fire at sea was a sailor's worst nightmare.

He scanned the horizon, but he didn't see any sign of the *Sea Wolf*, Bostock's cursed black-sailed schooner.

"Bring her smartly along the port side, if you please, Mr. Higgs." Nick smiled. This was going to mean a windfall for him and his crew.

"A sail, Cap'n," able seaman Tatem called out. "A point off the port bow."

Lights winked suddenly on the far side of the wreck.

"Bostock," Nicholas muttered. "The bastard's been running dark and crept in close without showing himself. But we can still beat him. Loose the t'gallants."

More canvas unfurled and the *Susan Bell* leaped forward, surging toward the wreck.

"Man overboard! Starboard bow."

Nicholas leaned over the rail, straining to follow the line from Tatem's outstretched arm. A wail soughed through the rigging, too high-pitched to be wind.

"A woman," Nick muttered. The dark form in the water disappeared as a wave crested over it.

"I make three souls there," Tatem said, his eagle eyes narrowed to slits. "Clinging to a spar."

And at least one a woman. If she was bleeding . . .

"Any fins in the water?" Nick demanded, looking back over his shoulder at the wreck. He was closer than

Bostock. By rights, the brigantine should fall into his hand like a ripe plum.

"Not yet." Tatem was so farsighted, Nick often relied on him more than his spyglass. "But if they keep up that caterwauling and thrashing about, it won't be long."

Nick had spotted a fourteen-foot tiger shark off Spanish Point a week ago but hadn't been able to spear the beastie. It faded into the Bermudian blue and disappeared in the deeper water off the shelf as soon as Nick's jolly boat hit the water. If that monster should be about now, it'd make quick work of a body adrift.

And it might have friends.

If Nicholas continued on to the wreck, the current would carry the castaways to Iceland before he found them again in these heaving seas.

Assuming they somehow managed not to become fish food in the meantime.

"Heave to," Nick roared, both to be heard over the wind and because his frustration wouldn't let him give the order without shouting. Why had the lubbers abandoned ship?

And why, by all that was holy, couldn't the fools be bobbing in the deep near Bostock's *Sea Wolf* instead of his vessel?

"Mr. Tatem, lower the boat."

As he climbed over the gunwale to take the tiller of the jolly boat, he saw mooring lines fly from the *Sea Wolf* to the wounded vessel.

He'd lost another prize to Adam Bostock.

Nicholas gritted his teeth. If sharks didn't get these idiots in the water, he might have to kill them himself.

Chapter Two

The broken-off hatch cover was barely big enough for the three of them to cling to without losing buoyancy. Sobbing and shivering, Sally tried to scramble up on it again, but Eve pulled her back.

"Just hang on," Eve ordered as a wave broke over the women. "It's not big enough to ride."

The frame of canvas-covered wood was only about four feet square. Eve Upshall didn't voice her fears about what might happen if they should lose this little bit of flotsam keeping them afloat. It might just push her friends over the edge. Penelope was lock-jawed and saucer-eyed. Sally was near hysteria already.

"But I can't bloody swim!" Sally wailed again.

"Shut it." Eve delivered a quick slap across Sally's open mouth. The stinging blow settled the girl and she subsided into moist hiccups. "You should have thought about that before you jumped in."

"But the fire," Sally sputtered between sniffles. "I'm mortally afeared of fire."

"Which hasn't spread a lick, thanks to this cursed rain." Eve hated being harsh, but panic would help no one.

"Here, let me untie your panniers," she offered. The horsehair and wire contraption was probably weighing Sally down. Eve reached under the sodden mass of Sally's broad skirts and jerked the knot at her waist free. Eve had kicked off her shoes and shed her panniers as soon as she hit the water.

"Penny, do you need help with yours?"

The question jolted Penelope out of her rigor. "No," she said, hooking an arm across the hatch. "I'll make do."

Grim-faced, Penny worked at her lacings until the system of hoops loosened and she wiggled free of them.

"Did anyone see Lieutenant Rathbun?" Sally asked.

"No, and I don't think we need concern ourselves with anyone else's welfare at present." Eve swiped her eyes, trying to clear the stinging brine. "Our plate of troubles seems quite full enough, thank you."

A wave surged by, high enough to obscure the wreck of the *Molly Harper* behind a wall of water. When the ship reappeared on the dark horizon, Eve saw that the current had dragged them surprisingly far from their vessel. Her belly roiled.

The women had been forced onto the open deck when the *Molly Harper* ran aground on the hidden reef and water began pouring into the tiny cabin they shared. Sally panicked at the sight of flames on the poop deck and had run heedless through a broken spot on the gunwale, dropping into the black waves below.

Penelope jumped in after her, knowing her friend couldn't swim. Eve watched from above for a helpless few heartbeats while Sally, stupid with terror, thrashed the water and tried to scale her would-be rescuer. Another minute and she'd have drowned them both.

The deck was alive with sailors running, hauling at the ropes and swearing the air blue. Every hand was busy trying to keep the *Molly Harper* from total ruin, with no thought to spare for three women, who everyone claimed were unlucky on a ship in any case. So Eve had grabbed up the loose hatch cover and followed the other two into the waves.

In retrospect, it was probably not the cleverest thing

she'd ever done. If her time in Newgate Prison had taught her anything, it was that the wise woman looks to herself. But the confinement of a small shared cabin had wrought a sense of kinship among the three of them. Eve couldn't let flighty, impulsive Sally or the steady, quiet Penelope come to grief if she could help it.

So now despite her best efforts, they were all in a pickle.

Sally squealed again. "Look! Another ship!" She waved a pale arm at the hull surging toward the wreck. "Why don't they stop?"

Another wave washed over them and Sally came up sputtering.

"They probably can't see us," Eve said. "On the count of three, we must all scream as loud as ever we can."

"You won't slap me?" Sally asked reproachfully.

"Not this time, ninny," Eve promised with a wry smile. "Ready? One, two, three."

Even Penelope shrieked for all she was worth.

For a heart-stopping moment, it seemed nothing was happening, that no one had heard them. Then suddenly sailors on the approaching vessel scrambled to spill wind from the sails to slow the ship and a boat was lowered over the side. A big fellow with what looked like a permanent scowl engraved on his face stood at the tiller as his men plied the oars.

"We're saved!" Sally shouted and waved her free arm.

Eve started to believe it herself, but a sudden movement caught the corner of her eye, something different from the rhythmic roll of the waves. When she turned her head, a long gray body stippled with dark patches passed by them no more than ten feet away. A sharp dorsal fin rose and then disappeared beneath the waves.

She swallowed hard.

Sharks had dogged the *Molly Harper* across the Atlantic, hoping for more scraps after that piglet fell in just off the Azores. Once, one of the sailors speared a big gray fellow, but before the men could haul the shark from the water, the other fish turned on the wounded one in a bloody frenzy. They boiled the water red devouring one of their own.

"Sally, dear, you must be quiet," Eve said, forcing an even tone. She prayed the other girl wouldn't catch a glimpse of the predator before the jolly boat arrived. "A lady is always calm and collected."

"Even now?"

"Especially now. Imagine how impressed the gentlemen who are coming to our rescue will be when they see how graciously you face difficult circumstances," Eve said. Lieutenant Rathbun had schooled them in decorum all the way across the long stretch of the Atlantic. Perhaps the lessons would come in useful now. "And keep your feet and legs as still as possible."

"They can't see my legs," Sally protested.

"No, but if your head is bobbing around they'll know you're kicking up your feet like a light-heeled trollop. And it will be quite as bad as if they could see them. Look at Penny." Eve nodded at their quiet friend. "She's being perfectly still."

The boat was drawing closer. The master growled an order, but the wind carried away his words.

The dorsal fin reappeared behind Sally and Penny's eyes flared with alarm.

"Quiet, Pen," Eve urged as the shark circled.

Penelope sucked in her bottom lip and worried it in silence.

The moon ripped through the clouds, silvering the black water. The shark glided by again. Its lidless eye flashed feral over rows of jagged teeth. It was closer on this pass. It seemed to be studying them, trying to decide what to do. Eve could almost hear its fishy thoughts.

Is they nice? Is they tasty? Shall we give 'em a nip then, ducks, just to see for ourselves?

The shark's imagined voice sounded like that disgusting bloke from Cheapside, the one whose unwanted attention she'd fended off during her nightmarish weeks in Newgate. She shook away the evil fancy.

Someone from the small boat shouted to them, but Eve couldn't yank her gaze from the monster. The sleek body was twice as long as she was tall.

Merciful God, it's big enough to swallow us whole.

White-knuckled, Eve gripped the hatch cover till her nails bit into the wood. Why hadn't she grabbed up something useful before she leaped into the sea? Like maybe a pike?

Sally caught sight of the shark and began to shriek like a lost soul.

"Suffering Christ," Nick muttered, then shouted. "Put your backs into it, men."

He hadn't given up a prize vessel just to see these stupid women butchered before his eyes, but the shark wouldn't wait much longer.

"Must be the same big bastard we seen off Spanish Point, Cap'n," Tatem said. "There ain't another un' like that in these waters, or I'll hope to shout."

Nick drew his pistol and tried to track the course of the fin around the women. The beast was so close, he couldn't be sure he wouldn't hit one of them. The hysterical blonde invited attack with her flailing and screaming. One of the others grabbed her and clamped a hand over her mouth.

"At least one of them has the brains God gave a goose," Nick conceded.

He aimed his weapon at the circling shark, gauged the distance and allowed for lead time. He squeezed the trigger, but instead of a sharp report, his pistol gave a disappointing click. The rain had wet his powder thoroughly.

"Damn."

There was no help for it and no way he'd order one of his men to join him in what he was planning. Lunacy was a dish best eaten alone. Nicholas yanked off his boots.

"Take the tiller, Mr. Williams," he ordered. "Tie off the line and make ready to haul away on my signal. Tatem, stick a harpoon in him if you get half a chance."

"Aye, Cap'n."

Nicholas looped one end of a rope around his waist, thrust a dagger between his teeth and dove into the surging sea. Once his sleek head broke the surface, he closed the distance between the pitching jolly boat and the women in a handful of powerful strokes.

When he surfaced beside them, he pulled the knife from his teeth and unfastened the rope, kicking to stay afloat. The shark passed slowly, eyeing him with a pitiless stare. He didn't dare look away until it disappeared, dissolving in the black water. Nick knew better than to feel relief. It would be back. Probably when least expected.

"Anyone hurt?" he shouted.

The screamer whimpered.

"Not yet," the one trying to pacify her said. "Get us out of here."

As if he wasn't trying.

"My men can pull two of you to safety at a time." The

weight of the three of them would likely drag the women under. "Grab this rope and hold on!" he ordered the most sensible one of the bunch. In addition to a level head, she had fine features and high cheekbones—a bone-deep beauty that would only ripen with age.

"Not bloody likely," she said. "You'll take Sally and Penny first." Her lovely eyes were wide, but her voice didn't waver. She looped the cable around the other two. "Pen, grab hold of the rope." She forced the screamer's hands around the line. "Sally, shut up and hold fast."

Nick wasn't used to being countermanded, but there was no time to argue.

"Whatever happens, don't let go," he said to the quaking pair.

He waved both hands over his head and the rope drew taut. The women shot across the surface like a corsair under full sail. Nicholas spotted a fin trailing them. The big tiger shark was back.

"Make some noise," he said to the woman clinging to the hatch beside him.

"What?"

"Scream, wench, or your friends are nothing but shark bait."

That got her attention. She yowled like a cat with its tail caught under a rocker. She flailed her arms and legs, splashing and whooping.

"Good. Keep it up," Nick bellowed.

As he expected, the fin slowed and turned. Given a choice, a shark would always pick an injured target over one moving smoothly through the water, and the beauty beside him seemed like she was mortally wounded all right.

The shark headed straight for them.

The woman stopped screaming and loosed an impressive string of expletives.

"What part of this is a good idea?" she demanded.

"This." Nick pulled her close and planted a hard, wet kiss on her mouth. His only regret was that he must be brief. *Nothing like a spot of danger with a beautiful woman who knows her way around profanity to make a man feel achingly alive.*

He flashed her a quick grin, then looked back toward the oncoming shark. She had enough grit in her gullet for two of his men, but her lips were butter soft. With any luck at all, he'd have time to explore that sweet mouth with greater leisure later. Who knew what outlandishly wicked things a grateful woman might do for a man who faced a shark for her?

Unless this night's work claimed him.

The fin sped up and sank.

He was out of time now.

"Tuck your knees to your chin and be still. Wait for my men to haul you to safety."

Nick took a couple quick breaths, then dove down to meet the shark.

"Wait!" Eve gasped as the man's feet disappeared with a final kick. A wave smacked her in the face and once it passed, she'd lost track of where he'd gone down. The shouts of the men in the jolly boat were louder now. She glanced up in time to see her friends being reeled in to safety.

She tucked up her knees, as the man had ordered. He might be a fool to attack a shark with nothing but a knife, but his advice made sense. Her broad skirts swirled in the water beneath her like jellyfish tendrils.

Something passed below her, catching and tugging at the trailing muslin. It sucked her down for a heartbeat.

Water shot up her nose and brine burned the back of her throat. Panic grasped her belly. Then she was suddenly free and bobbed back up, clawing at the surface. The hatch cover was nowhere to be seen.

The inky sea thrashed around her, the water mounding up. Then as a bolt of lightning jagged across the sky, the shark breached beside her, its body glistening silver in the moonlight, its mouth a gaping maw.

The man clung to one fin, his legs wrapped around the cylindrical body. His other hand sliced the knife along the shark's belly. Blood streamed black against its smooth skin. They slapped the surface and sank with a mighty flip of the shark's tail, disappearing so quickly Eve almost couldn't believe what she'd seen.

She searched the moon-speckled water for any sign of the pair. She was so intent she didn't even hear the approaching jolly boat over the roar of the wind and sea until a sailor reached under her armpits and hauled her aboard. She was dumped on her bottom without ceremony on the unforgiving planks of the hull while the crewmen turned their attention back to locating the missing man.

"Sing out if you see anything," the fellow at the tiller called.

Eve grasped the gunwale and looked out over the shimmering blackness. The moon scattered silver coins in a long broad path across the heaving waves. The small boat pitched and yawed in the rolling sea, but it beat a hatch cover by a long stretch.

She drew a deep shuddering breath.

A dozen questions speared her brain. How long could a man hold his breath? What was one knife compared to a mouthful of razors? What kind of lunatic took on a shark against such odds?

She only had an answer for the last one.

She fingered her bottom lip, still tasting the hard salty kiss that had smacked of farewell. "A brave lunatic," she muttered. "A bloody brave lunatic."

Chapter Three

His chest ached. His lungs burned for air. The last of his carefully hoarded breath had slipped away in tiny bubbles tickling across his cheek long ago. His ears threatened to explode. He fought the urge to inhale as he clawed toward the distant light.

The shark was dead.

Damned if he'd drown now.

His heart pounded like a smith's hammer.

How much farther?

His arms and legs were slowing down. He couldn't make them . . . he couldn't . . .

He'd lost the knife. He couldn't remember where.

His vision tunneled.

Then his head broke the surface and he dragged in a lungful of rain-sweet air. He sucked it in clear to his toes. Relief flooded his body. He lay back in the ocean's arms, satisfied just to let his chest rise and fall. Stars wheeled overhead, brittle pinpoints of light poking through the sky's black curtain.

Water muffled the sound of the dissipating storm. Nicholas drifted, closing his eyes in bone-deep weariness. How pleasant just to let the sea buoy him up, to let her rock him on her warm, wet breasts. How—

He jerked himself to full awareness.

The hull of the wreck loomed before him.

"As I live and breathe, what do we have here?" a sickeningly familiar voice drawled from above him. "I declare, I do believe it's Captain Scott gone adrift."

Adam Bostock was leaning over the gunwale of the wrecked *Molly Harper,* leering down at him. Bostock's angular face was lit with self-congratulation as he slapped the rail with his thick palm.

"This vessel and her crew are secure now, and let me tell you, she's a fine catch, but I still stand ready to aid another stranded mariner this night. Tell me, Nicholas, do you need my assistance?"

He wished for his lost knife with all his heart. Nothing would have kept him from hurling it at his gloating nemesis.

"Cap'n!" Tatem's graveled voice echoed against the wrecked ship's hull.

Nick pivoted in the water to see the jolly boat bearing down on him, the faces of his crew strained with worry. He glared at Bostock, then turned without a word. He wouldn't give the bastard the satisfaction. He windmilled his arms through the water, streaking a beeline toward the boat, determined not to let Bostock see his crew haul him aboard like a lost bit of baggage.

Nick was shaking with rage by the time he heaved himself over the side of the jolly boat.

"That's right. Best you hurry back to your ship, Nick!" Bostock cupped his hands around his mouth and shouted across the water. "I'd hate to see Higgs run the *Susan Bell* aground for you. But rest assured, if he does, the *Sea Wolf* will help you out."

And claim her as salvage. Not bloody likely.

Nicholas balled his fingers into tight fists. He'd see the *Susan B* on the ocean floor before he let Bostock set so much as the sole of his cursed foot on her.

"Your orders, Cap'n?" Tatem said.

His crew knew there was no love lost between Nick and Bostock. They just didn't know why. And Nick was determined to keep it that way.

"Home," he said simply before sinking onto the nearest empty slat seat. He dragged a hand over his face. His head pounded as if he'd been on a three-day drunk.

"Captain Scott." A feminine voice interrupted the anvil strikes in his head. "We'd like to thank you for your help. Words fail in expressing our gratitude."

But words proceeded to fall out of her mouth nevertheless.

He looked up into the lovely face of the woman who'd been the last one out of the water. Here was a welcome distraction. Between the shark and Adam Bostock, he'd almost forgotten about her, but now he was vaguely glad his crew had managed to fish her out. She was sitting between the other two, who huddled around her, shivering and sobbing softly.

Her mouth continued to move, but he'd stopped listening to her words, lost in the tantalizing play of her lips, teeth and tongue. Pity that kiss had been so damned short, but there'd been no help for it at the time.

It was hard to imagine that same soft, lovely mouth could wrap itself around such an inventive string of profanity. Her language would've made a bosun blush. It made no sense, but he'd heard her with his own ears. Here was a puzzlement worth untangling and a mouth definitely worth further investigation. His mood improved out of all reason as his gaze drifted down her neck to her low bodice.

It seemed to be a little known fact among womankind that wet muslin was well-nigh transparent. And this woman's dress was plastered to her form as if it had been troweled on. Her high breasts would make a pleasing handful and her tight nipples showed darkly through the wet fabric, two plump little berries.

"Mm . . . hmm," he said, his groin speaking to him

so loudly he had no ears for her words. Satisfied, she rattled on.

The planes of her long thighs, creamy and smooth, showed readily through the thin muslin.

Nick's attention was only diverted when the jolly boat arrived back alongside the *Susan Bell*. Higgs had kept her well beyond the ring of reefs while he waited for their return.

Without responding to the woman's running dialogue, Nicholas stood. "Prepare to make fast."

"Captain." A pair of deep grooves marred the space between her even brows when he didn't acknowledge her. "Captain Scott, will you agree to help us or not?"

"What did you say your name is?" he asked as he hauled away on one of the lines.

"Miss Upshall."

"How very appropriate." He looped a rope around her waist and gave a hand signal to the men above. "*Up* you shall go."

"Ooof!" Her feet left the pitching boat as the sailors heaved at the other end of the line, bearing her aloft.

Nicholas gave her an additional heft with a palm to her rump, enjoying the feel of her sweet flesh through the wet fabric, as his crew hauled their new passenger aboard. Her skirt billowed in the stiff breeze and gave him and the men in the jolly boat a fleeting glance up the muslin tent to the shadowy realm between her legs.

How delightful that women wore nothing at all beneath those yards and yards of fabric. Even if danger averted hadn't already given him an aching cockstand, Miss Upshall was quite enough to make him crowd his trousers.

"Enjoy what you can, boys," Nicholas said with a laugh. "It's the only prize you'll win this night."

His crew laughed with him. None of them questioned his choice to abandon the wreck in favor of these three women, even though the booty they'd lost in his decision was considerable. They knew if it had been one of them in the deep, he'd have made the same choice and saved their lives as well.

Some things were more precious than a bolt of Manchester wool or Welsh tin.

Or even a pound of tea.

The other two women were hauled up in similar fashion. Then the jolly boat crew climbed after them, up the rope netting that draped the ship's starboard side before the boat was raised.

As soon as Nick cleared the gunwale, Miss Upshall was there to meet him.

"Captain Scott, I must protest—"

"If you feel you've been ill-used, Miss Upshall, we'll be happy to drop you back where we found you." He pulled his shirt over his head and twisted the fabric to wring out the saltwater in a long stream.

"Sir! If you please!"

She stepped back a pace and averted her gaze as though a man's bare chest was uncharted territory for her.

Nicholas chuckled.

Her head snapped toward him and her gaze didn't waver this time. "There's no need to snigger at me. I'm not the one who's half-naked."

If she only knew that muslin was still wet enough to make her a liar. Her nipples stood out stiffly like proud little soldiers. She didn't even need to pinch them to attention the way Magdalen had.

"Even here at the edge of the world, surely there are standards, rules of decency and—"

"Indeed there are and they don't generally include ladies who are able to outswear old salts."

Her mouth snapped shut at that.

"Mr. Williams, relieve Mr. Higgs at the helm." Nicholas snapped his fingers for Higgs, who responded so fast, Nick wondered if his britches were afire. "Your names, if you please, so Mr. Higgs can enter you into the ship's log."

"I'm Sally Munroe," the blonde spoke up. "And this is Penelope Smythe."

Miss Upshall glared at him in silence.

"Mr. Higgs is waiting and your friends are dripping all over my deck. Your Christian name, of your kindness, Miss Upshall. A ship's log demands a certain thoroughness."

"Eve," she spat out. "Eve Upshall."

"Eve," he repeated. *The original temptress. How fitting.* "Mr. Higgs, take our passengers below and find them something dry to wear."

"This way, if you will, ladies." Higgs made a smart leg and started toward the aft stairs.

Nick grinned at the unusual display of good manners. His first mate's speech impediment rendered him shy and stammering with the ladies on dry land. Who'd have thought Peregrine Higgs had a courtly bone in his body?

Two of the women were quick to follow his first mate, but Miss Upshall didn't budge an inch.

"I'm not going anywhere until you and I come to an understanding, Captain."

Several of his crewmen were unable to keep their eyes to themselves as they passed Miss Upshall in her wet gown. Truth to tell, he couldn't blame them.

"Then perhaps you'd care to join me in my cabin,

where our understanding can be more complete." He glared at able seaman Tatem, who quickly averted his gaze and hurried on with his business. "And more private."

She glanced around at the loitering crew. "Accompany a man who obviously has no sense of propriety into a more private setting? How daft do you think I am?"

There was a question no sane man would answer.

But if he were king, Nick decided he'd declare wet muslin the height of fashion and demand all his female courtiers wear it every day. Too often a woman could pad and plump her way into a much more pleasing form with a man none the wiser till he was committed to a bedding.

Miss Upshall's charms needed no enhancements, her breasts as ripe a pair of pips as a man could wish.

Indeed, some of his men eyed her as if they were a wolf pack and she a lost ewe they'd like to have to supper. Nick didn't know how much longer they'd confine themselves to just looking. The last thing he needed this night was a brawl with his own men.

"Perhaps you'll allow that a lady would be better served in my cabin, where I can drape my greatcoat over her than on the open deck with no protection from the elements at all." He let his gaze wander pointedly to her breasts and then back to meet her eyes.

Miss Upshall looked down and instantly realized her state. She crossed her arms over her chest. "Very well, Captain. Let us remove to your cabin immediately."

She followed him down the companionway. He held the hatch open for her and gave her a casual leg, a much less elegant gesture than his first mate had sketched for the women.

If wrestling a shark wasn't enough to impress this woman, Nick couldn't imagine what would.

Chapter Four

Eve Upshall breezed past him into his sanctuary and lifted his greatcoat from its peg without waiting for his help. After she donned it, her sharp eyes swept his cabin. Like everything on the *Susan Bell*, it was spartan, but he was proud of it.

The small cabin held a narrow bed along one wall. A table that doubled as space for both his mess and a working desk was screwed to the floor in the center of the cabin. An oil lamp swung from one of the low beams. A row of windows canted over the stern, giving Nick a sweeping view of where he'd been. A narrow shelf held his charts and instruments and a few precious books that filled his infrequent idle moments at sea.

"Please, have a seat." He offered her the only chair in the room. In the lamplight, he noticed that her bedraggled dark hair had auburn highlights.

He'd always fancied redheads.

He reached over to brush an errant lock off her cheek, but she shied like a whipped pup.

"Easy, lass," he said, as he tucked the strand behind her ear. Her cheek was soft, but lightly grained with salt from her time in the sea. "Check your bearings. You're safe now."

Nicholas opened his sea trunk and pulled out a dry shirt. He thought about offering her one, but she'd been given an opportunity to find dry clothes and dismissed it. Besides, she was now thoroughly engulfed in his heavy oilskin coat. Pity. He'd have enjoyed the show till the muslin dried.

"I'm deeply grateful for your assistance this night, and in truth, I've never seen such a reckless display of courage. Nevertheless," she said primly, "you owe me an apology, Captain."

"Indeed? For what offense?"

Her cheeks flamed. "For kissing me without permission."

He laughed. "That was hardly a kiss, lass. It just seemed a shame to waste a pair of lips at the time."

He considered her for a moment. Fashion favored a little pink bow of a mouth, but this wench's red lips were a wide, full ribbon, slanting sensually across her oval face.

Nick decided little pink bows were overrated.

He leaned forward, bracing himself on the arms of her chair. "Now this," he said simply, "is a kiss."

She opened her mouth to protest, but it only made his job easier. He slanted his lips over hers, capturing her with ease. She was rigid with surprise at first, but he expected that. He also fully expected the way her mouth softened under his in the next heartbeat. Her lips were dusted with sea salt, but he slid his tongue past them to search out the honey inside.

Damn, she was sweet. She made some noises, but they didn't sound like the usual moans of pleasure he coaxed from Magdalen. He tried to tease her tongue into chasing his back into his mouth, but she played coy.

Her hands found his chest, raking her nails across his skin.

Encouraged, he deepened the kiss.

And then the little minx grasped a few of the dark hairs that whorled around his nipples and yanked them out!

"Ow!" He jerked away from her, rubbing his chest.

"The next time you force something into my mouth without my permission, I will bite it off," she promised with an evil glare.

Even fully enraged, she was a damned fetching bit of muslin. His stiff cock was wholly undeterred by the stinging spot of skin on his chest that was now bare as a baby's butt.

"Do you make a habit of trying to maim the men who save your life?" he demanded.

"Only those who seem to think a heartfelt thank-you is insufficient gratitude." She refolded her hands in her lap. "Captain, I ask for your promise that in the future you will refrain from attempting to kiss me unless I give my permission."

"Truth to tell, that kiss of yours was no prize and is hardly worth repeating." By thunder, no woman had ever refused to bed him, let alone kiss him. He crossed his arms over his chest and glared down at her.

"However, if I decide to kiss you again, I'll do it," he said with certainty. "And I'll not be asking for any permission then either."

"We'll see about that." She narrowed her eyes at him. They were the deep aqua of the Great Sound on a clear summer day, but now there was a definite squall brewing behind them. Then her gaze swept down his form and he could almost see her remembering that she was supposed to be upset about his bare chest. She lowered her eyes.

"For the sake of our shared danger, I shall try to overlook your unchivalrous behavior."

"Unchivalrous?" he said, thunderstruck. "I leaped into shark-infested waters for you. If that doesn't qualify as chivalrous in the extreme, I'd like to know what would."

"Captain, I will not be drawn into a debate. Of course, I appreciate that you rescued my friends and me. I simply will not be treated as though I owe you more than a lady ought to repay."

Nick's lips thinned. *I'll be buggered. A bona fide lady.* For the past few years, he'd avoided that rare species as if they carried the plague.

"However, it seems I also owe you an apology," she said, lacing and unlacing her fingers on her lap, while her gaze darted about the room, looking anywhere but at him.

"And what was *your* offense? Besides barbering without a blade." He chuckled, hoping to ease the tension between them, though he decided to take his time about donning a clean shirt since his state of undress clearly unnerved her.

"When we were in the water and the shark headed back toward us . . . well, my tongue seemed to act of its own accord. I said some unseemly things. I hope you'll allow that I was not myself for a moment."

"No, I suspect you were exactly yourself. At times like that, a body cannot be otherwise. Besides, the situation called for a few ripe phrases." He was about to commend her for levelheaded behavior in straits that might have undone many a man, but she plunged ahead with her agenda.

"But now that we are no longer in dire straits, I must insist that you and I reach an accord."

"Willingly," he said with a ready grin. "I'm always agreeable to an accord with a fine young lady."

"Young lady of good family," she corrected. "And as such, I entreat you to help us continue our journey."

Good family. He allowed that might be so. The lace at her bodice and wrists bespoke quality and she wore a silver necklace with a locket. He pulled his shirt on over his head and tied the tabs at his throat. It covered him to midthigh.

"And just where are the three of you going in such an all-fired hurry?" he asked.

"My friends and I are en route to the Carolinas."

He made frequent runs from the Turks to Charleston, delivering salt and other less legal goods in exchange for foodstuffs desperately needed in Bermuda. The island waters provided bountifully, but a man could only stomach so much fish. In Charleston, he would load up the *Susan B*'s hold with jerked beef, salt pork and much needed grain. Miss Upshall's plans might dovetail nicely with his.

Nicholas reached under the hem of his fresh shirt and popped the buttons on his slop trousers.

"Captain Scott!"

"I need to get out of these wet trousers." He let the broad-legged britches drop to his ankles and stepped out of them, frowning at her. "Salt water will gald a man in short order."

"But you're . . . you're . . ." Her eyes were round as a pair of sea urchins.

"Naked beneath my shirt? Aye, but I'm covered enough for decency," he said as he hitched up a clean pair of trousers. "Besides aren't you naked beneath your skirts as well?"

"A gentleman should not speak so."

"There's your difficulty, Miss Upshall. You're laboring under the misapprehension that I'm a gentleman when I'm only a humble sailing man." He grinned wickedly. "And one who knows full well you've naught beneath your skirts but a pair of fine long legs."

She fumed, but he smiled at the memory of her kicking beneath the yards of muslin as she was hauled aboard. He turned his back to her while he fastened the drop front of his britches. It might hurt his argument that he was sufficiently covered if his cock tented his long shirt toward her.

"Humble sailing man." He heard her mutter behind him. "There's nothing the least humble about you."

He decided to ignore the jab. "Now what's so urgent for three young ladies of good family in the Carolinas?"

"Our weddings, sir, if that's any of your business."

When he turned to face her again, she was studying her folded hands, settled neatly on her lap.

"My companions and I are all engaged to marry gentlemen of property."

"Really? And where did you meet these gentlemen of property?

"We haven't. Not yet, in any case."

"Then how did these astounding engagements come to be?"

She rolled her eyes at him. "Our marriages were arranged, of course."

"I've been to the Carolinas," he said. "They suffer no shortage of women there. Why do these gentlemen need to drag you and your friends across the Atlantic?"

"Perhaps the colonial women there will do for most men, but these are men of distinction who want their wives to be English-born," she said primly. "They wish to make certain their children have the proper sensibilities, closer ties to England and the Crown."

Nick laughed. "There are plenty in the Colonies who don't give a flying fig for the Crown."

She blinked hard, shock registering on her features.

"Surely you've heard of the agitators, the patriots, they call themselves?" Nick couldn't believe the Colonies' unrest wasn't common knowledge in London. "There's a rat's nest of them up in Boston, but their words are flying from printers' presses up and down the Atlantic seaboard, spreading sedition like cankerwort seeds."

The colonists' quarrel with the Stamp Act, the tea tax and laws requiring them to quarter British soldiers had smoldered for the last decade and now threatened to erupt into real violence.

But not everyone suffered for it.

By rights, Nick should kiss the feet of King George and his heavy-handed parliament. Laws requiring the colonists to trade only with England had made Nick's smuggled cases of French wine and Caribbean rum ridiculously lucrative.

A little rebellion was good for business.

"How can they sanction such treason?" She shook her head in wonderment.

"They don't see it so. They claim to want representation since they're subject to taxation." Nick frowned. Why was he talking taxes with a delightfully wet woman? Still, he felt bound to warn her that life in the Carolinas might not be what she was expecting. "It's not everyone, of course, but there are those who would cut all ties with the old order and launch out on their own."

"Surely the King's loyal subjects will not allow such a thing to happen."

"Loyal subjects like your prospective husband?"

"Exactly. Mr. Smoot Pennywhistle, Esq., of the Carolinas, gentleman and planter. He's even a deacon in the congregation near his home." She reached for the locket at her throat and popped open the compartment to gaze at the miniature inside. Her features fell. "Oh, it's ruined."

"If you will allow me?" Nicholas held out a hand. She unclasped the locket and dropped it into his palm. The tiny painting was smudged and waffled from its exposure to seawater, but he could still make out the profile of a bewigged gentleman with a hefty set of jowls.

Nick knew the type. Pasty-faced, dissipated with too much food and drink, and satisfied to luxuriate in the fine things provided him by the labor of others. Mr. Smoot Pennywhistle was certainly not a match for the lively, opinionated woman sitting before him now.

"Let your Mr. Pennywhistle bake in the Bermuda sun for a day or two and I'm sure he'll be as good a man as ever he was," Nick said with sarcasm as he handed the locket back.

"Oh, I hope so," she said, missing his meaning as she fastened the thin chain around her neck once more. "So, you see, if you help us continue on our journey, I'm certain our fiancés would see you handsomely rewarded."

"Not your good families?"

The question seemed to catch her by surprise. "Well, naturally they would be glad to learn of your assistance."

"Excellent," he said. "There's a packet leaving for Bristol in a week. We'll send word to your families with it. It may take some time, but at least news of your survival should arrive alongside reports of the *Molly Harper*'s wreck."

"That's not necessary. The important thing is—"

"The important thing is you don't know who your prospective groom really is and I suspect your family doesn't either." He couldn't imagine why a beauty like Eve Upshall didn't have a dozen suitors clamoring for her hand in England. Even if her dowry was less than impressive, what he'd seen of her so far would more than make up for lack of funds to any man worthy of the name. He crossed his arms over his chest and cocked his head at her. "Are the three of you running away for some reason?"

"Of course not!" she said, a trifle too quickly. "What a ridiculous notion."

"Almost as ridiculous as sailing across the Atlantic to wed a man you've never met," Nick said. "Your family had no part in arranging this, did they?"

"Not that it's any of your business, but no, they didn't initiate matters. Our fiancés sent an agent to England to locate suitable wives. It's all quite proper, I assure you. Biblical, even."

"Biblical?"

"Of course. Have you never read how the patriarch Abraham sent his steward back to his father's homeland to find a wife for his son Isaac?" She leaned forward, her expression earnest. "Lieutenant Rathbun reminded me of that at our first meeting. He says that accomplished gentlemen with many demands on their time have often deferred to the wisdom of a third party in the matter of choosing a bride."

"Who's Lieutenant Rathbun?" Nick was predisposed not to like him already. If he was spouting scripture, he might even be a Methodist.

"He's the gentleman who's escorting us to the Carolinas." She frowned. "But when the ship ran aground, we were separated from him in the confusion and I don't know how he fared this night."

Nick didn't know either, but he doubted Rathbun was a gentleman. The whole tale was a point off plumb. Eve Upshall didn't strike him as a fool, but in this instance, she seemed entirely too trusting.

"Please, Captain. Lieutenant Rathbun assured us our fiancés are the most deserving of men."

"Deserving, hmm? Well, there are far more deserving men on Bermuda." The island boasted a couple brothels, but several of the young bucks in his crew chafed over the lack of respectable women. Whores were fine on short notice, but there came a time when a man wished to settle down.

Since he'd lost the prize vessel, he figured the least he could do was give his men a chance to court three likely young ladies. Besides, the thought of watching the shy Higgs go a-courting promised to be more fun than Nick could resist.

"I won't take you to Charleston."

"Then you refuse to help us?"

"I didn't say that. My help will just be in an entirely different vein than you imagined," he said pleasantly. "Three unattached, available ladies will need someplace to stay while they sort themselves out. My home on St. Georges is spacious enough to accommodate you and your friends."

"You expect us to stay in your home?"

"I knew you were clever. We're in complete accord." He rubbed his hands together. "Now, it'll only be until such time as each of you chooses a husband from among the willing island lads, with preference given to my crew, you understand."

"You expect me to marry one of your sailors?"

"I don't see why not? A husband is clearly your aim. Why not an able seaman? Or at least an islander." He fished a clean pair of socks from his sea chest and leaned against the bunk as he changed out of his wet pair. "After all, you were going to marry a pudgy, gout-ridden stranger named Pennywhistle."

"Mr. Pennywhistle is an upstanding, God-fearing gentleman of property."

"Perhaps, but I doubt a God-fearing gentleman will take to an acid-tongued harpy whose knack for profanity is well-nigh an art form." He gartered the stockings and chuckled as he stood upright. "A sailing man is far more apt to appreciate that unique ability in a woman."

She rose slowly and he fancied he could see steam leaking from the shells of her pink ears. "Then I shall enlist the help of another captain once we make port. Perhaps the one who salvaged the *Molly Harper.*"

One of her delicate brows arched in challenge. Apparently she hadn't missed the antagonism between him and Bostock. He further revised his estimation of her pluck.

"I wish you luck of that, Miss Upshall. The *Sea Wolf* makes berth on a different island," he said, careful to keep his tone even. "And since you've naught but the wet gown on your lovely back, I doubt you'll find success. Not even Adam Bostock is daft enough to board passengers without demanding the fare aforehand."

"Captain Scott, this is wholly unacceptable."

Nick swore vehemently under his breath and she plopped back into the chair. "Miss Upshall, I sacrificed a chance to salvage a fully loaded brigantine to fish you from the waves. I nearly ended up in a shark's gullet. And now I offer you the protection of my sword arm and the warmth of my hearth while you and your friends make new lives for yourselves on as lovely an island as you could wish."

He braced his hands on the arms of her chair and leaned down to nearly touch noses with her. "If that's not acceptable to a fault, then I don't know what possibly could be."

Even drenched with seawater, her skin held an indefinably feminine sweetness. If she wasn't the most irritating bit of muslin he'd ever met, he'd have been tempted to kiss her again.

Her mouth opened to respond, but a rap on the cabin door made her close it as quickly.

Nicholas barked out permission to enter and Tatem peeked around the door, ducking his head and tugging his forelock in deference.

"Beggin' your pardon, Cap'n," he said in his sand-paper voice. He held out Nick's dry boots. "We're coming up on the mouth of St. Georges Harbor, sir. Mr. Williams asks will you be pleased to relieve him at the wheel?"

"I'll be there directly." Nicholas never let anyone else negotiate the narrow passage to the *Susan's B*'s final berth. The harbor was as snug a cove as a sailor could wish, but with its many little islands and shoals, he always passed through with an easier heart when his own hands were at the helm.

"Miss Upshall, I suggest you avail yourself of my sea trunk for some dry clothing while I'm gone," he said as he tugged on his boots. "Saltwater will gald a woman just as quickly as a man. If you're to be courted, you'll not want to be doctoring a nasty rash."

As soon as he closed the cabin door behind him, something thumped loudly against it.

Probably one of his books.

Why did women always feel the infernal need to hurl things at him?

In taking the three castaways into his home, he'd wrung the only bright spot of cheer from this night's work.

But as he piloted the *Susan Bell* through the last leg of her journey, it dimly occurred to him that Magdalen might not see things in the same light.

Chapter Five

"Pigheaded, louse-ridden, so full of himself he couldn't spoon in another drop! The man's naught but a prick with feet."

Eve loosed another string of muttered curses as she bent to pick up the infuriating man's dog-eared copy of John Locke. She knew she shouldn't throw something as precious as a book, even if it was beyond her abilities to puzzle out much more than the title. Her mother had started to teach her to read, so she knew her letters, but there hadn't been enough time for her to develop any fluency with the written word before her life was up-ended as a child. She knew she shouldn't swear either. No one would believe she was a lady if she did.

But it was difficult to shake the bad habit she'd picked up in the tavern and perfected further in Newgate. Hurling the book had helped, but nothing relieved her frustration like a few well-chosen phrases. Especially if they were ripe enough to curdle fresh milk.

If she were being fair she'd have to admit that part of her anger should have been directed at herself. She'd been weak-willed as a light-heeled trollop when the captain kissed her. She hadn't reacted quickly enough with the righteous indignation a lady should display when a man took such liberties.

The way she softened, yielded for a moment, he'd believe she hadn't a ladylike bone in her body.

Captain Scott would be of no help to her. Of course, she appreciated his rescue, but if he was going to keep

her a virtual prisoner, that canceled out his heroics as
far as Eve was concerned.

Now what was she to do?

She had to find a way to reach the Colonies, and
not for any pudgy planter named Pennywhistle either.
Her mother's brother lived in Richmond. At least, that's
where the last letter had come from all those years ago.
Surely Richmond wasn't too far from Charleston.

Her uncle would help her. He had to. He was the
only family she had left.

"First things first," she admonished herself. She
couldn't trust Captain Scott to give her privacy for very
long.

Eve unlaced her bodice, thankful she'd been wearing
the pale blue muslin when the *Molly Harper* ran aground
instead of the floral patterned sack dress she was saving
for the day they made landfall in Charleston.

Much good may it do me now. The sack dress was lost to
her. It was by far the most elegant bit of frippery that
had ever touched her skin, but the blue muslin's laces
were in front. Which meant she could manage getting
into and out of it alone.

And no one else would see her bare back.

She peeled herself out of the sodden gown, toying
with the idea of wringing it out on the captain's polished wood floor.

*No, that'd be too petulant by half and would only inconve-
nience the cabin boy.* Eve squeezed the water out into the
chamber pot in the corner. Then she draped her gown
and remaining stocking—she hadn't even realized she'd
lost one—over the chair, where it still dripped steadily.
She knelt to rummage through the captain's sea chest.

When she pulled the man's shirt over her head, she
was pleased to see that it reached below her knees. It
felt odd not to have her breasts pressed up and to-

gether, imprisoned by whalebone and stiff fabric. The fine lawn teased her nipples as her breasts swung free beneath the fabric.

Eve could only find a pair of sailor's short slop trousers, the wide baggy-legged type favored by mariners. Sadly, these left a scandalous amount of her calves on display even if she could keep them up. She remedied the problem by knotting a length of coarse rope around her waist and pulling on a pair of thick woolen stockings. She had no shoes. Even if the captain had left a spare pair of boots in his cabin, she'd have clomped right out of them with every step.

She was by no means decently attired, but at least she was more modestly covered than in her wet gown. The ship canted into a sharp turn and then righted itself. Dawn broke through the stern windows.

Eve ventured out of the cabin and onto the deck to see for herself just where she and her friends had landed. Sally and Penelope were leaning on the starboard rail, heads together in conversation while the sailors went about their business. Since the women were dressed more or less in the same unorthodox fashion as she, more than one of the salts cast lingering glances at their ankles.

Since there was no help for it, she might as well put on a bold face. Ignoring the crew's leers, Eve strode across the deck to join her friends.

"Oh, Evie, isn't the island beautiful?" Sally gushed.

"Compared to bobbing in the deep, I'd expect any place would be," Eve said sourly. But truth to tell, the dense tangle of rhododendron and oleander beneath graceful palms and towering cedars was easy on the eyes. Especially after weeks of nothing but endless sea. The sweet scent of hibiscus wafted past her nose and the breeze held the heady breath of green growing things.

"We've landed on our feet and no mistake," Sally went on. "Why, the captain is taking us into his own home. And Mr. Higgs says he's all but lord of Devil Isle."

"Devil Isle," Eve repeated. How fitting for a black-eyed devil like Captain Scott. "And him the lord of the place. Well, he would be, wouldn't he?"

"Not really. There's a governor, but Mr. Higgs says folk generally pay him little heed unless there's a visiting delegation from England," Sally rattled on with scarcely a breath. "It's Captain Scott they look to. And it's noised about that the captain is a gentleman of high birth."

"And low sensibilities," Eve muttered.

As if she hadn't heard her, Sally breezed on. "Likely a second son, they say, because he don't bear no real title, 'cept the town folk here do call him Lord Nick."

"What else did Mr. Higgs say?" Eve figured it would do no harm to learn more about the place and the people in it.

"He says Devil Isle is the old name of the place, o' course. Seems when folk first came here there was naught but a flock of birds and a herd of wild hogs, of all things! In any case, the sailors thought their calls and grunts were the cries of demons, up from the pit." Sally shivered in horrified fascination. "Now Mr. Higgs says the islands are called the Bermudas."

"Seems Mr. Higgs is quite a fount of information," Eve said dryly. She cast a glance toward the first mate, who stood near the rail, his hands clasped behind his back. His gaze darted toward the women, then away almost immediately when she caught him looking. His face reddened with a quick flush. Tall and lanky, with his pale hair pulled into a neat queue beneath his tricorne, Mr. Higgs reminded Eve of a long-legged colt, skittish and wary. "He seems shy."

"Do you think so?" Sally rested a plump cheek on her

palm. "I was worried about how we might seem to him in these clothes, but he said as we were the picture of English womanhood, no matter what we wore." Sally sighed in a thoroughly besotted way. "Wasn't that kind?"

"The Captain seems kind, too," Penny said. "And brave."

"But far too accustomed to getting his own way," Eve said. "He refuses to take us on to Charleston."

"That's just as well." Sally's head bobbed in a satisfied nod. "St. Georges will do me fine. Once I set foot on dry land again, it'll take the devil himself to force me onto another ship."

White-roofed houses came into view. Neat and clean, the village of St. Georges was a welcome dash of civilization, as if a snippet of England had reached across the Atlantic's gray waves. The ship's bell began to sound news of their approach.

Eve looked back up to the helm, where Captain Scott stood behind the wheel. Legs spread, muscles bulging beneath his open-collared shirt, he strong-armed the ship into its berth. Instead of wearing a wig, as any gentleman would, or a tricorne over a neat queue like Mr. Higgs, the captain let his long dark hair fly free. It teased his broad shoulders as if he were some barbarian prince.

Eve turned away from him in frustration. Too bad the civilization of St. Georges had not tamed the master of this vessel.

The *Susan Bell* sidled up to the wharf, rubbing her hull against the dock like a tart toying with her lover. Nicholas supervised his men as they made her fast.

An enterprising wharf rat had evidently heard the ship's bell as they approached. The boy had nipped up to Nick's big house on the hill and fetched an empty wagon in anticipation of the goods Nick should have been hauling back from the wreck. The lad had even thought to tie Nick's horse to the back of the wagon bed.

"Mr. Higgs." Nicholas snapped his fingers and his first mate came to heel immediately, following him to the head of the gangplank. "Bring our guests up to the house in the wagon. I'll be along directly."

"Aye, Cap'n."

"Oh, and fetch that lad along as well." Nick pointed at the boy who stood at the stallion's head. "Make a place for him in the stables for now. If he continues to show promise there, we'll see about a berth for him among the crew."

"Aye," Higgs said, a worried frown beetling his brows. "But aren't you going to be there when we arrive? I'm thinking Miss Magdalen may not welcome our . . . guests as warmly as we might like."

Nick laughed. "Astute as ever, Higgs," he said. "Which is why I'm making a stop by the milliner on the way. Never go into battle unarmed, lad. And if your opponent is female, the best weapon is a new bonnet and a handful of ribbons."

"B-but if we arrive before you, what shall I say to Miss Magdalen?" Peregrine's stutter was back as soon as the deck stopped rocking.

"Don't worry." Nicholas clapped a hand on his shoulder. "Women are always curious as magpies. Take our guests for a slow turn around the town and I'll make sure to beat you home. It'll all be sorted out by the time you arrive."

He strode down the gangplank, tossed tuppence to the lad by the wagon and told him to wait for Higgs. Then Nick mounted the stallion and dug his heels into its flanks, launching into a quick trot along Water Street.

An image of Magdalen's face shimmered before him. Perhaps *two* new bonnets might not be amiss.

"Oh, what cunning little things. Nick, they're beautiful," Magdalen exclaimed over the new fripperies. She pulled herself away from the hatbox long enough to plant a quick wet kiss on his mouth before she turned her attention back to the bonnets. "I take it all back. You were so right to salvage that wreck."

"I don't know about that."

"I do." She slipped on the pink one and knotted a jaunty bow under one ear, admiring the effect in Nick's looking glass. "Why, this is every bit as fetching as that lot at Mistress Atwood's shop down on Water Street. I'll wager it came straight from Paris. Was the ship French?"

"No." He wondered how much longer he had before Higgs arrived with the wagon.

"What else were they hauling? Bales of cloth?" Her eyes sparkled like a deep emerald cove. "Better yet, were there any ready-made dresses?"

"I don't know." Nick sank into his favorite chair, flanking the hearth. "Look Magda, those bonnets didn't come from the salvage vessel."

She looked askance at him.

"They're from Mistress Atwood's."

"But—"

"I didn't make it to the wreck in time."

"Oh, no." She skittered over and sank to her knees before him, resting her skillful fingers on his thighs. "Never say it went down with all hands."

"No, not exactly. Bostock beat me to it."

"I'm so sorry, Nick." She raised herself up and leaned to kiss him again, but he turned his head. No mere kiss would make up for losing the *Molly Harper*. "He must have had a head start. No one can outsail you."

"He didn't outsail me, but Bostock had the better luck, which is ofttimes more telling than skill. I was the nearer salver, but I veered off to pick up some souls already in the water. And so Bostock reached the wreck first. That makes it his, fair and square according to the laws of salvage."

"Well, if they'd abandoned ship already, Bostock didn't get much, I'll warrant." She ran her thumbs along his inner thighs, teasing close to his groin but not touching. His body roused to her.

May as well get this over with, he thought, *before I stop being able to think with my big head.* "They hadn't called for all hands to abandon ship."

Magdalen reared back on her heels and frowned. "Haven't you always said going into the sea is the last resort? If someone was addlepated enough to leave a ship still afloat, you should have left them there till you made sure of the prize."

Nick shook his head. "If I'd done that, they'd be dead now, and I didn't want their blood on my head."

"It wouldn't have been. You should have let the fools meet their fate." She rose to her feet and began to pace in frustration. "Oh, Nick, was it a big ship?"

"A fully loaded brigantine," he admitted, wishing he hadn't spent the extra for a second bonnet. This no longer seemed like an argument he cared to win. "It was three women in the water, Magdalen. I couldn't let them die."

"Male or female, it makes no difference. You owed it to me—I mean, your crew, at the very least, to capture that wreck."

"None of the men have complained." For a blink, an image of Eve Upshall demanding he save her friends first flashed through his mind. Magdalen would have grabbed the lifeline away from them, and devil take the hindermost.

She sighed. "Men are so impractical sometimes."

"I suppose we are." He'd never much considered what went on in Magdalen's lovely head. Now that he'd gotten an eye-popping peek, he didn't find it quite so lovely. He'd suspected she was mercenary, and she certainly loved fine things—her monthly bills at the shops along the St. Georges waterfront proved that. But he hadn't expected her to be such a coldhearted bitch. "They have no place to stay, so I offered to let them live here."

"Here?" Her eyes bulged like a grouper's. "You're bringing three strange women into this house? No, Nick, I'll not have it."

"You have nothing to say about it. This is *my* home, Magdalen."

"But I've been living here with you for—"

"For as long as I care for you to, I'm thinking."

"Oh, Nicholas, you don't mean that." She changed tactics in a heartbeat. She crossed her arms beneath her breasts to better emphasize them and thrust out her lower lip in the pout he used to find fetching.

He refused to be distracted from his purpose. He'd made up his mind, and there was no point in dillydallying.

"We've had a good run, you and I, but we've reached an end. For the sake of what we've had, I'll have Higgs deposit a goodly sum in an account for you at Butterfield's bank," he offered. She'd never be able to say he wasn't generous. "If you should ever be in want, do not hesitate to come to me."

"Three women, hmm?" She narrowed her eyes at him. "If you wanted another woman in your bed, you should have told me. I have a friend who would jump at the chance. She and I have pleasured a man together before and—"

"Tempting as that sounds, I'll pass," he interrupted, regretting she hadn't suggested it before now. The idea held all sorts of tantalizing possibilities, but unfortunately, he'd lost interest in bedding Magdalen, with or without a second woman under the covers. "You may take everything you've acquired while in my household. Send a list to Higgs and he'll see it delivered to you. You do still have that little house over on Paget's Island, don't you?"

She nodded, mute but dry-eyed. There had never been any question of love between them as far as he was concerned and he was glad to see the indifference was mutual.

Lust was an exceedingly pleasurable thing, but once it burned out, it left nothing but dead gray ash in the heart. Not terribly satisfying, but easy to sweep clean.

"Good." He turned to leave the room, then had a second thought and snapped his fingers. "Oh! Since they lost everything in the wreck, my guests will need something to wear. I ask, of your kindness, that you spare them a few necessaries from your wardrobe."

"Of my kindness? Why, you bastard!" She launched herself across the room and pummeled his chest. "You'd take the clothes from my back and put it on your new tarts."

He grabbed her hands and held them behind her back. She stopped struggling and pressed her breasts against his chest, peering at him from under her long lashes.

"Is this a new game, Nick? Trying to get me angry so you can hold me down?" One corner of her mouth tilted up. "All right. I'll play."

"But regretfully, my dear Magdalen, I won't." He would miss her. She was as adventurous in bed as she was conniving of heart. But he'd never be able to swive her again without hearing her wish three innocent strangers dead so she might have a few more things. "Be gone before my guests arrive or you may forget about my generous congé. I suspect you have less than a quarter hour."

He released her and strode from the room without a backward glance.

Chapter Six

Being alone with three strange women would normally be enough to turn Peregrine Higgs into a stammering puddle.

Thanks be to God for Reggie Turnscrew, Higgs thought as he drove the wagon through the narrow and increasingly steep streets of St. Georges. Perched on the seat beside Higgs, the lad twisted around to face the passengers in the wagon bed. He kept up a steady stream of conversation, entertaining the ladies with tales of the islanders' doings, telling them who lived in which houses and where the likeliest handouts were to be had.

As if ladies would be interested in such things!

"And as near as folk can figure, there be about one hundred seventy islands in the Bermudas all together, give or take," Reggie was saying. "O' course, some of 'em ain't hardly big enough to set your foot on, but if it ain't touchin' another bit o' land, I reckon it counts, don't it?"

Like the ladies they obviously were, they listened politely and made appropriate comments whenever Reggie gave them half a chance.

Which meant Peregrine didn't have to utter a single syllable. Good thing, since single syllables were about all he suspected he was capable of at the moment.

Had there ever been a finer flower of English womanhood than Miss Sally Munroe?

He swallowed hard. And him not trusting himself to say a bloomin' thing!

They'd left the main streets of the village and started up the narrow track that led to the captain's house. A gig with a single horse came flying down the hillside toward them. The driver plied the whip to its withers with a heavy hand. Peregrine reined his team to the far left side of the road to allow them to pass.

The driver was a woman, her dark hair streaming behind her, a scowl making her face an angry mask. Peregrine hid his smile and doffed his tricorne as she flew by. She didn't give him a second glance.

Looks as if the captain sorted things out like he promised. He chirruped to the team with a light heart and they jolted into a trot. Peregrine had never much cared for Magdalen. She lost no opportunity to make fun of his stutter whenever the captain wasn't about.

"Oh, I say!" Miss Munroe exclaimed. "Who was that?"

"That's Magdalen Frith, that is," Reggie supplied helpfully. "Off on a right proper tear, too, by the looks of it. She'd be Lord Nick's regular lady."

Reggie winked hugely as he pronounced the word "lidey," but Peregrine wasn't in a position to throw stones at the lad's unschooled speech. By gum, he wished he could do as well by half.

"Lord Nick's regular lady?" Miss Upshall asked.

"You know, 'is lady friend, 'is doxy, 'is—"

"Th-that's enough," Pere muttered to the boy. The captain hadn't ever made a secret of his relationship with Miss Frith, but there was no need for the lad to go blabbing everything he knew.

"Is it much farther to the captain's home, Mr. Higgs?" Miss Upshall asked.

Higgs shook his head.

"Just on the other side o' that rise," Reggie added, evidently unaffected by Peregrine's rebuke. "Whispering Hill be one of the finest houses on the islands, you'll be pleased to know. Even better than the guv'nor's place, if you're asking my opinion."

"Why's it called Whispering Hill?" Sally Munroe asked. "Goodness! I hope it's not haunted. It's not, is it?"

Peregrine chuckled. What an imagination she had! Along with shining blonde locks and the merriest brown eyes Pere had ever had the pleasure of gazing into.

" 'aunted? Go on wi' you! Ain't that a thought!" Reggie said. "Naw, it's called Whispering Hill on account of the way the wind moves through the palms. Folks say it sounds like the island's telling all its secrets, if a body were of a mind to sit still long enough to listen."

"How charming," the quiet one said.

What was her name? Oh, yes, Miss Smythe. Higgs remembered now, though her Christian name escaped him. He'd have to go back and check the ship's log on the morrow.

As the wagon cleared the rise, there was a collective gasp from the women behind him as Whispering Hill came into view. Seeing it afresh through their eyes, Higgs had to admit it was a fair treat.

Long and low, with a number of little courtyards and curves, the house draped itself over the hilltop as if it had grown there. Its pale yellow walls peeped from behind curtains of bougainvillea and vining hibiscus beneath its starkly white roof. The bottle green jalousie shutters were all propped open a bit, like heavy-lidded eyes, to let the prevailing breeze cool the interior.

"Mr. Higgs, do you live here, too?" Miss Munroe asked.

Peregrine nodded, feeling the tips of his ears heat. He hadn't even thought that far. He'd be living under the selfsame roof as this blonde goddess.

He might never get another lick of sleep.

"And now I live here, too!" Reggie proclaimed. "Leastways I live in the stable, I'd expect. There's a snug corner or two there for the likes of me, I'll be bound."

Peregrine drew the team to a stop, hustled himself down from the driver's seat and nipped around to hand the ladies out of the wagon. Each murmured her thanks to him, but his fingers tingled when Miss Munroe slipped her small hand into his for a brief moment.

"Oh, Evie." Miss Munroe hugged her friend as she surveyed the house. "It's not exactly a castle, but it is rather like a fairy tale, isn't it?"

The captain appeared in the open doorway to welcome them.

"Complete with a dragon," Miss Upshall said under her breath. Then she squared her shoulders and strode toward the door. Miss Munroe followed her.

Miss Smythe started after them, but then stopped and turned back to Peregrine. Her gaze met his for a heartbeat and then settled on the ground before his feet. Several strands of her long brown hair fell forward to obscure her face.

"Good day, Mr. Higgs. And thank you again."

"My pleasure." He doffed his hat. "Good day to you, Miss Smythe."

She looked back up, her face dimpling in a shy smile. There was a smattering of freckles across her nose and apple cheeks. Miss Smythe bobbed a quick curtsey, and then scurried to catch up with the other women.

Peregrine led the team to the stable to show Reggie Turnscrew what was what. The boy fully appreciated the opportunity he'd been offered and was keen to make himself useful. Peregrine set him to polishing the brass on the fancy carriage the Captain seldom used. Higgs tended the horses himself.

He'd been brushing down the bay mare for a full

twenty minutes before he realized he hadn't stam-
mered when he answered Miss Smythe.

What to make of that, he had no idea.

"You may choose whichever empty chamber you wish
for your own," the captain said expansively.

He led them down a whitewashed corridor. Alternat-
ing windows and lantern recesses were buried in the
outer wall, which appeared to be several feet deep. On
the other side of the hall, highly polished doors opened
onto the interior rooms. Eve had to admit Whispering
Hill was beautifully and exotically appointed. Captain
Scott even had a table whose base was fashioned from
an Indian elephant's foot, but she saw no need to fawn
over him about it.

A cage might be silk-draped and gilded, but it was
still a cage.

"There seem to be quite a lot of available rooms,"
Sally said, clearly overawed.

"I like to entertain," Captain Scott said with a shrug.
"And frequently my guests come great distances and
need to stay for a long visit. It happens when you live on
an island."

"England is an island, but I've never been in a house
with so many rooms," Penelope said.

"Then you've obviously not visited the right sort of
houses back home." Puzzlement made his eyes narrow.

Eve needed to warn Penny and Sally to be more careful with their words or the captain would never believe
they were ladies.

He led them into the second to last room off the long
hall and opened the double doors of the large wardrobe.

"You may each have your own room, but at present I
have only these garments available for you to divide

among yourselves." He waved a hand toward the impressively large number of gowns. "Of course, if you need something else—and since you are female, I suspect you will—we can send for a modiste to come take measurements and arrange for whatever is required."

"Thank you, Captain," Penelope said.

"Oh, yes, thank you ever so." Sally started pawing through the dresses.

"Am I right in assuming these gowns, gaudies and gewgaws once belonged to Magdalen Frith, your 'regular lady'?" Eve asked.

"Ah, Miss Upshall." He turned to face her with an unabashed grin. "Just when I had despaired of ever hearing your sweet voice again."

So, he *had* noticed she'd remained silent throughout his self-congratulatory tour. That pleased her so much, she didn't protest when he took her elbow and guided her through the open French doors leading out to a small private garden. Sally and Penny were too engrossed in the contents of the wardrobe to notice their departure. Eve could still hear them in the room behind her, exclaiming over their new treasures.

"Aye, the garments once belonged to Miss Frith. Aye, she was my mistress, which means the gowns are of the highest quality." He raised a quizzical brow at her. "And in case you're wondering, aye, the post as my mistress has been vacated. Would you be interested in applying for the position?"

"Captain Scott!" She raised a hand to slap him, but he caught her wrist and held it fast.

"Miss Upshall, you are far too highly wrought," he said silkily. He brought her wrist to his lips and brushed them across her pulse point, never taking his gaze from hers.

She tried to pull away, but his grip was firm and

persistent. Like a bird charmed by a snake, she lost the will to resist and allowed him to continue to hold her hand.

He stroked the back of it with his thumb. Tendrils of pleasure followed his touch, ebbing and flowing like a rising tide. She knew she shouldn't allow it, but it felt amazingly good.

"In my experience," he said softly, his voice a low rumble, like a lion's purr, "when a woman protests this much, it means she hasn't had the attention of a man recently and is in desperate need of it."

That broke the spell.

"You conceited swine! Perhaps if you consorted with women other than barmaids and trollops, you'd recognize a lady's revulsion when you see it."

His gaze dropped to her breasts, where the hard tips showed like a pair of raised buttons under the man's shirt she was wearing.

"Believe me, Miss Upshall. I can read the signals you're sending, and revulsion is not in evidence."

"Why, you—"

His mouth swallowed the rest of her response. True to his word, he'd asked no permission to kiss her again.

She knew she should fight, but his lips were firm and demanding and despite her best resolve, her insides melted like a dish of butter left in the sun.

It made no sense. He was everything she despised in a man—arrogant and cocksure and totally in control. He was holding her against her will, for pity's sake, and yet, his body spoke in some hot secret language and her body yearned to answer him in kind. When his tongue teased along the seam of her lips, she ached with the urge to open to him.

She had to be strong. She had to win free before he

shattered her will completely. She pressed against his chest, but he was unyielding as English oak.

Two can play at this sort of game, she decided and abruptly switched tactics. She was no match for him in strength. She stopped struggling and let her arms and legs go suddenly slack. She was dead weight in his embrace.

"What's the matter with you, woman? Are you insensible?" He pulled back from their kiss, alarmed. "You're limp as a jellyfish."

She straightened and stomped down on his foot as hard as she could. He released her and stepped back a pace.

"Jellyfish carry a sting, I'm told," she said with vinegar in her tone.

"Eve! Oh, there you are!" Sally appeared at the double doors. "Come and choose before all the best gowns are gone." She disappeared as quickly as she came amid a shower of giggles.

"If you'll excuse me, Captain," Eve said, with a mocking curtsey. "I believe I need to try on one of your old mistress's gowns. Do not construe that as an application for the position. Truth to tell, I'd sooner run around naked."

"I can arrange that," he said darkly.

"Not and play the gentleman you're pretending to be." She turned to go but he stopped her with a hand to her forearm.

"There's something between us here, Eve."

Her name on his lips sent a shiver of pleasure through her. She tamped it down.

"Miss Upshall to you," she corrected.

"Blast and damn, whatever you want to call yourself, so be it. But you can't deny you feel it, too." His features softened and he looked at her with hungry intensity. "When you change your mind, my chamber is at the end of the hall."

"I won't change my mind."

"Your body will change it for you," he said with eerie assurance. "Trust me, lass. I know my way around a woman's body and yours is ripe for the taking. Come to me and you'll not regret it. I promise."

"Careful, Captain." She shot an evil glare at his groin. "Jellyfish know several effective places to sting a man."

She turned on her heel and rejoined her friends with her head held high. But inside, she was quaking, thinking about what might happen the next time she found herself alone with the cursed man.

Jellyfish had no spines. No spines at all.

Chapter Seven

Nick rolled over on the bed and looked around. He could've sworn he hadn't sought his mattress alone.

"Nicholas," a feminine voice called.

Ah! There she was, wearing his shirt and slop trousers again. They'd never looked better.

"Oh, dear." Eve glanced down at herself and then back at him with a heavy-lidded gaze. "The knot in that rope belt has come undone again, and I greatly fear I'm about to lose my trousers."

"You'll look all the better without them, luv," he said, rising naked and rampant from his bed to go to her.

She greeted him by wrapping her arms around his neck while he rucked up the hem of the shirt and made short work of the rope. He thumbed her navel for a moment and then slid his palm inside the waist of the loose trousers, over her sweetly rounded belly and down to her damp curls.

She gasped in pleasure and lifted her face to him for a kiss. She parted her legs to allow him better access and leaned into his hand as he cupped her sex. He lowered his mouth to nip hers. She squirmed, trying to thrust her secrets toward him.

"Patience," he murmured as he toyed with her lips. He slanted his mouth across hers, tasting her, teasing her with his tongue, till she made another noise of frustration.

He slid his fingers along the slick cleft between her legs, and she moaned into his mouth. Her little nub of pleasure swelled up to be stroked. He spread her with two fingers and slid back and forth over her sensitive spot with long slow strokes.

The trousers dropped over her hips and she stepped out of

*them, moaning with frustration when she had to move away
from his touch for even a moment. Then she hooked a leg over
his hip and rocked against his palm, rubbing herself on him.
She was hot and ready.*

*The air was sweet with the musk of her arousal. His mouth
was suddenly at her breasts, sucking her nipples through the
thin cotton. His cock glided against the smooth skin of her
belly, searching for a darker, wetter home.*

*She stood on tiptoe, pressing herself against him. He reached
around and cupped her bottom.*

"Now, Nick," she panted in his ear. "I want . . ."

*Someone was knocking at the door. He ignored the inter-
ruption.*

"I want—"

*He bit down on her nipple and she cried out in aching
joy. His balls drew tight.*

*Nick hefted her up and then lowered her slowly onto his wait-
ing cock. He watched her intently as her mouth went passion-
slack. He'd never grow tired of looking at her.*

*She wrapped both legs around his waist as he lovingly
impaled her by finger widths. When at last he was completely
sheathed, she rocked against him once and came in shattering
waves. She threw her head back and a delightful tapestry of
profanity poured from her mouth at the same time.*

The knocking grew louder.

*Eve raised her head and looked down at him, doe-eyed. "I
want . . . TO GO TO CHARLESTON NOW."*

Nick jerked awake to find that Higgs was indeed
pounding on his chamber door. But nothing else was
the same as his dream. He was very much alone in his
big bed. The linens were balled in a disheveled mass and
one corner of his pillow was sodden where he'd been
sucking on it in his sleep.

Damnation! That's what happened when a man went
without a good hard swive for too infernally long!

"Come," he barked to Higgs. His enraged cock still throbbed. *Better not say that again.*

"B-beggin' your pardon, Cap'n," Higgs said. "You've a number of callers. They're lining up again already. I thought as you should know."

Male ears had pricked at the news that three likely young ladies fresh from England were in residence at Whispering Hill. Every day, shopkeepers and sailors alike called on "Lord Nick" under some pretext or other, but it was an open secret that they were only there to snatch a look at the new lovelies.

"W-we'd make out like highwaymen if we charged admission," Higgs observed sourly at the end of the day as the last of the long line of potential suitors finally headed back down the hill to St. Georges. "They'll be coming from the other islands as w-well before you know it.

Nick nodded absently. He should have been glad interest ran so high. It meant his guests' stay would be relatively short and he could forget about maintaining the façade of gentility. He could return to his former libertine ways.

It was difficult to get roaring drunk each night knowing he'd face three accusing faces at breakfast the next morning.

He was setting a new record for going without a woman in his bed while on dry land. Probably why he'd wakened sucking his pillow with a cockstand stiff enough to pitch a tent over.

He'd never been one for brothels. As master of a trim ship, he'd never seen a bordello clean enough to suit him—either the girls or the linens.

But he couldn't even think of replacing Magdalen as long as he was acting as guardian for three marriageable young ladies.

Unless, of course, he could lure Miss Upshall into the post. He'd never met a woman he couldn't seduce, but this one was leading him quite a dance. Evidently, she didn't remember the man was supposed to lead.

Nick was used to women falling into his hand the moment they caught his eye. Eve Upshall avoided his gaze.

He suspected he could convince her if he could only catch her alone long enough. He'd felt her yield when he kissed her. His fingers had brushed her quickening pulse. She wanted him. He was sure of it.

She just wouldn't admit it.

And Nick would know no relief until she did.

The infuriating Miss Upshall was careful never to be without at least one of the others by her side at all times. Now the three of them entered his dining room arm in arm, their broad hoops filling the arched entry.

"Good evening, ladies."

Nicholas made an elegant leg to his guests as they all settled in their places for the evening meal. He held out the chair next to him for Eve, but she breezed past it and sank into the seat opposite his first mate at the far end of the Bermudian cedar table.

Miss Munroe giggled and took the proffered chair instead. Nick slid her close to the table, determined not to recognize Eve's slight. He took his seat, thrusting a corner of his napkin into his collar.

"I trust you all passed a pleasant day," he said.

Nick certainly hadn't. The troop of men filing in and out of his study on the flimsiest of excuses, angling for introductions to the ladies, wore thin after a very short while.

And he'd been at it for several days.

"If by 'pleasant' you mean to ask if we enjoyed being ogled as if we were prize heifers, then yes. By all means, we had a jolly good day," Eve said with a poisonous smile.

Santorini, Nick's cook, had ratcheted up the quality and diversity of his menus in deference to the new members of the household. He'd really outdone himself with the shellfish bisque that started their meal. Nick ignored Eve's sniping comment and spooned it up heartily. The white soup would have done credit to a duke's table.

"Everyone seems friendly and polite," Miss Smythe observed so softly Nick had to strain to hear her.

"Yes, indeed, polite to a fault. I confess myself over-awed by the islanders' mannerliness," Eve said. "I was particularly gratified by the way they restrained themselves from checking our teeth."

Higgs nearly spewed the bisque out his nose.

"Miss Upshall, my purpose is to see the three of you suitably wed. In order to do that, you need bridegrooms and a man usually wants to see what he's getting into before he allows himself to be leg-shackled for life," Nick said, grasping his spoon as if it were a dirk. "How else would you suggest we proceed?"

"You already know my sentiments on the subject." Eve placed her spoon on the table with icy precision. "I suggest we proceed to Charleston, where bridegrooms who are willing to make that commitment without benefit of inspecting us first await our arrival. You may even stay on as witness to our nuptials, since our welfare seems to concern you so gravely."

"Oh, Evie," Miss Munroe said. "You know I can't bear to set foot on another ship."

"Penny, you still want to go on, don't you?" Eve said,

peering down the table at her friend. "Remember how Lieutenant Rathbun described your intended as the kindest and gentlest of men."

Miss Smythe glanced from Eve to Miss Munroe, then at Peregrine and finally at her own lap.

"We'll put it to a vote," Eve said.

All of them began to speak at once, arguing the merits of staying or going.

"No, by thunder, we will not!" Nick snatched the napkin from his throat and slammed it to the table. He couldn't drink, couldn't sleep without dreaming of rutting her and now the wench was even stealing away his appetite for fine food. "This is no damned democracy. I decide where and when the *Susan B* sails. I'll not take you to Charleston and there's an end to it."

His outburst shocked them into silence. They all stared at their soup till Santorini came to clear the table. The cook muttered in Italian under his breath, obviously dismayed over how much they'd left in their bowls.

The next course was a succulent baked sole with mango glaze. Miss Upshall forked up a healthy bite, shot Nick a mocking grin and slipped it between her luscious lips, making appreciative noises.

"This is truly splendid, Mr. Santorini," she said while his cook balanced the used crockery in his arms.

"Grazie, signorina, mille grazie." Santorini nearly turned backflips bowing and scraping his thanks. Then he hightailed it to the kitchen, which was in a separate building behind the main house. Santorini, like the rest of the servants at Whispering Hill, was overanxious to please the three women as far as Nick was concerned.

Everyone at the dining table followed Eve's lead, and began to relax. Even Higgs smiled and fell to his meal with relish.

Power trickled steadily from Nick's end of the table.

Usually his word alone was enough to ensure instant obedience. His men certainly never questioned him.

But he wasn't on the deck of the *Susan Bell*. He was adrift in the shadowy realm of respectable femininity, a place he'd heretofore avoided as if it was laced with uncharted shoals. He didn't understand the rules of engagement, but he recognized his position in a heart-beat.

Eve Upshall had the wind of him, and he'd never catch her if he continued on this heading. A change of strategy and a course correction were definitely needed.

He retrieved his napkin, tucked it back under his chin and decided to give the matter a think.

Eve led the group in harmless chatter, which he easily ignored. In the candlelight, the gentle curve of her graceful neck drew his eye. Once again, she was wearing the blue muslin, the same dress she'd been wearing when he fished her from the sea. He'd noticed she avoided wearing Magdalen's castoffs. But now the muslin was freshly laundered and starched, and the lace at her bodice led his gaze around its deep scoop.

Her breasts were trussed up into fashionable "rising moons." Her creamy skin glinted with the luster of satin. Respectable matron or slattern, fashion dictated they all emphasize their femininity by baring a good deal of skin from the nipples up.

Nick wondered what it would be like to rub his cock along the valley between Eve's delightful mounds till he spewed his seed all over them.

He moved his napkin to his lap to hide the aching bulge in his breeches.

If the little minx didn't want him to ogle, why display everything but the pinks of her nipples on that narrow shelf of fabric?

And just the thought of those strawberry buds gave him even more astoundingly tight breeches.

And an epiphany.

He realized immediately where respectable women enjoyed seeing and being seen. Where they delighted in flaunting themselves and their charms with reckless abandon. All through the meat course, he refined his idea, envisioning her possible countermeasures and marshaling his own forces.

"I have a thought," he said after he finished a remarkable slice of pork loin in silence. "I'm thinking I haven't made any opportunity for you to become acquainted with the other ladies who live on the islands."

"Do you mean we should have them for tea?" Miss Smythe asked.

Eve narrowed her eyes at him, obviously recognizing his opening gambit for what it was.

"That's a fine idea, Miss Smythe," he said genially, "but I confess I'd not want to leave the gentlemen out entirely. Maybe something with card playing and music and—"

"And dancing?" Miss Munroe leaped in just as he'd hoped.

"Assuredly, if you wish. I suppose we could shove back the furniture and hire a fiddler for an evening or two." He snapped his fingers as if the thought had only just occurred to him. "You see, I'm considering hosting a house party."

"A house party!" Miss Munroe clapped her hands.

"Yes, a weeklong affair, I'm thinking. We could send out invitations to some of the best folk." A house party would allow the women to feel completely relaxed in his home since there would be a few matrons about. When the event was spread over a number of days, a party always broke up into smaller groups catering to divergent interests. While her friends played at Blind Man's Bluff or sang around his clavichord, Nick would divide and conquer. There'd surely be another opportunity for him to find himself alone somewhere in his rambling home with Miss Upshall.

He leaned back in his chair as Miss Munroe and Miss Smythe carried his idea forward as if it were their own. Eve had no way to gainsay it. Picnics, archery and lawn bowling were all debated and approved. Then when their ideas for the party seemed to sag a bit, he tossed in, "And I'm thinking a new gown apiece for you ladies would not come amiss."

As soon as the words were out of his mouth, Miss Upshall's eyes flared with delight. He realized he'd made a tactical error, but he wasn't sure where.

"Why, Captain Scott, what a generous gesture. But on top of the expense of a long house party, that seems unfair to you," she said, leaning her cheek on her palm in thought. When she snapped her fingers, he recognized the gesture as a parody of his own. "What about a ball?"

Nick frowned. "A ball?"

"Oh, yes!" Miss Munroe now slid firmly into the opposing camp. "Is there anything more romantic than a ball?"

"I like to dance," Miss Smythe added shyly.

"Even though your home does have many guest rooms, it can only accommodate so many. But a ball, which shouldn't require you to provide lodging, would allow you to invite many more people," Eve said, her logic flawless. "And your stated purpose is for us to meet as many eligible men as possible, is it not?"

"There's the rub, Miss Upshall," he said with a triumphant grin. She'd run herself into a narrow inlet this time with no clearance to turn around. "My home is spacious, but I have no ballroom. Even if we cleared out the dining room"—he waved a hand around the largest room in his home, which he'd designed around the cedar table that expanded to seat twenty when all the leaves were in place—"we'd still be hard-pressed to make space for more than a half dozen couples or so to dance at once. A reel is quite vigorous, you know."

"Then we must choose a different venue," Eve said, neatly closing the trap on him.

"I-I could inquire about hiring the town hall," the traitorous Higgs offered.

Around the table, ideas for the ball bounced from one woman to the next, the plans zipping beyond his control, like a hooked marlin diving for deep water. Eve's new scheme quickly escalated past the point of reeling it in.

"Oh, Captain—" Eve finally deigned to include him in the discussion. "Since this ball constitutes a savings for you over your original plan, I do trust you'll still be willing to provide new ball gowns for us."

All the feminine heads turned expectantly in his direction.

"Of course," he said in resignation. Nick glared at his first mate. "I expect Higgs can see to the arrangements for new ball gowns and all the necessary accoutrements while he's off hiring a hall tomorrow!"

Sometimes, in the smoke of battle a promising action turned south when a man least expected it. A wise man had to know when to withdraw from an engagement, so he might regroup and fight another day.

Nicholas wished them good evening and excused himself before Eve Upshall forced him to wave his napkin like a white flag.

Chapter Eight

"I think I'm far too flat in back, don't you?" Sally twisted her neck before the long looking glass, trying to catch a glimpse of her own derriere. "Give it a look, then, won't you, Evie?"

The women all enjoyed their own chambers, but frequently met in Sally's, since hers was the middlemost and boasted the largest looking glass. Usually the face-sized mirrors in their own rooms were fine for Eve and Penny, but they were preparing for "Lord Nick's Ball" that evening. Being able to view the full effect of their new gowns was an important consideration. And for Sally, it seemed critical.

Her pale brows scrunched into a frown. "Evie, don't you think I need a bumroll?"

"I think your bum is adequate for all normal purposes," Eve said, briefly glancing up from the book in her lap. "Without an additional roll."

Eve returned to her book. Think what she might about "Lord Nick," the wicked devil knew how to stock a library. She'd found a relatively easy book on the history of animal husbandry and was using it to hone her limited reading skills. The subject matter wasn't exactly riveting, but she was able to cobble the letters into intelligible words much quicker now than when she'd started.

"Eve's right. You're lovely, Sally," Penelope said. She was already trussed into her new lemon yellow sack dress. Penny perched delicately on the edge of a straight-backed chair to avoid creating any wrinkles in the yards of silk. "I expect the men of these isles have never seen the likes of you."

"You, too, Penny," Eve said. "That yellow makes your skin glow and against your dark hair, why, it's enchanting. You'll catch plenty of masculine eyes."

"Doubt he—they'll even notice I'm there." Penelope looked toward the open window, where the setting sun was fractured by the rectangles of multiple panes.

"Nonsense," Eve said. It hurt sometimes to see how little Penelope thought of herself. "Besides, tonight is just a chance to have a little fun at the captain's expense. Remember that you have a fine, respectable gentleman waiting for you in Charleston."

"I don't want a fine respectable gentleman in Charleston," Penny said softly.

"Pen has her eye on someone here already." Sally hitched up a bumroll under her panniers despite Eve's opinion. Once she tied off the tabs, she smoothed down the pink silk panels of her gown and ruffled petticoat. She turned sideways and eyed herself critically, then gave her cork-enhanced bottom a wiggle. Sally smiled at her reflection with a satisfied nod. "Our Penelope's been mooning around over someone for the last fortnight, but she won't tell me who he is."

"Is this true, Penny?" Eve closed the book. She didn't think she could persuade Sally to continue to Charleston. Her fear of another wreck was just too great, but Eve was counting on Penelope to join her.

Penny shrugged and smiled. "You know Sally. If nothing interesting is happening, we can always count on her to make something up."

Before Eve could pursue the matter further, their new maid, Daya, appeared in the doorway with news that Eve's bath was ready. "Lord Nick" hadn't ever kept any female servants before. Mr. Higgs had let it slip that the captain's previous mistress wouldn't tolerate any other women in the house, but Daya lived with her husband Sanjay in the small caretaker's cottage on the edge of the captain's land. Sanjay was a brilliant gardener and kept Whispering Hill's expansive grounds in pristine condition. So when Eve and her friends needed a lady's maid, Daya was close at hand to help and glad of the work.

Eve thanked Daya and hurried back to her own chamber where a jasmine-scented hip bath waited.

As usual, Eve allowed Daya to loosen her stays, but declined help in disrobing. She didn't want even this calm, silent East Indian woman to see her naked.

Just before Daya slipped away, Eve called out. "Oh! The modiste is supposed to be delivering a second petticoat for me. Could you watch for it and bring it to me as soon as it arrives please?"

Daya nodded and sketched her exotic gesture of farewell before closing the door behind her.

Once the maid was gone, Eve reached under her skirt and untied her panniers. The wire contraption fell to the floor and she stepped out of it. She toed off her slippers. Then she wiggled the rest of the way out of her gown, peeled off her chemise and rolled off her stockings.

With satisfaction, she sank into the hot water. She closed her eyes for a moment, drinking in the fragrant steam before she picked up the jar of soap and sudsed her hands.

She reached as far as she could over her shoulders, lathering her back. The awful bumps and ridges of the scars were still there. She wondered if they were still angry and red. She wet a cloth and let the water sluice down her back.

The scars on her soul were angry. Why shouldn't the ones on her back be as well?

As Nicholas strode through the foyer on the way to his study, he noticed Daya squatting in that inexplicable Indian fashion of repose by his open front door. She rose as soon as she saw him and templed her hands before her.

"Please do not think me idle, Lord Nick," she said with a deep salaam. "I but wait for a package for Miss Eve. Ah! There it must be."

A gig shuddered to a stop in the circular drive and a man hopped down with a large parcel under his arm. Daya skittered out to retrieve it and hurried back.

"This must be something of supreme importance," Nick said with a grin.

"Assuredly so. It is her new petticoat."

"I paid for it, so that makes it mine. Why don't I deliver it to her?" He tried to take the package, but Daya didn't release it instantly as he expected. "Where the devil is she?"

"In her chamber, but she is with her bath, sir, and would not be liking you to come in." Daya tugged on the parcel, but he managed to snatch it away finally.

"Her bath, hmmm?"

His imagination treated him to a rakish vision of Eve rising from her ablutions, rosy-skinned and glistening, like Venus rising from the waves. Desire denied was leaving him with an almost perpetual erection. If this kept up, he'd need to see his tailor for some permanent alterations to his breeches. He held the parcel strategically before him. He'd be happy to let Eve see the evidence of his arousal, but he didn't want to embarrass his gardener's wife.

"Didn't anyone ever tell you that cleanliness is next

to godliness, Daya? Godliness is beyond me. Perhaps I should settle for the next best thing."

"Oh, she will not be happy with me," Daya said, trying to reach for the package.

"You work for me, not Miss Upshall. If I'm pleased, that's all that need concern you." Nick turned and headed for the wing that held the row of bedchambers. "Don't worry," he called over his shoulder to Daya. "Surely you've heard the ugly rumor that I'm acting the gentleman now. I'll knock first."

It wasn't his fault Eve answered his knock with, "Come in, Daya."

He turned the knob and pushed the door open slowly. A gentleman would announce himself at once, he knew.

Fortunately, he was not really a gentleman. He was a smuggler at heart. Cunning and stealth had served him well in the past. He peered around the door.

Blast and damn! She had a privacy screen set up around the hip bath, but he could hear water splashing on the other side of the thin shield of silk.

"Just put the package on the bed," Eve said. "I'll unwrap it myself. That'll be all, thank you."

He trod across the room, careful to keep his footfalls as soft as possible and laid the parcel on the end of her bed. From this position, he made the happy discovery that the privacy screen did not wrap completely around the bath. Moreover, there was a well-placed mirror above her dressing table which canted at an angle that gave him a partial view of her.

He was treated to the sight of her soapy knee rising from the copper bath. If he bent down a little, he could make out the swell of her breast. The knee blocked any chance of spying a wet nipple. There was a bit of a slender arm. The teasing glimpse made his whole body ache.

He made a mental note to furnish her room with a larger looking glass at the first opportunity.

"I said, that'll be all, Daya." She half rose, enough for him to see her belly button peeping between her up-raised knees in the small glass.

He tiptoed to the door and, without going through, opened and shut it quietly, just as Daya would. For good measure, he slid the bolt, taking care not to make the slightest sound. The bathwater sloshed as she settled back into it.

The screen was low. He should be able to see over it, provided he could get close enough. With agonizing slowness, he toed off his boots and then crossed the floor on silent, stockinged feet.

Boldness had always yielded rich rewards in his past. The present was no exception.

Eve was faced away from him, but she reclined in the bath so he looked down on the crown of her head. She'd pulled her auburn hair into a topknot, baring her neck. A few tendrils had escaped and were teasing her tender nape.

He ached to taste her skin just there at her hairline.

His position gave him a full view of her delectable breasts. They were all he'd imagined they'd be—creamy, rose-tipped mounds just begging to fit a man's palm. He could drown in the well between them and not care a whit.

His gaze traveled southward, over her ribs, past the indentation of her navel to the water's edge. Her secrets were obscured by a layer of soap bubbles.

He inhaled silently. Sweet jasmine. Spicy and exotic, the scent spoke to him of hot summer nights and sweat-slick bodies tangled up in inventive ways. His travels had taken him to places in the world where the giving and receiving of physical bliss had few restrictions.

Oh, how he'd love to school this prim English rose in a wide assortment of primitive pleasures.

She took up the jar of soap and dipped her fingers into it. Then she lathered her body, touching all those places he longed so to touch. When her fingers passed over her breasts, scrubbing across her nipples, bringing them to pert tightness, he fervently wished, like Shakespeare's Romeo, to be a glove on that hand. He nearly groaned aloud when her knees parted and her legs fell slack. Her hand dipped between them to wash her intimate folds.

And stayed to dally in those wet curls.

Nicholas swallowed hard. Magdalen had let him watch once while she pleasured herself. That time wasn't anywhere near as exciting as this stolen glimpse into a wench's private desires.

He'd thought to school Eve Upshall in the carnal arts. Perhaps she had a few things to teach him as well.

The soapy layer on the water parted and he saw, in wavering shadows, her fingers slipping between those tender nether lips. She stroked lightly. She circled. She spread herself wide with her other hand.

He was near to spilling his seed in his breeches.

Then she made a noise of frustration and stopped, planting both hands on the sides of the hip bath.

He bit his tongue to keep from urging her on.

Her head lolled to one side. She sighed and loosed a muttered string of invectives. He didn't catch the name attached to the curses, but she questioned someone's parentage back several generations, accused this person of copulating with various farm animals, invited him to "sod off" and ended with a heartfelt plea for the Prince of Darkness to "damn the man all to hell."

Nick grinned, hoping the curse was meant for him. The way she said it almost made the tirade an endearment.

She loosed a long sigh. Then she pulled her legs under her and rose from the bath, water streaming down her curves. Little soap runnels disappeared in the crevice of her heart-shaped buttocks.

But instead of being titillated, Nick frowned. He was no longer interested in that lovely bum. His attention was riveted on her slender back.

It was covered with recently healed scars. Diamonds of healthy flesh between the angry crisscrossed weals told him the stripes had been laid on by a master of the whip. None of the marks had been overstruck, but each had broken her delicate skin. The bastard who'd administered this punishment had placed the lash with exquisite care for every stroke, not a jot out of place. No doubt, he was someone who fancied himself an artist and liked to leave distinctive marks on his victims.

Nicholas had witnessed plenty of floggings in his years at sea. He'd ordered it done once when a seaman was caught red-handed stealing water from the scuttlebutt when the ship was under drought rations. Even when it was necessary, flogging a man was a nasty business.

He'd be the first to admit Eve Upshall was a sorely trying woman, but nothing she might have done could possibly warrant punishment like this.

"Bloody hell," he said softly. "Who did this to you?"

Chapter Nine

She whirled around to face him and her eyes flared wide. Her lovely mouth formed a gasping "Oh!" as she grabbed up the towel to cover herself.

"What the devil do you think you're doing here?"

"I should think that's obvious." His gaze swept slowly over her exposed wet skin.

Then his eyes narrowed, refusing to be distracted by the glistening tops of her breasts and the length of her shapely bare legs. He thanked God for small towels as he strode around the privacy screen and grasped her shoulders. He turned her around to get a closer look at the devastation of her back.

"Who did this?" he demanded again, yanking the towel down so he could see the full extent of the damage.

"If you don't leave this instant, I'll scream," she threatened over her shoulder as she tried to wiggle free of his grip.

"If you were going to scream, you'd have done it already." He shook his head at the way her perfect flesh had been marred.

He ran a fingertip along one stripe that started below her left shoulder blade and ended at the bottom of her right rib cage. Tiny muscles shivered under her skin. She'd been put through hell and her ravaged flesh retained a memory of the nightmare in its very fibers.

Rage boiled through his veins. A muscle ticked at his jawline.

"Name the man who did this, Eve." His tone was silky and even, but laden with menace. "Wherever he is, I'll find him. And I'll take great pleasure in gutting the bastard. Slowly."

"I don't know his name."

She twisted out of his grasp, leaving only her towel in his hands. Naked, she skittered around to the other side of the privacy screen and wrapped her fingers over the top of it.

"Don't come any closer."

As if that thin piece of silk could stop him if he was determined to follow.

He looked at her lost towel and then back to her, raising a quizzical brow. "Why haven't you screamed, by the way?"

"I . . . I'm not the excitable sort. I didn't scream about the shark, did I?"

"No, you didn't," he admitted, but he'd wager the *Susan Bell* she'd screamed while those stripes were being laid. He'd seen men he judged to be tougher than he try to keep mum during a flogging. To a man, they'd ended up wailing and pleading, their spirit completely broken along with their flesh.

"Now, please leave and I'll not mention this to—"

"Oh." He snapped his fingers as the realization dawned. "Now I know why you don't scream. You don't want anyone else to see your back."

She looked away from him and he knew he was right.

"That's why you insist on wearing gowns that lace up the front," he said. "That's why you don't have Daya attend you in your bath as the others do. I'll have you know she came to me the other day very concerned that you were unhappy with her service."

Eve worried her bottom lip.

"You need privacy, even from your lady's maid, so you can keep your secret."

She glared at him. "Expecting others not to invade my bath doesn't seem an unreasonable demand."

"I didn't invade," he reminded her. "I knocked and you invited me to enter."

"I assumed you were Daya."

"My dear Miss Upshall, I cannot be held to account for your assumptions." He leaned toward the privacy screen till he caught a whiff of her clean, jasmine-scented skin. She smelled good enough to eat. "Just as you are not to blame for my assumption that you were a gently bred lady. But I won't hold the truth against you."

"I've told you the truth."

"Perhaps," he allowed. "However, I can think of no reason why a lady of quality would bear the marks you bear."

She turned her face away, unwilling to meet his gaze.

"Unless you are not the lady your dress and demeanor proclaim you to be," he said, dipping his toe in the un-explored water of that new idea. If she weren't a lady of good family, the impediments to her becoming his mistress dwindled by the moment. He took a step toward the edge of the privacy screen. "Shall we test that notion?"

"Another step and I *will* scream, I promise you."

"No, you won't and we both know it," Nick said. "So as long as you're in this delightful state of undress, we'll remain unmolested because you can't chance anyone else seeing your back."

"So you intend to take advantage of a lady's misfortune," she accused, her eyes narrowed to slits. "You loathsome toad. You're absolutely despicable."

"Alas, dear Eve, you have no idea." His hand shot to

his chest as if her barb had struck home. Then a wicked grin tilted his mouth. "However, even the depths of my depravity do not extend to forcing myself on an unwilling woman."

"What do you call this then?"

"Negotiation," he said with a grin. "A parley over the terms of surrender, if you will."

"I am not yours to be had for the asking."

"No, you're actually mine for the taking." He stepped around the edge of the screen and panic contorted her features. There was no cloth close by, so she covered her breasts with one arm while her other hand shielded her sex from his view. Tears trembled on her dusky lashes.

If he listened to his cock, he'd cheerfully toss her on the bed and swive the living lights out of her. She was clearly in need. With only a little skillful bedplay, she'd remember that her body was clamoring for a man's touch. Hadn't he caught her with her cunning little fingers trying to satisfy the ache between her legs in the bath?

But while his cock spurred him on, his conscience flayed him. He wanted this woman. Wanted her with a desperation that bordered on madness, but not like this.

He wanted her soft and willing. He wanted her begging for him. He wanted her to need him just as desperately as he was coming to need her.

He ran a feverish gaze over the hills and valleys of her form. A pleasing arrangement of soft and slender, she was all that was woman. A joy to his eyes and a siren's call to his throbbing cock.

But there'd be no joy in forcing her. He'd take her willing or not at all.

"Fortunately for you, I do possess a few scruples," he

said softly as he draped the towel over her shoulders and turned around to give her privacy. "But only a few, so don't tempt me further."

He heard the padding of her bare feet on the polished heart-of-pine floor and the rustle of fabric. When he turned back around, she'd pulled on a wrapper and knotted the belt at her waist. Since the sight of her body was still burned in his brain, the thin fabric offered her no shield from his imagination.

But the disturbing image of her scarred back reared up to slap him.

"Flogging is a serious punishment, reserved for serious crimes," he said, propping a hip on the edge of her bed. "What did you do?"

"Nothing." Her chin quivered, but she raised it slightly. "I did nothing to merit the lash. And I did not lie to you. I *am* wellborn. My father was Sir Anthony Upshall of Kent. I am a lady born and I expect to be treated as one."

"If that's the case, the insult done to your back must have carried a double sting," he said. She'd have been bare-breasted while that sort of punishment was administered, he was sure. Stripped to the waist and paraded to the stake with a crowd of onlookers jostling for the best position. His fingers itched to strangle the lot. "What were you accused of, then?"

Her lips thinned into a narrow line. "If I'm innocent, what does it matter?"

"It matters to me." The words slipped out before he thought better of them. They were dangerously close to a declaration that she meant something to him. "I mean, your pain matters. Um, naturally when someone . . . anyone really . . . is unjustly accused . . . it should matter to . . . all civilized people."

Christ, that was eloquent.

She had him as tangle-tongued as Higgs. He did *not* have feelings for this woman. He would not allow it.

This was just about the bedding he richly deserved from her. Nothing more.

"In this instance, you are an exceptional case, Captain. You'd be surprised how little people care for another's pain if it affords them a bit of entertainment."

"I wish I'd been there to stop them," he said through clenched teeth. Anger and lust coursed through him so hotly and so intermingled that he was at a loss to separate them.

"I wish you had, too." She turned away from him and leaned on the open French door, looking out onto the little private garden. She sighed and breathed in the perfumed air.

He hoped the riot of flowers gave her solace. Hannah had certainly loved them.

Where the devil did that come from? He'd often gone for months without thinking of his dead wife. He banished her quickly to the back of his mind. No point living in the past when there was every chance he might soon coax this warm, vibrant woman before him into his bed.

"You seem to enjoy my gardens," he said, coming up behind Eve. Her hair was tumbling from its topknot in beguiling little tendrils along her nape. He brought one lock to his lips and inhaled deeply. Her skin looked so soft, his hands were on her shoulders before he realized it. "I'm glad the flowers please you."

She flinched under his touch, but surprisingly, she didn't pull away.

"It is beautiful here," she admitted.

Was it his imagination or did she lean into him by the slightest of measures?

"Beauty for the eye has a way of healing the soul, I'm

told." Encouraged, he kneaded her shoulders softly. She sighed again and bent her head toward first one, then the other shoulder, as if working out the cricks in her muscles. "Perhaps being here will ease your pain. I can help you forget. Let me try, Eve."

The wrapper slipped off one shoulder and he lowered his lips to taste her flesh. Her breath hitched as he delivered a string of baby kisses up to her ear before he took the soft lobe between his lips and sucked. He considered it a minor miracle that she didn't pull away.

Instead, she made a small noise of pleasure, so faint he couldn't be sure if he'd only imagined it.

His cock sprang to jubilant life, just in case.

Nick could scarce believe his luck. He ran his hands down her arms and then slid one around her to pull her closer to him. Surely she could feel his desire pressing against her bottom, but she didn't object. He purposely positioned his hand beneath her breast, poised to cup it. Nick teased along the lower crease with his thumb instead of grasping her immediately. Rushing this woman had been ineffective. Perhaps a campaign of stealth would yield the reward he sought.

He nibbled back down her neck, noticing the way her breath caught. When she reached up a tentative hand to ruffle his hair, he nearly whooped in victory, but settled for a love bite on her neck instead.

She moaned softly.

It was time for a strategic advance.

He moved his hand up, brushing her breast lightly. She arched her back, pressing her softness into his palm. Her nipple was already tight, but when he parted the wrapper to touch her bare flesh, he purposely avoided that taut peak. Instead, he circled it slowly, tormenting that needy bit of flesh with the anticipation of his caress.

"You're beautiful, Eve." He slid the wrapper off on

one side and bent his head to place a soft kiss on her scarred shoulder blade.

A muffled sob escaped her lips when his lips touched her ruined back.

He'd intended to claim her nipple with his fingers at the same time that he kissed her back. But before he could capture that tight bud, Eve turned in his arms and palmed his cheeks. Without seeming to notice or care that her robe was open and nearly off, she raised herself on tiptoe, never taking her aqua eyes from his. She tilted her mouth up and kissed him, softly at first and then with an urgency that thrilled him to his toes.

She'd struck her colors and run up the white flag. Eve Upshall was as good as his.

Chapter Ten

Foolish, foolish, foolish, Eve chanted to herself even as she chased his tongue with her own. She knew it was beyond folly to give in to the terrible cravings this man stirred in her. Every ounce of reason argued against it. But reason was no match for the urges of her body.

He'd seen her back and still called her beautiful.

He'd pressed a healing kiss to the horrible scars.

Something inside her she'd thought shriveled and dead rose up. Her battered heart sang.

His mouth found her breasts, tugging and suckling. Desire streaked from her nipples to her womb. The deep call of need that she'd started to assuage in her bath and then denied in frustration and loneliness, began afresh in a low drumbeat between her legs.

His hands were everywhere. Her skin danced where his rough calluses nicked it. The stubble of his cheek against her ribs, his tongue, warm and wet as it dipped into her navel—she was drowning in a wash of sensation.

Then he dropped to his knees before her and covered her with his mouth. Her knees nearly buckled, but his hands massaging her buttocks kept her upright.

His tongue found her cleft and sweetly divided her. He found her aching nub and teased it.

She was dimly aware that words were pouring from her throat, profane and earthy words, slipping out in tender tones as if they were endearments. He seemed encouraged by them, for he positioned both her legs over his shoulders, hefted her up and carried her to the bed, still tonguing her. She grasped his head to stead herself, giddy with pleasure. When he dropped her on the feather tick, she laughed aloud for pure joy.

Nicholas grinned down at her, his face flushed, his lips glistening wetly.

"So you can laugh! And a right pleasant sound it is, to be sure." He chuckled. "I'll have to make sure you do it more often."

He dived onto the bed with her and settled his hips between her splayed legs. Taking her head gently between his palms, he tipped her mouth to his. She tasted herself on his lips, musky and hot. She groaned with need.

Pound, pound, pound.

No, wait! That wasn't her heart.

The loud knocking on the door was a dash of cold water. She wrenched her mouth away from his.

"Evie, are you all right?" Sally's voice came through the heavy pine.

"I'm fine," Eve called back, squirming under his weight. He took the hint and rolled off her.

"Why is your door locked?"

Eve's gaze snapped to Nick.

He shrugged. "A prudent man plans ahead."

"Keep quiet," she hissed before climbing out of bed and hurrying to the door. She pulled her wrapper up over her shoulders again and belted it closed. The desperate ache between her legs still throbbed. "I'm just finishing my bath."

"Is someone with you? I thought I heard voices."

Eve balled her fingers into fists. "You must have heard me . . . talking to Daya."

"Well . . ."

There was a long pause and Eve fervently prayed to whatever God protected liars that Daya wasn't currently standing at Sally's side.

"Tell her to hurry with your toilet," Sally said. "We need to be leaving soon or we'll be late! Do you want help with your hair?"

"No, dear. I can manage."

Sally had already helped her more than she knew. The madness was passing and Eve was thinking clearly once more.

Giving in to Captain Scott would have been just as weak as giving in to that cockney jailer at Newgate in exchange for a ration of unmoldy bread. She'd resisted then when her very survival hung in the balance.

Surely she could resist now, even though only her maidenhead was in jeopardy.

She glanced over at Nick, who still lounged full-length across her bed. He smiled lazily at her, but his eyes were lit from behind with a dark fire.

The cockney jailer had been missing several teeth and had sported a bad case of head lice, so even his appeal to her empty belly hadn't made her succumb.

But Nicholas Scott was enough to tempt a nun.

Still, Nick was using her own body against her, too. He was just aiming a bit lower than her stomach to accomplish his seduction. Not only was he more devilishly handsome than any mortal had a right to be, his bed skills promised to be beyond her wildest imaginings. Was there anything more wicked than that man's mouth on her—

Eve snipped off that thought before the memory of his tongue on her delicate private parts began to heat her blood once more. She leaned against the door.

"Why don't you see if Mr. Higgs has brought around the coach?" Eve suggested to Sally. "I'll be along directly."

"All right. If you're sure. But please hurry. This is my first ball and I don't want to miss anything."

Eve listened at the door till Sally's footfalls faded away completely.

"Come back to bed, Eve," Nick patted the space beside him. "Poor Miss Munroe. She doesn't realize the party has already started right here."

"No, Sally's correct. I need to get dressed if we're to arrive at the ball in a timely manner."

Nick frowned. "I'm the host of that blasted ball. They're not likely to start without us."

She didn't budge.

He sprang from the bed and closed the distance between them, pinning her between his body and the stout door with his long arms cutting off any escape.

"Eve, I want you."

His words made her throb. She'd never felt so empty, so achingly needy. So sure he could still the madness coursing through her. All she had to do . . .

His hot gaze seemed to peek into her soul. "And I know you want me."

"It's not that simple." She couldn't bear to look at him any longer.

"It is if you let it be." He cupped her chin and forced her to meet his gaze. "As I suspected, you're a passionate woman, Eve Upshall. It's wrong to deny your own nature."

She laughed again, this time with no joy at all. "I don't think I need look to someone like you to tell me what's right and what's wrong."

"Pray tell, what do you mean by 'someone like you'?"

He leaned close so she could feel his hard maleness pressed against her. Her belly clenched with renewed desire, but she tamped it down.

"A rogue, a smuggler, a drunkard, a scoundrel—"

"I see Higgs has been bragging about me again." His ribs jiggled against hers with a deep chuckle. "Eve, this is simply about pleasure."

His fingertips slid down her arms and found her hands. He brought one to his lips and placed a lover's kiss in her palm. Then he hooked one of her fingers in his mouth and sucked. She closed her eyes as her body wept fresh dew between her legs.

"If you say I wasn't giving you any pleasure, I'll know you for a liar."

Her body throbbed in response to his rumbling tone. He could make her entire being sing, but she had to stop before things moved past the prelude.

"Pleasure is beside the point." She shrank back, pressing her spine against the door.

"On what continent?"

"A lady—"

"A woman," he corrected, running his fingertips along her cheek, down her neck and over the swell of her breasts. She drew a shuddering breath. "A woman knows when her body will be well served. That should trump any notions of 'ladyness' all to hell."

"Well, it doesn't." She straightened her spine and met his gaze squarely, willing her body to keep from melting into him. "I am sufficiently covered now, Captain, so believe me when I tell you that I'll scream my bloody head off if you don't release me right this moment."

He covered her lips with his, trying to lure her back into his lusty fantasy. Warmth pooled in her groin, but she fought not to answer his summons to that dark hot place.

It took every ounce of will she possessed not to respond.

Just when her last shred of self-control was frayed to the breaking point, he pulled back and narrowed his eyes at her.

"Very well, Miss Upshall." He threw back the bolt on her door. "I shall leave *your ladyship* to diddling yourself in your bath. Though I noticed that you don't seem to have much talent for self-gratification. But since I've helped you along the way, there shouldn't be much further to go. I wish you a happier conclusion on the next go-round."

"Why, you—"

He was out the door and slamming it behind him before she could find a sufficiently foul oath for him. His voice came through the door to her.

"But there's no time to dawdle. Be quick about your diddling this time," he snarled. "We have a damned ball to attend."

Peregrine Higgs wanted to drive the coach down the steep track toward town, but the captain wouldn't have it. Instead, Pere rode beside his employer on a sorrel mare. They formed the rearguard of the coach, which lurched far too quickly around the tight corners for Peregrine's peace of mind. He'd have taken the slowest pace possible, mindful of the precious cargo traveling inside.

The only liberty he'd been allowed was handing the women into the waiting coach.

Miss Upshall was a fetching sight in her emerald gown, but a pair of deep grooves marred her brow. By rights, she ought to have been delighted with the world this night. After all, the ball was her idea, wasn't it?

The woman's a squall waiting to happen or I'm a Chinaman, Higgs thought. He tossed a glance at Nicholas Scott, who was riding in silence beside him. *Come to think of it, the captain don't look much sunnier than Miss Upshall.*

When two wicked weather fronts threatened to collide, a prudent seaman charted a course for the nearest port.

Miss Smythe had been surprisingly comely in her yellow gown. She was so quietlike, it was hard for a man to take much notice of her when a beauty like Miss Munroe was about, but this night Penelope Smythe was pretty as a buttercup in a meadow. She'd thanked Higgs in her soft tone as he handed her into the coach. He predicted Miss Smythe would not sit out any dances unless she pleaded that her feet were wore slick.

But Miss Munroe had looked like a bit of spun sugar in her new pink gown. She was rosy and fresh, as sweet a treat as any confectioner could fashion. Peregrine's mouth watered when he caught a fleeting glimpse of her neatly turned ankle as she climbed into the coach.

He'd shut the coach door, sealing the ladies in, feeling agreeably male after the sight of so much feminine folderol. He was justifiably proud of himself for making at least two of them very happy. He had been instrumental in shepherding this ball into existence, after all. Peregrine figured he'd laid the groundwork for his assault on the affections of Miss Sally Munroe.

Once they reached the town hall, he realized he was sadly mistaken.

Men from all over the islands, some from as far away as Irish Isle, had made the trip. The finest families were there, even the Tuckers, though Peregrine was grateful the captain's former friend, Saint George Tucker, was safely in the Colonies. "Saint" gave no quarter when it came to charming the ladies, which might have been why the captain and Saint George parted ways. Higgs wasn't sure.

But all those in attendance hoped to meet and suitably impress the three women Captain Scott had "snatched from the jaws of death." Word of their beauty had been stoked by the retelling of their harrowing experience in the deep. Now it seemed half the unattached men on Devil Isle fancied themselves taken with one—or all three!—of the newest additions to their pink-sand shores.

In the few minutes it took Higgs to see to the horses, the ladies' dance cards were completely filled. He couldn't have bought a reel with a single one of them, even if he'd had a chest full of doubloons to offer as payment.

So he helped himself to a cup of grog and moped by the open double doors. All he could do was watch as Miss Munroe tossed her golden curls, flirting and laughing with her dance partners. Each one of them seemed to believe that smile was especially for him.

Blast! There went gravel-voiced Tatem sashaying by with Miss Munroe beaming on his arm.

The captain came and stood beside him in silence for a while. Lord Nick watched the festivities with such a grim face, folk might think he was presiding over a hanging instead of the merriest ball the islands had ever seen.

"Belay that lubberly grog, Higgs." The captain pulled a silver flask from his vest pocket and handed it to Peregrine. "This night's work calls for sterner stuff."

Higgs noticed Captain Scott's gaze rarely left Miss Upshall as she performed the intricate steps of a minuet. She was paired with Archibald Snickering, the governor's pasty-faced secretary. Miss Upshall smiled politely at her partner, but turned her head to the side when the dance called for a stylized kiss on the lips.

Miss Munroe did not turn hers.

Peregrine tipped the flask and let the whisky scald his throat in several eye-watering gulps.

"Y-you were right, sir," he admitted. "A house party would have been the w-wiser course."

"That ship's already sailed, Higgs." The captain clapped a sympathetic hand on Peregrine's shoulder. "Give it no more thought."

But it was hard not to wish back the moment when he'd offered to arrange this ball. He'd thought to win Miss Munroe's favor by it, but instead the woman who tormented his dreams was flaunting her charms before every man in the place except him.

He took another pull on the flask.

"Easy, lad. Check your bearings." The captain relieved Higgs of the spirits. "You've a long night before you."

The captain nodded at several other guests. "It seems I'm expected to act as if I'm the host of this debacle, so I'll leave you now." He started to push his way into the crush of people, then turned back. "Pace yourself, Mr. Higgs. And don't do anything foolish."

Too late.

Higgs was already doing something foolish. He couldn't seem to keep his eye from following Miss Munroe around the dance floor.

She never glanced his way once.

Higgs had stood night watch in the pouring rain with more cheer.

After the fiddler played three reels in a row, suddenly Peregrine found Miss Smythe standing before him, red-faced and fanning herself.

"Mr. Higgs." She bobbed a quick curtsey. "I'm so glad I found you."

He leaned toward her in order to hear her soft voice over the din of so many people, all talking and laughing at once. She wrinkled her nose as her gaze darted about the room, and he realized that beneath the heavy perfume worn by almost everyone, not all the bodies pressed into the hall were terribly clean. Being a sea-man had dulled his sensibilities somewhat in that department, but he did catch a fresh whiff of vanilla wafting from the lady before him.

Along with clean feminine skin.

". . . and so I'm afraid with all this dancing and so many people . . ." she was saying. Her hands fluttered at her sides. "I'm fair done in."

"Would you be needing some fresh air perhaps?" he asked politely.

Her smile carved a deep dimple in her left cheek. Peregrine wondered why she didn't do it more often.

"If you'd be so kind," she said shyly. "I don't feel I know any of these new gentlemen well enough to take the air with them."

"Of course," Peregrine said, making a smart leg and offering her his arm. "It would be my pleasure, Miss Smythe."

Perhaps Miss Munroe would see him escorting her friend out into the soft island night and think better of him, he reasoned. A little jealousy, he'd heard, wasn't necessarily a bad thing and might lead to a realization of the heart's true condition. He resisted the urge to crane his neck to see if Sally Munroe was watching.

As they entered the small foyer, Higgs ground to a halt.

Adam Bostock, the captain of the *Sea Wolf*, stood in his path, feet spread shoulder-width, hands fisted on his hips.

"Hello P-P-Peregrine. Nice p-p-party," he sneered. "Tell your master I'm here."

Bostock's pale-eyed gaze raked Miss Smythe's form with a slow intimate appraisal.

Peregrine could take the insult to himself. His ship-mates teased him about his speech with such regularity, it no longer stung. He'd normally let Bostock's jab roll off him like water off an oilskin, but the jackal had no right to ogle a lady as if she were some doxy.

He shifted to place himself in front of Miss Smythe.

Higgs had sent open invitations to all the islands, but he'd never expected the man who despised his captain, and was hated with vehemence in return, to consider himself welcome.

Bostock wasn't going to enter the hall if Higgs could help it.

And he certainly wasn't going to ogle Miss Smythe again.

But it seemed Miss Smythe had other plans. She peeked around Peregrine toward the open door.

"Lieutenant Rathbun! Please excuse me, Mr. Higgs, but I know this gentleman." Miss Smythe padded smoothly around Peregrine to greet the man standing behind Bostock. "Oh, I'm so glad to see you. We feared you lost when we became separated during the wreck of the *Molly Harper.*"

She extended a hand to the newcomer and he bowed low over it.

"My dear Miss Smythe." His tone was proper, and he patted her hand like some long-lost uncle, but his gaze lingered at her bodice a trifle overlong for Peregrine's liking. "I, too, am delighted to find you unharmed. Are the others here as well?"

Before she could answer, the voice Higgs had heard thundering over many a gale stopped the music, causing the hall to go suddenly silent.

"Bostock!"

Captain Scott strode across the large room. The

crush of people parted like the Red Sea before Moses. Good thing. The captain would have trod over them if they hadn't skittered out of his path.

Murder glinted in his eye.

Peregrine swallowed hard. The captain had urged him not to give in to foolishness earlier.

Now Higgs feared he wouldn't be able to convince his captain to take his own advice.

Chapter Eleven

Nicholas pushed in front of Higgs to stand toe to toe with Adam Bostock.

"I don't recall issuing an invitation to any offal with feet, do you, Higgs?" Nick said, spoiling for a fight. "What are you doing here, Bostock?"

"Looking for some of my lost cargo, Nick." Bostock's gaze swept the room in unhurried fashion; then he raised a hand and examined his nails for some imagined bit of dust. He blew on them, and glared at Nick from under lowered brows. "It fell off the *Molly Harper* and I want it back. I understand you have it here."

Nick's fingers curled into fists. He'd sworn an oath not to kill the man, but that didn't mean he couldn't beat him to a bloody pulp if he got half the chance.

"I have nothing that belongs to you."

"You're probably right." Bostock nodded, a rakish smile tilting his thin lips. "You can't say the same about me, can you? Pity. I've had plenty that belonged to you."

Nick would have lunged, but Higgs grabbed his shoulders and held him back with a surprisingly strong grip.

Bostock laughed. "Good thing your first mate has you on such a tight leash. You might start something you can't finish."

Nick jerked out of Peregrine's grasp, but the moment's delay had given him a chance to control his fury and gather his wits. There was no way the bastard could know about his promise to Hannah.

Was there?

"Besides, I'm only doing you a favor. Keeping three women as your private playthings is overreaching, even for you, *Lord Nick*." Eve and Miss Munroe pushed through the crowd toward Bostock. His icy eyes warmed to burnished pewter as he swept the women's forms. He doffed his tricorne to them, tucking it neatly under his arm. "My, my, an embarrassment of riches to be sure." His steely gaze shot back to Nick before the ladies were within earshot. "Keep up this delicious brand of hedonism, my friend, and you'll die of the pox."

"Not likely," Nick said, his voice silky with menace. "So long as I avoid *your* mistress."

Bostock emitted a low growl and went for his blade. The shining steel cleared its scabbard with a metallic rasp.

A gasp went through the crowd pressed around them.

Nick had removed his sword belt earlier. It was customary for civilized men to lay aside their weapons for public events. Now Nick's sword stood useless in the stack of blades shed at the door by the revelers, too far away for him to reach, even with a lunging grab. The tip of Bostock's blade wavered before Nick's chest, poised to strike like an adder.

"As you can see, I am without means to defend myself at present." Nick spread his arms and did a slow pirouette. "With all these witnesses, running me through would mean a short rope and a long drop. There's no doubt you deserve hanging, Adam, but are you in that much of a hurry to meet Madame Hemp?"

Bostock didn't budge. Nick bared his teeth at him. No one would mistake the expression for a smile. "Come, Bostock. I'd count it worth dying so long as I knew you'd be fitted with a necktie when the magistrate convenes the next assizes."

His enemy wavered a bit. "In deference to this festive occasion, I might be inclined to more tolerance than usual."

"Your forbearance is noted." Nick lowered his arms and his voice. "However, if you feel the need for satisfaction, Adam, I will be more than happy to accommodate you at the time and place of your choosing."

Challenge me, you bastard. I beg you. Surely a promise not to do murder did not mean he couldn't defend himself.

"Now, now, gentlemen. This has all been a simple misunderstanding, I'm sure." The man holding Miss Smythe's hand dropped it and stepped forward with alacrity. "Please, Captain Bostock, I urge you to desist. I'm certain we can settle this dispute amicably."

The newcomer made an elegant leg to Nick and topped it with an intricate flourish, waving his cockaded tricorne before him. Nick kept his gaze trained on Bostock. This other popinjay's antics might be just the distraction Adam was waiting for.

"Allow me to introduce myself, Captain. I do have the honor of addressing Captain Scott, do I not?" Without waiting for a reply, the man hurried on. "I am Lieutenant Fortescue Rathbun, lately of His Majesty's Royal Navy. Once a military man, but now devoted to the gentler pursuit of seeing fine young ladies suitably wed to deserving gentlemen in the Colonies. Your servant, sir."

Rathbun seemed to expect a similar speech in return, but Nick was damned if he'd scrape and bow to such a fop. After all, this was the weasel who'd convinced Eve to agree to marry some planter named Pennywhistle.

Ignoring him, Nick spoke to Bostock, who still hadn't lowered his blade. "Well, Adam? What's it to be?"

Lieutenant Rathbun sent Bostock an urgent glance, his lips pulled in a tight line.

A muscle ticked in Bostock's cheek, but he sheathed his blade. Then he unstrapped the sword belt and deposited his weapon with the others that had been surrendered near the door.

Nick signaled to the musicians to begin playing again. The merriment started afresh, but the dancers were in danger of neck cricks from craning to keep the group at the door in sight, just in case more sparks should fly. Music, dancing, spirits and the possibility of mayhem. The island had rarely seen such entertainment under one roof.

"It seems you're fitted with a rather tight leash yourself, Adam," Nick said, flicking his eyes to Rathbun and back. If he goaded Bostock hard enough, he might yet receive the challenge he was angling for.

"Pity." Nick spat the word.

The corners of Bostock's mouth turned down in disgust, but before he could respond, Eve pushed around Nicholas and took Rathbun's arm.

"Lieutenant Rathbun, how lovely to see you looking fit and well after our ordeal. I assume this gentleman"— she nodded to Bostock—"is the one who came to your aid on that dreadful night of the wreck."

"Indeed, he did." Rathbun introduced Captain Bostock all around. Bostock bowed and preened for the women he'd recently referred to as "cargo." Nick wanted to knock him into the next world.

"And the best part is Captain Bostock stands ready to assist us once again," Lieutenant Rathbun said. "Ladies, you'll be relieved to know I've arranged passage for all of us to the Carolinas on his good vessel, the *Sea Wolf*. Your bridegrooms will only be inconvenienced by an additional few months' wait at most."

"Noble intentions aside, I'll wager Lieutenant Rathbun hasn't two coins to rub together. Did you demand the fare up front?" Nick asked his enemy.

Bostock shot him a death's-head grin. "No. As soon as I heard it might inconvenience *you* to remove these lovelies from your home, I agreed to payment upon delivery." He shrugged his massive shoulders. "It was the least I could do."

Nick glared at him. "You can always be counted upon to do the least."

"But, Lieutenant Rathbun," Miss Munroe put in. "What if we no longer want to go to the Carolinas?"

"Not want to go?" The man's mouth gaped as if he was totally flummoxed. "How could you not want to go to a prosperous and deserving bridegroom?"

"After that horrible storm, I never want to set foot on a ship again," Sally said with conviction.

Eve scurried to her side. "Now dear, I'm sure you don't mean that. It was only one storm and—"

"And it was naught but a wee squall, at that," Nick finished helpfully. "You've not seen a storm worthy of the name till you've seen your first hurricane."

Sally turned the color of parchment. "You mean there's worse than what we went through?"

"Assuredly," Nick said. "Why, one season, the *Susan Bell* was driven before a storm for the better part of three days near as we could reckon it. There was no morning or night to be seen. Only wind and waves and a leaden sky."

"And us b-battened down with not a stitch of canvas flying, b-bilge pumps manned round the clock." Higgs jumped into the fray with Nick like the excellent first officer he was.

"Even seasoned crewmen were sick as babes," Nick said. "Remember that, Higgs?"

"Aye, sir." His first mate nodded, fighting back a grin. "S-seaman Tatem was green as an oyster."

"That settles it. I won't go." Sally shook her head. "And Penny won't go either, will you, dear?"

Miss Smythe glided over and took Sally's hand. "No, sir. I would prefer not to leave St. Georges."

Eve's jaw dropped in dismay. Nick could've kissed the pair of them.

"Shall we put the matter to a vote, Miss Upshall?" he couldn't resist asking. "Ah! It appears we just did. Sorry to disappoint you, Rathbun. The nays have it—the ladies will not be leaving with you."

He'd figured Rathbun for a dandy, accustomed to using sweet talk to persuade and wheedle his way, but now the man's face went hard as iron.

"Miss Munroe, the decision to continue on is not open to question. We are not a democracy. We have a sovereign and the rule of law," Lieutenant Rathbun said. "Setting aside an engagement of marriage is no light matter. There have been agreements made, moneys expended, and I needn't remind you of certain issues best left undisturbed. It would be a shame if I were to have to uncork that unsavory barrel of fish, if you take my meaning."

"I don't know what you're talking about, but I certainly take your meaning," Nick said. He'd made no promise to his dead wife not to kill smarmy coves like Rathbun. "You've just threatened ladies who are under my protection. You will withdraw immediately, sir, or I'll be forced to demand satisfaction."

"I'd be honored to be your second," Higgs spoke up, without a stammer for once, and took his place at Nick's left side.

Rathbun lowered his brows. "This is not your affair, Captain Scott."

"I'm making it mine."

"Very well, though I should warn you that throughout my military career, I was regarded as a master of the blade," Rathbun said through clenched teeth. "Captain Bostock, may I count on you as my second?"

Bostock hesitated. "Ordinarily, I'd jump at the chance of anything which results in blood spilled, especially when it mostly belongs to Nicholas Scott."

Nick cocked his head and sent his enemy a wry smile in acknowledgment of the swipe. "Go ahead and accept, Bostock. And I'll do for you, too, once I'm done with this macaroni."

"You tempt me, but I'm not in the habit of taking ladies on a journey they clearly don't care to make." Bostock folded his arms over his chest. "With regret, Rathbun, I must decline."

Rathbun's nostrils flared. "This matter is not concluded."

He turned on his heel and stalked into the night.

Adam Bostock made a leg. "Good evening, ladies." He shot a glance at Nick and turned to Eve. "Miss Upshall, I believe you are still in favor of continuing your journey. I will be happy to place a cabin on the *Sea Wolf* at your disposal, should you desire it."

Eve dropped a low curtsey. "I thank you, sir, but without at least one other woman on board, it is impossible. No lady's reputation could survive such a voyage."

"Of course. My mistake." He cocked his hat at a rakish angle while Nick seethed at him. "If there should be a change in circumstance, I'm at your service." Bostock gave one more tip of his hat. "Nicholas, another day."

"I'll count on it." Nick returned his pleasantry with a wooden smile.

If they'd been a pair of hounds, both their ruffs

would have been on end. Bostock turned and stalked into the balmy night.

The fiddler put the final flourish on a gay reel and the dancers swirled to a stop behind Nicholas. Then the music started again, a stately minuet. Its slower pace was a welcome respite.

Nick's body had been denied the chance for a fight. It was still primed for action of some sort. His cock led him in a new direction.

And the steps of the minuet require a kiss, Nicholas recalled.

He captured Eve's hand and began leading her to the floor. "Come, Miss Upshall. This is our dance."

"I'm sure you're mistaken, Captain," she said, flashing a cat's smile while trying to pull surreptitiously out of his grasp. "I'm certain my dance card designates a different partner for this minuet."

"As host of this ball, I'm entitled to one dance of my choosing, so I am altering your dance card," he said, smiling and nodding to his other guests as he led her into position.

He snugged her against his hip for an instant before he allowed her to twirl into a shaky curtsey. He bowed in response. With any luck at all, he'd alter her entire evening.

Chapter Twelve

Eve's heart pounded against her gown's whalebone bodice.

There hadn't been this much hostility in Nick's eyes when he faced that shark. She sensed his seething fury was directed at that Captain Bostock for some reason and not her, but it still made her pulse race.

"Have a care, Captain," she warned softly as he led her through the intricately controlled steps of the minuet. A muscle ticked along his jaw and a vein had popped out on his forehead. "You'll have a fit of apoplexy if you don't calm yourself."

He laughed as if she'd uttered a witticism, and the dancers around them smiled. Only she seemed to hear little mirth in the sound.

"My dear Miss Upshall, I find your concern for my health deliciously ironic." His lips scarcely moved as his silky tone continued. "Especially since you are principally responsible for my life's reversals of late."

"Indeed?"

"Shall I catalog them for you so you may gloat?"

"I'm surprised you think my arrival has made a speck of difference to you. It would mean admitting someone with less than gale force winds behind them can turn you from your purpose."

The dance steps required them to raise their joined hands and step toward each other. Nicholas lengthened his stride to make sure his body was flush with hers for an instant. The vein disappeared from his forehead.

Even through the layers of silk, she felt his hardness and her breath caught in her throat. He'd obviously channeled his bloodlust into animal desires of a different sort.

She felt suddenly as if her temperature had spiked several points. The blood in her veins sang a hot, seductive tune beneath the violin's melody.

"If my presence has been of any real consequence to you whatsoever, I confess to utter surprise," she said, determined not to allow him to sense her body's response to him.

"Let us see." He executed a turn with masculine grace and raised his other hand for her to palm. "Since I met you, I've lost the chance to claim a prize vessel, dismissed my mistress, spent a small fortune at the modiste and milliner—with no return on that investment, I might add—and lost virtually all control over my own household. Is that not consequence enough?"

"Then you should be anxious to be rid of me instead of creating obstacles to my departure," she countered as she made a slow turn under his arm.

His raised brow acknowledged her point. "I really should. And yet, it's because I see great potential for you to redeem yourself that I do not."

When Nicholas leaned to deliver the prescribed kiss, she turned her head to avoid his lips and immediately wished she hadn't. His warm, whiskey-laced breath tickled her ear.

"You may start by allowing me to watch you bathe again," he whispered.

More heat spread up her neck.

"I could wash your back," he mouthed when the dance called for them to be close enough for another whispered suggestion. "Or your front. Your choice."

Her cheeks flamed, but it wasn't from embarrassment. She was strangely pleased. He liked seeing her naked.

All of her.

Eve had never thought a man would be able to bear her horrible disfigurement. Even if someday she married, she expected to hide her scars from her husband. She didn't think it should be too hard since respectable women never undressed completely before a man, even during marital relations.

Her belly offered its approval to the captain's lewd suggestions with a couple of slow backflips. But her knowledge of society's dictates rose up to counter her body's weakness.

"I have greater plans for my life than being a convenient object for your lust." She turned a graceful pirouette.

"Somehow I suspect Mr. Pennywhistle of the Carolinas is not at the heart of those plans."

Drat the man! Can he read my mind?

"But back to you being the object of my lust. There are those who could assure you it is a high calling, with many pleasurable benefits." He bent over her hand and brushed his lips across her knuckles with perfect correctness. "For example, I feel certain I could satisfy *your* lust better than these lovely fingers seem able to."

The urge to curl those very fingers into a fist and pop him in the nose was almost more than she could bear. But so many eyes were upon them, and the dance was nearly over. She could surely last a few more measures, but only if she refrained from speaking or even looking at him more than necessary. The sight of his wickedly handsome face infuriated her.

"You could do much worse than becoming my mistress," he said when the dance allowed him to bend close enough again.

"I take leave to doubt that. In fact, I could hardly help but do better."

"Smile, Eve," he said, the corners of his own mouth forced upward. "People will think you aren't enjoying yourself with me."

"They'd be right."

"Liar."

She narrowed her eyes at him and dropped into the final curtsey of the dance. The last note of the tune faded into silence. "Pray, excuse me, Captain. I find I need a change of air."

"Then you will require an escort." He offered his arm.

She ignored him and strode away. He was beside her in a heartbeat, placing her hand on his arm and covering it with his other palm, so she couldn't yank it away without causing a scene.

"Captain, I do not wish to take the air with you."

"Check your bearings, Miss Upshall. You dare not go alone." He continued walking her toward the door, smiling and nodding, as if they were having a pleasant conversation. "We may dress ourselves in the outward trappings of civilization here on the island, but it's a thin disguise at best. Most of the single men in this hall and half of the married ones would love to catch you by yourself someplace and indulge in a quick game of hide the sausage, whether you were willing or no."

"And you don't count yourself in that number?"

"Of course, I do." He cocked his head at her as if he thought her daft. "But I'm not likely to play until you're ready for the game. And besides, I'm the one you want."

"You conceited swine," she murmured through clenched teeth.

"Now you've the right of it," he said pleasantly. "Show me a man who doesn't think himself the center of his own universe and I'll show you a man without the brass to accomplish anything."

They passed through the open double doors and into the fragrant night. Once clear of the hall, she pulled her hand away from him and lengthened her stride.

"On the contrary," she said over her shoulder. Eve hoped to put some distance between them, but found him flanking her handily, "Not all men think the sun rises and sets on their own . . . brass."

He laughed and plucked a hibiscus blossom from a nearby bush. "Eve, that's what I like about you. Stand still for half a moment." He tucked the bloom behind her ear and then caught up both her hands. "You play at being a lady with great conviction and do it as well as I've ever seen. But sometimes, the real Eve slips out and the jig is up."

"There's no need to insult me." She jerked away from him and quickened her pace across the cobbled square, past the empty stocks toward the wharf.

"How is it an insult that I enjoy who you are?"

That stopped her short. He didn't think less of her for her stripes. He was amused by her lapses into vulgarity. It was tempting to lean into his casual acceptance of her faults. If only his acceptance wasn't also a prelude to seduction. For an unmarried woman of no great dowry, a maidenhead was her only real wealth. She'd fought like a wildcat to keep it in Newgate. It would be pure folly to surrender it now, just for his asking.

She started walking again.

"Haven't you ever wanted to be more than you are?" she asked.

"Aye, but I got over that notion fairly quickly." He caught her hand and held her fast. "Stay a bit, Eve. There's no need to chase the night. The air will come to you."

She drew a deep breath, a lungful of night-blooming narcissus, the fishy-tar scent of the wharves and the brisk tang of the sea. A breeze whispered through the nearest palms, sending the fronds fluttering in soft sibilance.

"The island whispers its secrets," she murmured, remembering little Reggie Turnscrew's tales.

"What's it saying to you?" Nicholas thumbed her wrist, sending little waves of pleasure up her arm.

"It's saying I shouldn't trust you farther than I can throw you, Captain Scott."

"Then the island lies, because if I give my word on something, it's good." He took a step closer to her, so she had to tip her head back to meet his gaze. "I fought off a shark for you, Eve. Don't you think you might find it in you to call me Nicholas?"

She tested the name on her tongue. "Nicholas."

He smiled down at her and for the first time, his eyes smiled, too. "I was just wondering how we might put the notion of my trustworthiness to the test."

She arched a brow at him.

"I've an hourglass in my chamber," he said. "It keeps excellent time."

"How nice for you."

"Will you let me finish?"

She drew her lips in a tight line and nodded.

"I propose that you come to my chamber and allow me to touch you in any manner for the duration of one hour—"

"But—"

He put a finger to her lips. "You were supposed to let me finish."

"And you were supposed to tell me how you could prove yourself worthy of my trust. So far, I've heard nothing that leads me to that conclusion."

"Then listen. If at the end of one hour, you do not wish to remain with me for the rest of the night, I will see you back to your chamber and trouble you no more."

"And all you would do is touch me?"

"For one hour." He brought her hand to his lips and pressed a kiss between her first and second knuckles. "If you enter my chamber as a virgin, you will still be one when the last grain of sand falls."

"Very well," she said softly.

"You agree?" He started to pull her into an embrace, but she straight-armed him.

"Aye. On the day you show yourself in church, I'll come to your chamber by night." Eve smiled smugly at him.

That agreement was safe as houses. On their first Sunday on the island Mr. Higgs had squired the three women to services alone. After some wheedling questions from Sally, Higgs admitted that the captain would sooner swallow tacks than darken a church door.

Strains of a fiddle wafted toward them.

"Now walk me back in, if you please. I owe someone a gavotte," she said taking his arm and glancing at the dance card dangling at her wrist in the moonlight. "And it is not you."

Chapter Thirteen

Twenty-six steps led up to the broad double doors of St. Peter's. Nick knew for a certainty how many there were because he'd counted them himself the last time he attended a service at the little Anglican church.

The coach he trailed stopped at the base of the steps. He dismounted and tied his horse to the rear of the conveyance. Then he nipped round to hand the ladies out.

Only two ladies.

"There you go, Miss Munroe," Nick said as he helped her alight. Peregrine was at his heels ready to assist her up the steep steps.

When Miss Smythe popped her head out of the coach, her mild face was marred by a worried frown. "This isn't like Eve at all. Even on the crossing, she never had a moment's illness. I wonder if I ought to have stayed with her."

"Don't trouble yourself," Nick said. Eve had taken unaccountably ill with a sudden sick headache when he announced his intention to accompany them to church this morning. He'd called her bluff and she'd thrown down a losing hand. It had been all he could do to keep a straight face as he expressed his sympathy and hoped she'd be on the mend by nightfall. "Daya will tend her. I'm sure it will turn out to be nothing. Mr. Higgs, kindly escort Miss Smythe also and I'll be along directly."

Higgs stopped where he was, about ten steps up. With a nod to Miss Munroe, he left her side and hurried back down to collect Miss Smythe. It wasn't often Peregrine squired around even one young lady. His gangly frame seemed to stretch all the straighter for having one on each arm.

Nick rapped on the coach's side and the driver pulled away, leaving him alone at the base of the steps. He looked up at the whitewashed structure, its steeple stabbing the lowering sky. Higgs and the ladies disappeared into the church.

Thunder rumbled in the distance. By rights, he supposed lightning should strike him down. Never had anyone attended St. Peter's with a less pure motive.

"All right, Lord," Nick said, taking a deep breath as he scanned the darkening clouds. "Let us see if You have a sense of humor."

He mounted the steps, taking them two at a time.

And arrived at the top unscathed. The Almighty either didn't notice or didn't care that Nicholas Scott had come to call.

He removed his tricorne and entered the sanctuary as the pipe organ began its wheezing prelude. A bass pedal seemed to be stuck and droned on unchanging beneath the wandering melody. No one had bothered to fix it since Hannah's funeral.

Or maybe no one but he noticed it. The continuous low rumble set his teeth on edge.

A whispered murmur followed him as he trod down the aisle. The good folk there were undoubtedly surprised to see him, but as far as he could tell, nothing had changed in St. Peter's since he was there last.

The same families huddled together in the same boxed pews. The gallery overhead was filled with the same black faces, the faithful servants who were expected to attend, but were not allowed to sit on the main level with the white congregants.

Nick had never understood such divisions. His black crewmen were seaman same as the whites, with shares in keeping with their abilities instead of their skin color. Surely the Lord God didn't divide his flock on the basis of the hue He gave them.

Nick found his assigned box. He'd endowed the church handsomely enough at Hannah's death. Pews were set aside for his household even though his own attendance was scarce as hen's teeth. Higgs and the ladies were already seated.

On the cushions Hannah had lovingly embroidered and donated to the church before she and Nick were married there.

Was it really only five years ago?

He took his seat next to Higgs, choosing not to face the altar. He hung his tricorne on the peg Hannah had insisted they should put there. Was it his imagination or did a little of her lilac fragrance still linger?

No, that was impossible.

The organ stopped. The priest began intoning the liturgy, but Nick barely heard him.

There was a swirling knot in the cedar pew between Miss Munroe and Miss Smythe. His gaze chased around that little wooden maze, just as it had during Hannah's interminable funeral. Curving back on itself like a sea snake, the knot wound around in tight loops. He never could find the end of it.

Memories he'd thought buried with Hannah rose to life, clawing their way through his mind.

He realized suddenly why God had chosen not to cut him down on the church steps. Memories of losing Hannah were far greater punishment than a mere lightning strike.

Two mortal hours later, the last chord of the postlude finally died away. The stuck pedal sighed on for another heartbeat or two before it faded into the open beams over the sanctuary.

The worshipers filed out in silence, but Nick remained seated. He had no desire to engage any busybodies in conversation on the front steps. Everyone would be abuzz about the prodigal's supposed return to the fold. He was determined not to give them any more fodder for their gossip.

"Captain?"

Higgs's voice pulled him out of himself.

"Go on, lad," Nick said. "See the ladies safely home. I'll bide here awhile."

He rose a few minutes after they'd left and made his way out the side door that led to the little churchyard.

The topsoil was too thin for burial belowground in most places, the rocky bones of the island barely covered by its stretched skin of dirt. Stone vaults lined the narrow walkway. Violets wept in profusion along the path. He ducked under the low-hanging branch of a mimosa and continued around the building, dragged inexorably toward her grave.

When he rounded the corner, he ground to a halt.

Adam Bostock was there.

Damn the blackguard! Wasn't it enough he'd stolen her in life? Did he think to claim Hannah in death as well?

Nick ground a fist into his other palm. The rain that had threatened earlier finally arrived, first as a fine mist, then pelting him with the relentlessness of a thousand tiny hammers. As he watched, Bostock removed his hat and tucked it under his arm. His shoulders sagged and he swayed unsteadily on his feet. Then he sank to one knee.

Probably drunk. Adam Bostock could cast up his accounts someplace else.

"You there!" Nicholas bounded across the grave-yard. "What do you think you're doing here?"

Bostock scrambled to his feet, swiping his red-rimmed eyes.

He'd been weeping, Nicholas realized with a start, not just wiping away rain.

"Come to finish our quarrel, Nick?" Bostock asked. His voice was less booming than usual, but his bluster nearly covered for it.

"If you're spoiling for a fight, you've picked a poor spot," Nicholas said. "This is holy ground."

Adam jammed his black tricorne back on his head, blinking at the rain. "I never figured you for a praying man, Scott."

"I'm not. But this is my wife's grave." Nicholas emphasized "my wife" more loudly than he intended. He was still furious with Hannah, but he owed her that much respect. "That makes this place holy."

"And your child's," Adam said with a curl of his lip. "Let's not forget it was your spawn that killed her."

Nick looked at the small ossuary pressed up against Hannah's vault. His lips clamped tight. If ever there was a place for truth, a graveyard was it.

"The child was yours," Nicholas said, his tone as flat as the great organ's stuck note. "She confessed it as she lay dying."

"You lie!"

Bostock grasped Nick's collar. Nick was ready for him and swung. Bostock ducked, but managed to throw a counterpunch that landed squarely in Nick's belly. Nick bent double as the air rushed from his lungs, but he regathered himself and rushed Adam.

Nicholas lifted his enemy up and promptly lost his balance because of the slick moss under his feet. They rolled together across the wet grass and the mud of a newly worked flower bed.

A blow connected with Nicholas's jaw, and stars careened in his head, but he landed a few good licks of his own. When they finally came to rest, Nick was astraddle Bostock's chest with his fingers around his enemy's throat.

Bostock's body bucked under Nick, but couldn't shake him off. His enemy tried to roll away, but Nicholas continued to squeeze the life out of him. Bostock's pale eyes bulged as he shoved the heel of one palm against Nick's chin. Nick turned his head and bore down all the harder. Adam's arms flailed and he tried to work his fingers under Nick's grip. Nick held on like one of the alligators he'd seen in a Carolina swamp. Bostock's eyes rolled back in his head.

He was dying.

"Damnation," Nick swore as he released him. He stood over his enemy as Bostock rasped in a deep breath and put a protective hand to his throat. "I promised Hannah I wouldn't kill you."

A pained expression passed over Bostock's face. His complexion was pale as he staggered to his feet. "She made . . . me promise . . . the same damn thing."

"Women," Nick said simply.

Bostock nodded.

"Hannah told me she was carrying your child." Bostock sank onto the stump of a huge cedar. The rain was coming down harder now, muffling all sounds but its own steady percussion. Neither man seemed to notice. "I figured the babe was why she broke it off with me. I would have taken her away, but she wouldn't go. She said she wouldn't separate you from your heir."

"Perhaps she didn't know for certain which of us

fathered the child," Nicholas said through clenched teeth. Hannah had played him false, but she'd chosen him at the last. That ought to count for something.

It didn't.

"If I'd thought the child was mine, I'd have taken her from you, whether she wanted to go or not," Bostock admitted. "I should have taken her anyway."

For a moment, Nick wished he had. Then Bostock would've had those haunting memories of the birthing chamber in *his* head.

The screaming had gone on for hours. But when it stopped, Nick found the silence even worse. The midwife turned him away countless times during the labor, but he finally pushed past her.

Christ, there was so much blood. Pools of it in the rumpled bedclothes. It dripped steadily onto the pine floor. He never thought a body could lose so much and yet live. Hannah was as pale as the muslin sheets, but her eyes burned with fear.

"I'm going to God," she whispered. "I must unburden my soul."

She told him all in shuddering gasps, how she'd found comfort in Adam's bed while Nick was on his last triangular run from the Turks to the Carolinas and home. Then Hannah begged his forgiveness, but he was too stunned by her revelation to say the words she wanted to hear. As the stillborn child finally slipped from her body, her spirit left with it.

Along with any chance to ever make it right.

"Was it a boy or a girl?" Bostock asked.

Only SCOTT was carved on the small vault. There was no need to shame the dead. Nick claimed the child as his, so far as the world knew. But he hadn't wanted to think about the child more than necessary. He'd taken

Hannah's word that it wasn't his. Now he wondered if he should have given it a proper name.

"It was a boy."

A son. A legacy. A piece of himself every man hopes will live on after him. The wee lad might have been his.

And he hadn't even given the child the simple recognition of a Christian name.

Bostock walked over and placed a palm on the top of Hannah's vault. "God rest you, love."

Love. Why hadn't Nick ever been able to say the word? If he had, maybe Hannah wouldn't . . . he shoved away the thought. There was no going back. No way to undo the past.

"It appears we won't be killing each other today," Nick said as he stood across the vaults from Adam. He didn't want to touch the cold limestone of either raised grave, but Bostock stooped to rest his hand briefly on the child's stone as well.

"No, not today." Adam strode away, then stopped and turned back. He shot Nick a grim smile. "But cheer up. There's always tomorrow."

Nick watched him go, surprised that he'd been thinking along the same lines. Perhaps he and Bostock were more alike than not. Maybe that was why Hannah had turned to the bastard . . .

He'd never know for sure. He settled on the cedar stump and kept silent watch over his dead till the rain stopped and the warm Bermudian sun began to turn the puddles to steam.

Eve startled at the rap on her door. The rest of the churchgoers had returned long ago. Penny had brought her some clear broth and offered to sit with her till the headache passed, but Eve sent her away. She hated to lie to Pen. Her head was fine.

Her heart was not.

It galloped wildly as she rose from her chair by the hearth and went to open the door. She was certain it was Nicholas on the other side.

Come to gloat. Come to claim his winnings.

She could usually count on her clever tongue to get her out of trouble. It had doomed her this time. The Captain had shown himself in church. And she'd all but dared him to do it by declaring she'd come to his chamber on the day that he did so.

Why, by all that was holy, had that thought even popped into her mind, let alone out her mouth?

The sharp rap at the door was replaced by a demanding knock.

Eve slid back the bolt and opened the door a crack.

Captain Scott had propped himself against the frame with both arms. His gaze was fastened on the floor.

"Nicholas, what's happened to you?" Eve pulled the door wide. His hair had escaped its tidy queue and hung in wet strands across his face. His fine suit of clothing was drenched and plastered with mud. The white stockings would never come clean even if Daya scrubbed them for a week and he'd all but ruined his silver-buckled shoes.

"Miss Upshall," he said, working his jaw back and forth as if testing its alignment. A fresh bruise purpled one cheekbone. "I have come to discuss—"

"I hardly think the hallway is the place to discuss the indecent agreement in which you've trapped me," she whispered furiously, and waved him in, but he didn't budge.

"It is if I'm calling it off."

Eve flinched as though he'd slapped her.

He straightened to his full impressive height. "In light of my attendance at services this morning, you may feel yourself compelled to certain actions this evening. Do not, I beg you. I release you from whatever obligation you may feel you've incurred."

He turned to go, but she stopped him with a hand on his soggy arm.

"What sort of trick is this?" she demanded. What had happened to him? He didn't seem the type to embrace religion. And the filthy condition of his clothing suggested he'd spent the afternoon drinking and brawling.

"No trick." He laid a mud-caked hand on hers. "I've just realized a few things."

"Such as?"

"Coercion is the worst sort of prelude to shared pleasure. If one party is determined not to be with another party, no power on earth can make them come." He pulled away and shuffled down the hall. "Or make them stay."

Chapter Fourteen

Eve threw back her sheets and cursed the moon. Silver light fingered its way through the jalousie shutters and across her bed. It wouldn't let her sleep. She swung her legs over the side and toed on her slippers. She drew back the long drapes that obscured the door to the small private garden off her chamber. *Perhaps some fresh air.*

It wasn't just the moon that disturbed her.

There was something blooming outside her door. Something wild and forbidden and indescribably sweet. The fragrance wrapped itself around her, bidding her to come away, to surrender, to lose herself in its exotic scent.

It wasn't just the seductive perfume of some unpronounceable flower, she realized with a sigh. It was nothing she could smell.

It was the man. The man whose chamber door was mere steps from hers.

Nicholas Scott wouldn't let her sleep.

She'd tried to reason with herself all day. Tried to convince herself that she dreaded keeping her bargain with the black-eyed devil. Telling herself that *if* she made good on her debt, and a lady had to live up to her word, she'd only be doing so out of duty. She'd grit her teeth and submit to his touch till the last grain of sand was gone from the hourglass.

Then she'd laugh in his face and return to her own room, her honor intact, her point made. He'd have to take her to Charleston once he saw there was no sense in continuing his pursuit of her maidenhead.

If she could only reach her mother's brother in Richmond. Whether she married eventually or lived out her days as a spinster at her uncle's hearth, she'd do whatever was necessary to live a life beyond reproach. She'd never be at the mercy of strangers. Her family would see to it.

No one would ever whip her again.

And if to accomplish that goal, she had to allow Nicholas Scott his moment of triumph, so be it. She'd endure it and come away unscathed.

She'd developed a real talent for lying while in Newgate Prison. But now even she couldn't swallow her own golly-whoppers.

It was more than curiosity about what Nicholas would do to her. She wanted to be touched with gentleness, not malice.

And, blast it all, she wanted Nicholas Scott to be the one to touch her. Only touch her. He'd promised.

What had happened to make him decide he didn't want to now?

She had to know. Eve pulled on her wrapper over her cotton chemise and pushed through her door before she could talk herself out of it.

The latch sounded unnaturally loud to her ears. But when she stood rigid in the hall, listening for another soul stirring, she heard nothing. Before her courage flagged, she padded down the hall to Nicholas's chamber.

She raised her hand to knock, but stopped herself.

What if someone besides the captain heard it?

She tested the knob. It turned in her hand. She pushed the door open and slipped in.

There was no one in the large bed that commanded

the center of the masculine space. But the bedclothes were as rumpled and mussed as her own.

"If you've come for the silver, you're in the wrong room."

His voice made her jump. She saw him then, his broad-shouldered frame silhouetted against a long window. He was backlit by the moon, but Eve could tell he was naked. She should have expected it.

How else would the Lord of Devil Isle sleep?

Every curve of muscle stood out in stark definition, every long line of him kissed by moonlight. He leaned against the windowsill with both hands, still looking out to sea. Her mouth went dry.

"But you're not here for the silver, are you, Eve?"

"How—" Her voice cracked and she swallowed hard. He hadn't even bothered to look. "How did you know it was me?"

"I know the sound of your footstep," he said, turning to face her slowly. "I know the smell of your skin. What else would you like me to know?"

She wanted him to know every inch of her body and not flinch from the hideous parts. But she couldn't bring herself to say it. "I would like you to know that I honor my debts."

He began to walk toward her. It was too dark for her to see everything clearly, but the brief glimpses of him were magnificent. She'd visited a menagerie once when she was small and seen a real live lion from Africa. Mane flying wild, rippling strength in each movement, rampant maleness exuding from every pore—the lion in his prime was nothing compared to this man. She couldn't tear her gaze from him.

"I released you from that foolishness. You owe me nothing." His voice was a low rumbling purr.

Would she even care if he ate her alive? "I owe you my life."

"And you've thanked me." His teeth flashed white in the darkness. "Are you come to thank me again, Eve?"

"I came because . . . because you have an hourglass and . . . because neither of us seems able to sleep."

He stopped an arm's length away. She'd been an unwilling witness to all manner of sexual congress in the big common cell at Newgate, but she'd never seen a finer example of a man than the one who stood with his cock straining toward her now.

"What do you want?" he asked. The tension in his voice stretched so tight. She'd swear he could launch an arrow with it that would fly clear to Bristol.

"You promised you would . . . only touch me."

"And you want me to touch you?" He took a step closer.

She nodded, not trusting her voice.

He took another step toward her. She planted a palm on his bare chest. His heart galloped under it.

"The hourglass," she whispered.

"That's how it's to be?"

She nodded, starting to remove her wrapper.

"Don't," he ordered. "I'll do that myself."

Then he strode across the room and upended the hourglass that sat on his bedside table. He walked slowly back to her.

"Remember, you are here because you want to be. You asked for this." The serrated edge of something dark and dangerous crept into his tone.

"If I want to leave—"

"You won't." His voice fell to a whisper. "But if you do, I'll not stop you. On all that's holy, I so swear."

He stood stock-still. She didn't even think he breathed. Then, though his lips barely moved, she heard one word.

"Stay."

It reverberated deep inside her head. But the anguish in that one word was so complete, she drew in a sharp breath. For that slice of a moment, she seemed to feel a little of what he was feeling.

The man was in torment.

He was on the edge of some precipice, his balance teetering wildly.

"What would you have me do?" she asked.

Relief rolled off him in palpable waves. "Nothing. Just be. I will do what's needed."

He didn't move, but the muscles in his bare forearms twitched beneath his skin. His gaze locked with hers as if he feared looking elsewhere.

His mouth lifted in a brief smile. He raised his hands to her face, gently pressing his fingertips to her forehead, her temples. Her eyelids closed as his hands traced over them and on to her cheeks. He brushed a thumb across her parted lips.

He'd bathed before retiring. His hand smelled of soap and of him. Eve breathed him in. His hands moved down. She opened her eyes and looked up at him as his strong fingers encircled her throat.

She was totally at his mercy and she knew it. He could snap her neck and dump her body over the cliff behind his home. The tide would bear her away and no one would ever be the wiser. Panic curled in her belly.

She'd sworn never to let herself be in another person's power again. And yet, there was something in his face, a look of such tenderness that made her certain he didn't intend to hurt her.

He slid his hands down to her elbows and forearms, taking her wrapper with him as he went. Her skin rioted with pleasure in the wake of his touch. The wrapper slid off and pooled at her feet.

When he reached her hands, he grasped one and pulled it between them, tracing around each of her fingers with his forefinger. He was completely absorbed by each of her parts, as if he were committing her to memory.

When her right hand had been explored, front and back, her knuckles and palm caressed with unhurried thoroughness, he placed it on his shoulder and met her gaze for a moment as though checking to make sure she agreed with its placement. Against her better judgment, her lips curved up and she gave his shoulder a slight squeeze.

He smiled back at her and the moonlight seemed to shift around him, flaring silver with his pleasure.

He gave her other hand the same leisurely attention. When he was finished, he brought it to his lips, uncurled her fingers and placed a soft kiss in her palm. Then he took two fingers in his mouth and sucked them.

Her belly clenched. If Nick started a riot in her insides just by making love to her hands, Lord help her when he moved on to more sensitive spots.

Once her left hand was firmly placed on his other shoulder, he met her eyes squarely once more. His hands found the drawstring at the neck of her chemise and untied it. He parted the thin cotton, shoving it out of the way. Her breasts were bared.

Then his gaze drifted lower. She held her breath as he stared intently.

"You're so beautiful."

Her heart leaped.

He grazed a nipple with his knuckle and it drew up into an even tighter knot. A white-hot message streaked from her breast to her womb. She closed her eyes and felt his heat as he ran his fingertips along the crease beneath each breast. Then he hefted their weight in his palms and dragged his thumbs across her taut nipples. She bit her lip to keep from arching into him.

When she opened her eyes, he was still looking at her breasts. The hunger in his face made her ache. She drew a shuddering breath.

"Raise your arms," he ordered.

She lifted them in the time-honored gesture of surrender. He bunched her chemise in his fists and drew the garment over her head.

Nicholas dropped to one knee and brushed his lips over her ribs. He circled her belly button a couple times before inserting a fingertip in the indentation. He smoothed his palms over her hips. His warm breath feathered her abdomen and made the small hairs over her crotch sway with each exhalation.

"Spread your legs." His voice was ragged.

Grinding her teeth, she complied and he invaded her softly, teasing a finger into her most intimate crevice. He explored her gently, discovering each little fold and circling her most sensitive spot with maddening slowness. Her body answered him with fresh dew and a deep throb. She almost cried out when he pulled back and moved his hand on down her thighs.

This is madness, she told herself. She should not be flirting with ruin just because the moonlight wouldn't let her sleep. Still, he was keeping his promise only to touch her. As he ran his palms down her shins and ankles, she scented a whiff of her own arousal, musky and sweet.

The wanting grew keener. Nicholas was touching her in a far deeper place than just her skin, that place where her soul hunkered, where her closely guarded heart sheltered behind rules and propriety and "oughtness." He cut through her defenses and made her rouse to him with a deep, throbbing ache.

And if she could smell her arousal, he surely could, too. She pressed her lips together in embarrassment.

"Don't fret, Eve," he said softly. "I think you smell wonderful."

"How do you know what I'm thinking?"

"I can't hear your thoughts," he said as he rose to his feet and looked down at her. "But you have my complete attention. I sense how you're feeling with each breath and shiver of muscle. I have to know how you feel in order to know how I should touch you. I can make a good guess at your thoughts."

In that case, she was truly at his mercy.

He leaned toward her slightly. The tip of his cock grazed her belly and she thought he was about to kiss her, but he caught himself and straightened.

"Turn around," he ordered, his tone gruffer than it had been. She realized that he was bridling himself and it was proving a struggle.

Perhaps she could guess at his thoughts as well, and just as accurately.

She flinched when he first touched her back. Then his hands smoothed across her shoulder blades and traced her spine. She began to relax. With a featherlight touch, he visited every stripe, setting the undamaged skin between the ravaged bits dancing.

"Can you feel that?"

She shook her head. He must be skimming the tops of the scars themselves, she reasoned. Part of her back was dead. He lowered his mouth to her shoulder.

That part of her was joyously alive.

He began kissing his way down her back. For every stripe her tormentors had laid, he laid on his mouth a dozen times. By the time he reached her waist, tears were streaming down her cheeks.

Her shoulders quivered and he must have heard

the catch in her breathing as she tried to stifle her sobs.

He rose to his feet and wrapped his arms around her, pulling her back against his hard chest, snugging her bottom against his harder groin.

"There are to be no tears between us. Only pleasure. Only bliss is allowed." His voice was a rumble by her ear while one of his hands reached around to toy with her nipple. "There is no place for the past. No thought for the future. There is only now."

He was so warm, feverish almost, against her skin. She narrowly resisted melting into him.

"I want you only to feel." His hands slid down and cupped her buttocks. He massaged her flesh, lifting and spreading, teasing the sensitive crease.

She wondered if she might burst into flames.

"Do you know how fine you are?" he whispered as he knelt to run his palms down the backs of her thighs and dally at the ticklish spot behind her knees.

She only knew how fine he made her feel.

He moved his hand, drifting up to her buttocks and back down. His touch sent pleasure rippling over her.

"So smooth," he said. "So cool."

She could almost feel her own skin through *his* fingertips.

And his delight in what he felt.

Eve shivered. She was giving herself over to him completely. Was there some drug in the fragrance of that flower blooming by her door? She shouldn't be surrendering so utterly that she was losing sense of where she ended and he began.

He slid his hand between her legs to tease her little point of pleasure again. Heat pooled in her groin. If he turned her around and put his mouth on her again as he had in her chamber, she'd be lost this time.

"Stop," she pleaded.

He removed his hand and stood behind her. "The hourglass isn't spent yet."

She glanced over at it. The bottom half of the glass was two-thirds full. She'd lost all sense of time passing as he kissed away her hurts and lavished tender care on her skin with his hands and mouth. If she could only last a bit longer, she'd be able to leave with her self-respect intact. She'd have proved that she was still in full possession of herself.

"Are you afraid of me, Eve?" He picked up her plait and brought it to his mouth for a kiss. He inhaled deeply, then used his teeth to tug at the ribbon that bound her hair. The knot slid free.

"No," she said. "I'm not afraid of you."

I'm afraid of me. If he'd tried to take her like the louts in Newgate, grabbing and thrusting, she'd have fought him, tooth and claw. None dared try it more than once, especially once she sharpened her spoon into a deadly weapon and nearly emasculated one of them.

But against Nick's unexpected and unrelenting gentleness, she had no defense.

"You're trembling." He began to massage her scalp, then he separated her plait and spread her hair over her shoulders. "I'm treating you like the lady you are, Eve. You've no cause for complaint, have you?"

"No." Then bald curiosity made her ask, "If I weren't a lady, what would you do?"

He made a noise, a sort of low groan and lowered his lips to her ear. "If you were no lady, I'd do something like this."

Nicholas wrapped an arm around her waist and bent her suddenly over. Her slim fingers splayed on the pine floor to catch herself. He covered her sex with his whole hand, sliding a finger into her, stopping at the thin shield of her purity. Her hair brushed the floor. Only his hand covering her kept him from ramming his big cock into her.

"This is what a lady misses out on," he said raggedly. "A good hard swive."

"You swore . . . only to touch me."

"Aye, and I'm only touching you," he snarled. "And my cock will touch the places my fingers cannot reach."

"Please, no."

"Don't deceive yourself. You want this. You can't lie to a man who's holding your wet little puss in his hand. I've a quarter hour left. Plenty of time to rut you blind, wench."

His grip around her waist tightened and she felt him tremble. Her body still screamed out its need in aching pulses.

"Not like this," she whimpered.

He emitted a low growl and released her.

Eve's knees buckled and she dropped to all fours. Then she plopped her bottom on the floor and twisted around to face him.

Nicholas was still standing there, nostrils flared, dragging in deep, ragged breaths. When he looked at her, it was with the wild-eyed gaze of a stallion, rutting-mad and ready to mount anything that came near.

Fear raked her spine.

"Nicholas?"

"Get out of here," he said, his lips barely moving. "For Christ's sake, if you don't intend to stay, get out now."

She didn't need to be told twice. She grabbed up her chemise and wrapper and ran to his door. Heedless of her nakedness, she threw it open and bolted down the hall to her own chamber.

She didn't stop until her door was shut and locked behind her. She moved a chair over and propped it under the knob for good measure. Then she collapsed onto the cool heart-of-pine floor and covered her face with her hands.

There was no way to lie to herself. She had not a shred of dignity left. She'd teased Nicholas Scott. Had pushed him to within an inch of his endurance and only escaped through his good graces, not her moral rectitude or ability to remain cool and aloof.

She might try to fool the world, but she was no lady.

And now they both knew it.

Chapter Fifteen

The moment Eve slammed his door behind her, Nicholas strode to his water closet. He was powerless to stop what was about to happen. His mind went blank and his body took over.

He stood over the chamber pot, his cock angry and aching. He took it in his hand and stroked himself hard. Once. Twice.

His release surged in hot pulses into the small china receptacle. His whole body trembled with the force of his climax. Nick leaned a hand against the wall to hold himself upright as the last of his spunk splatted into the pot.

Playing with a goddamn cock-tease after weeks of abstinence. What did you expect?

He drew a shuddering breath. It wasn't nearly enough, but at least the madness faded to an empty ache. He poured water from the pitcher into the ewer and dashed a handful on his face. Blood surged hotly through his veins, pounding in his temples. He upended the pitcher over his head and let the water sluice over his form.

It wasn't cold enough.

He'd never wanted a woman the way he wanted Eve Upshall. He wanted her tender. He wanted her hard. He wanted her begging and helpless with need. His mind tumbled with a dozen inventive ways to join his body to hers. She'd been right here. He'd held her in his hand.

And he'd let her go.

He was done with women who didn't want to stay.

Nick had never felt so lonely in all his life. Not even when Hannah died.

Back then he'd simply gone numb. To lose a woman to death in the same breath he'd learned he'd already lost her to another man—it was too much to deal with in one heartbeat. Nick tucked it away into a quiet eddy in the back of his mind.

Sometimes he'd drag out the old hurt and worry it, like a dog unburies an old bone. But it was no use. He'd never know why Hannah had betrayed him.

Love was a wicked fickle beastie. Just when a man thought he might have it safe in his net, the damn thing slipped through a tear or leaped out over the top. Perhaps the whole idea of love was nothing but a bunch of smoke and oakum.

Maybe keeping a mistress was the best a man could hope for. At least there was no confusion. He'd get what his body needed and the wench would get hers. All neat and tidy and businesslike.

But he hadn't reckoned on the aching tenderness he felt when he pressed his lips to Eve's ruined back. Or the red-eyed haze when he sensed her pulling away from him. Or the pure lust that made him double her over and come nearer to ravishing an unwilling woman than he'd ever been in his life. He had no name for what he felt. He simply knew he had these feelings for her.

All of her.

He didn't know what he wanted from the woman, but whatever it was, he knew he couldn't force it from her.

His cock resurrected itself merrily at the slightest thought of Eve. His chin sank to his chest as he turned back to the chamber pot.

Looks like I'll be there awhile.

* * *

The sun refused to show its face the next morning. The whole island was shrouded in low-hanging clouds, which spit rain and threatened to birth a squall on the eastern horizon.

Nick noticed that Eve likewise didn't emerge from her chamber for breakfast.

But the Misses Munroe and Smythe were at his table, fresh as daisies and as damnably cheerful.

"I declare, I do believe I danced with every available bachelor on this entire island," Miss Munroe said. "Leastwise, my feet still seem to think so. I daresay, my slippers were too small to begin with, but I simply couldn't resist the cunning little things. Thank you again, Captain."

He grunted noncommittally into his parritch.

"Did you fancy any one of the men in particular?" Miss Smythe asked. She stirred her bowl several times without lifting the spoon to her lips once.

"How can I choose one star in the sky? One pebble on the shore?" Miss Munroe gestured as she spoke, then leaned forward. "But there are quite a number I wouldn't mind dancing with again, I'll tell you that."

Higgs pushed back from the table. Peregrine hadn't managed to wangle a dance with Miss Munroe even once, Nick knew.

"W-we are scheduled to sail for the Turks," Higgs said. "Are we going ahead, s-sir?"

"Let us see what the day brings. I don't much like the look of the horizon, but see to the *Susan Bell*'s provisions, in any case," Nick said. He was loath to leave without setting matters to rights with Eve. And how to accomplish that he had no clue, as yet. Still, he was due to make a run. "That salt won't take itself to the Colonies, will it?"

"Th-then if you'll excuse me, sir, I'll see to my duties."

"Carry on, Mr. Higgs."

Nick turned a weather-eye toward the eastern window. Clouds boiled on the horizon. The glass was falling precipitously last time he checked his barometer.

The women chattered on about the events of the ball for several more minutes while Nick scraped out his bowl. Finally he laid aside his spoon and said, "Has either of you spoken with Miss Upshall this morning?"

"I did," Miss Smythe said. "Eve asked for a tray to be brought to her chamber. She's still feeling poorly. It must be the change in the weather."

"And yet you said she's not the sickly type." Nick gulped down a mouthful of tea, even though it was hot enough to scald his tongue. Sipping was for fops. "I gather you've known each other long. Do you all hail from the same region?"

"Yes," Miss Munroe said.

"No," Miss Smythe said.

At the same time.

"Which is it?"

The pair exchanged a guilty glance.

"Oh, I thought you said *religion*," Miss Munroe amended quickly. "Of course, we're all Christians. We're English ladies, aren't we? But we're not from the same region, no. I'm from Surry and Penelope was reared in Suffolk."

"And Miss Upshall?"

"London," Miss Smythe said. "I think."

"But you aren't sure. Where did the three of you meet?"

"At . . . Mrs. Torrington's School for Young Ladies . . .

of Good Family," Miss Munroe said, casting her gaze up and to the right.

"Sally, you know that's not true."

"Penny!"

"I ask your pardon, dear, but I can't lie to the captain any longer," Miss Smythe said. "Not after he's been so kind." She turned to face him, then lowered her eyes. "Though I would not blame him if he decides to change his disposition toward us."

"There's not much danger of that," the captain said.

"Hear me out before you commit yourself," Miss Smythe said. "You see, we're not ladies in the strictest sense of the word."

"Don't tell me I'm harboring three well-spoken strumpets?" he said with a laugh.

Miss Smythe's eyes went round and he almost regretted teasing her. She was his best hope of learning the truth about Eve.

"Of course not," Miss Munroe chimed in. "We weren't convicted of anything like that."

"But you were convicted of something?" He'd always suspected there was something odd in Eve's story about why the three of them were headed for the Carolinas. People generally stayed put unless something drove them from a safe haven. "All of you?"

"Truth to tell, yes." Miss Smythe nodded sorrowfully. "And rightfully so, but please don't think we are women of loose character. I only stole a loaf of bread because my little brother was hungry and my parents sick."

"Ain't you a saint?" Miss Munroe rolled her eyes at Miss Smythe, then looked at Nick squarely. "And I stole a bit of ribbon because *I* wanted it, but hadn't the coin to pay for it. The frippery weren't worth more than a few pence hardly, but it was enough to land me on a ship bound for Australia, all the same."

"And what of Eve?" he asked, forgetting he should call her Miss Upshall.

"You'd have to ask her," Miss Smythe said. "I promised not to tell. But of the three of us, she's the only one who truly was wellborn. That much is certain."

"You've told everything else, haven't you? And now you've ruined everything. May as well kiss any more new gowns good-bye." Miss Munroe's face had turned the shade of poached salmon. "For your information, Captain Scott, Eve was convicted of public lewdness. So there."

Lewdness! But the wench was a virgin. He'd proved it with his own hand. Feeling that thin membrane against his fingertip last night was the only thing that had made him stop long enough for her to choose to leave him.

Miss Munroe stuck her tongue out at her friend, then stood and flounced from the room. Nick rose when she did and settled back into his chair once she was gone.

Miss Smythe burst into tears.

"Lord, deliver me from weeping women." Nick fished out his hanky and handed it to her. "I'll forget the whole tale if you'll only do me two wee favors."

"What?" she blubbered into his handkerchief.

"Number one—Stop crying."

Miss Smythe blinked several times, blew her nose loudly and sniffed. "And number two?"

"Tell me how the three of you wound up on the *Molly Harper* with that scoundrel Rathbun." When she offered his kerchief back, he waved it away. "Keep it."

"Lieutenant Rathbun's no scoundrel," Miss Smythe insisted. "He saved us."

"How?"

"Before the ship bound for New South Wales pulled away from the dock, Lieutenant Rathbun made a deal with the captain of the vessel. He's a progressive thinker, you see. He doesn't believe in punishment. He favors reformation."

"Hmph!" It sounded like snake oil to Nicholas, but he motioned for her to continue.

"At any rate, the captain agreed that any women who met Lieutenant Rathbun's requirements should be transferred to his safekeeping."

Nick figured that along with those high-sounding sentiments some coin had also changed hands. "And what were those requirements?"

She blushed as bright as the fuchsia azaleas by his front door.

"Lieutenant Rathbun required a certain level of comeliness and . . . purity. He brought a midwife with him to . . . make certain."

"On the theory that only comely virgins may benefit from reformation?" Nicholas asked with a grim smile.

"He said it was virtue's reward." Her puzzled frown told him she hadn't considered the matter from that angle before. "In any case, the three of us were the only ones he redeemed from the prison ship."

"Redeemed?" Nick repeated. "You make him sound like some sort of savior."

"If you'd seen that hold we were pulled from, you'd agree with me." She folded her hands on her lap to still them. "But after that, Lieutenant Rathbun continued to show his worth. He said we were to be brides of fine gentlemen in the Colonies. We were taken for fittings for two gowns a piece and boarded in a snug little private cabin on the *Molly Harper*."

"And you didn't question his motives?"

"The man saved us from a horrible fate. And I don't think Eve would have survived the journey on that other ship what with her—"

Miss Smythe clamped her lips together. She'd already said more than Nick had heard from her in all the weeks she'd lived under his roof. Apparently, she could still keep some secrets.

"Her wounds?" Nick prompted. When Miss Smythe stared at him in wonderment, he nodded. "Aye, I know about the flogging. Never mind how. Tell you about it, did she?"

"No, Eve is a very private person," Miss Smythe said. "But you must remember, we three shared a very snug cabin. And those sorts of wounds take a long time to heal."

To say nothing of the wound to her spirit, Nick thought darkly. He'd still relish the chance to kill the piece of dung who'd marked Eve's back with his whip.

"At any rate, Lieutenant Rathbun schooled us in all the refinements a lady should display. He's helped us ever so much, almost as much as yourself, Captain." Miss Smythe worried her bottom lip. "I know you must think poorly of us for lying to you all this time, but we didn't know what else to do. The world is a difficult place for a woman without a man's protection." She sighed. "I suppose you'll want us to go on to the Carolinas with Lieutenant Rathbun now."

"Not as long as there's breath in my body." Wherever Rathbun was intent on taking them, Nick would bet the *Susan Bell* it wasn't to a trio of deserving bridegrooms. He took one of Penelope Smythe's hands and kissed her knuckles as reverently as if she were a duchess. "In the gorgeous East, when a man saves another's life, he is responsible for that life from then on. You and your friends are under my protection for as long as you require it. And your secret is now mine, your lie on my head. Let it trouble yours no more."

Her little face crumpled and tears welled along her lower lids.

"But no tears. I forbid it," he said with mock sternness.

Miss Smythe gave him a shy smile.

"Captain! Captain Scott!" Miss Munroe came running back into the dining room, her cunning little slippers slapping against the wide-planked floor. Her lovely face was drawn with concern.

Nicholas rose to his feet. "What is it?"

"It's Eve."

"Is she truly ill?" Nick pushed past her toward the wing where the bedchambers were clustered.

"No, no, it's not that," Miss Munroe said as she dogged him down the hall. "She's gone."

Chapter Sixteen

Eve tramped down the dirt track as fast as she could go without attracting undo attention from the other islanders who were making their way to the market in St. Georges. If the rain grew worse, the track would turn to mud and her footing would grow more treacherous. A horse would have made her flight much easier, but if she'd taken Nicholas's horse, he might claim later that she'd stolen it.

She couldn't chance it.

During the time she'd been on Bermuda, she'd seen a few poor souls in the stocks outside the courthouse. Sometimes in England, such a sentence resulted in death or loss of an eye if the crowd turned vicious and decided to throw stones. At the very least, the victim's ear was nailed.

But here the islanders only hurled insults and pelted the condemned with rotting fruit. Shame, it seemed, was enough deterrent for the local miscreants.

Still, she'd never let herself fall into the hands of the law again if she could help it. She should have run when she was first accused back in London, but she'd been so sure her innocence would win out.

Now she knew better.

A pebble lodged in her slipper and stabbed at the ball of her foot. She stopped to take it out, the sudden pain stirring memories she'd rather not call up.

Shame was a miserable punishment. She thought she'd die of it when they stripped her to the waist and dragged her half-naked before the assembled crowd. Loathsome and foul-breathed, the rabble pressed in on her, grabbing at her and hurling insults, as she was led bound to the stake.

Then at the first taste of the lash, shame burned away in searing pain. With each stroke, she lost a bit of herself. She ground her teeth and tried to hold back, but ended up screaming herself hoarse. Her muscles contorted in arching spasms. She was a broken marionette whose puppet master delighted in watching her dance to his cruel tune. She'd have done anything to make it stop.

Anything.

When it finally did, her spirit was as shattered as her flesh. She burned for five days with fever and three more with cold fury in the filth of Newgate's big common cell.

Then her natural robust health returned and her back began to heal.

And with the newly formed scars, came her determination never to lose control of her own body again.

That's what made Nicholas Scott so dangerous. Even without bonds, he made her want to surrender. With no lash but pleasure, she was near to losing herself in him. She couldn't give herself over to another person so completely.

She didn't think her spirit would survive it a second time.

Eve reached the outskirts of St. Georges and hurried down the narrow ways toward the wharf. She didn't know if Captain Bostock's vessel was still in port, but even if it wasn't, she'd slipped a pair of silver spoons in her small bag. Surely that would induce some fisherman to ferry her to the island where the *Sea Wolf* made its berth.

She hoped Nick wouldn't miss a pair of spoons.

Wind whipped her skirts and she heard the sound of hoofbeats behind her. She turned in time to see Nicholas Scott barreling down on her atop his black stallion. She turned and ran, but it was no use. He leaned over and scooped her up with one arm.

"No! Put me—oof!"

She landed on her stomach across the horse's back in front of him, her bottom bouncing skyward. All the air whooshed from her lungs and she fought to draw more as he kicked the horse into a full-out gallop across the cobbled square.

He hadn't taken time to saddle the beast, she realized as her hands searched for something to cling to. She finally had to settle for Nick's booted leg since falling off at this speed was sure to result in a broken bone.

When they reached the wharf, he reined in the stallion so hard, the horse nearly sat on its haunches. Nick slid off, tossing the reins to a wharf rat along with terse instructions for the horse's care.

"What do you think you're—" she started.

He cut off her question by dragging her from the horse's back and flopping her over his own shoulder. "Put me down this instant."

Nick didn't answer her, but he doffed his hat pleasantly and spoke to everyone they passed on their way down to the *Susan B*'s gangplank.

Her pleas for help from the townsfolk were met with laughter and knowing grins. They howled with mirth when she pounded his back.

Nick waggled his brows at the islanders. "I deserved that."

They chortled even louder. It was Punch and Judy without the strings. They decided her fury was merely part of the show.

Lord Nick was just having a bit of fun.

His pleasant tone disappeared once the deck of the ship was under his feet. "Sound the ship's bell, Mr. Higgs. Is the crew aboard?"

"All but Digory Bock. Seems he's in his cups again, sir."

"At this hour? Strike him from the roll permanently. I've no use for a rum pot on my crew. Prepare to make sail within the hour."

"But, this weather, Cap'n . . ."

"What do you intend I should do about the bloody weather, Higgs?" he demanded with a snarl. "I'm not God Almighty, am I?"

"No, but he thinks he is," Eve said, still draped over his shoulder and too breathless to pound his back any longer. "Doesn't he, Mr. Higgs?"

Nick gave her bottom a swat, which was largely deflected by her panniers and yards of fabric.

"Oh! That was becoming to a gentleman, *Lord Nick*." Her voice dripped irony.

"As silence is to a lady," he fired back.

"But sir, the storm—" Higgs began.

"Higgs, you're whining like an old woman. Once we clear the channel, we'll outrun it. The wind will push us ahead of the storm," he explained as he strode toward the companionway that led down to his cabin. "We've done it countless times."

"Aye, sir, but never shaving things this close."

Nick turned back to face him down. "Your objections are noted, Mr. Higgs. If you feel yourself unequal to your duties, I shall have you relieved."

Eve twisted around to look at Higgs over her shoulder. The first mate's mouth twitched with indecision; then he straightened his shoulders, but he didn't drop his gaze a whit.

"No, sir. I'm fit for duty."

"Then see the carpenter about a bolt for the outside of my cabin door and step lively. Carry on, Mr. Higgs."

And Nick carried on as well, heading for the companionway door once more.

Eve briefly considered grappling with the doorjamb and trying to fight passing through it, but the *Susan B* was Nick's ship. Just as St. Georges was his town.

She might as well try to fight the wind.

So she ducked her head as they disappeared belowdecks and decided to pick her fights when there was a chance she might win.

He kicked open his cabin door and dropped her on his narrow bunk. "Now stay there."

"I am not your hound, to stay or go at your word." She popped to her feet. "Nor am I a member of your crew to be ordered about."

He pulled her close and covered her mouth with his in a hard kiss. He trapped her arms between them and ravished her mouth, demanding she open to him. When her lips parted slightly, he pressed his advantage and invaded. She couldn't fight him. He was too strong.

And her body was his willing ally. Part of her welcomed him in with aching abandon. He made rough love to her mouth, pulling her down into his dark desires. She sank like a swimmer caught in a riptide.

Drowning was actually said to be quite pleasant once a body gave up.

Finally he released her and she drew a shuddering breath. With a fresh breath came fresh resolve.

"I need to get the ship underway, but I'll be back," he promised. "You and I began something last night that we haven't finished yet."

"Yes, we did," she said. "You just didn't like the conclusion."

His head snapped toward the sound of a soft knock and he strode toward the door. "That'll be Higgs with the bolt. I'm locking you in for your own safety."

"Not your own convenience?"

One corner of his mouth turned up in a lopsided grin. "That, too. There's some bread and cheese on the shelf. Get something in your stomach. This is apt to be a wild ride."

Panic clawed her throat. Her last storm at sea had been harrowing enough to last a lifetime.

"Perhaps Mr. Higgs is right. Can't the journey wait till the squall passes?" she asked, ashamed of the quake in her voice. Out the stern windows, the eastern horizon was the nasty yellowish purple of a week-old bruise. "You don't have to do this to impress me with your seamanship."

"No, it appears I have to do it to make sure you can't run away again until we have this out." His eyes softened for a moment as he searched her face, then his nononsense attitude reasserted itself. "And the lock is to keep you from folly. You have a history of leaping from perfectly seaworthy vessels, remember."

He closed the door behind him. She heard a few sharp raps of a hammer and then a bolt slid home with finality.

Mr. Higgs had the crew well in hand when·Nick reappeared on the quarterdeck, but seeing their captain at the wheel made the seamen leap even more smartly to their duties.

Nick had sailed the *Susan Bell* in plenty of dicey weather.

"The wind is her lover," he liked to say, "and occasionally, the old girl likes it rough."

He intended to outrun the coming storm. It was a

measure of his crew's faith in him that spirits were high and there was nary a grumble from any save the cook, who was unhappy that Nick ordered a cold supper to avoid having a fire in the galley.

As soon as they cleared the harbor, he commanded all her canvas laid on and the *Susan B* bounded over the waves like a fox fleeing before the hounds.

Once they left the ring of reefs and shoals, Nick turned her nose south by southwest. She nearly lifted from the water and took flight.

"Mr. Tatem, did you bring along that wheezy old squeeze box of yours?"

"Aye, Cap'n."

"Fetch it out and step lively man, we need some music to speed us on our way." Nick looked up at the rigging, where every sail strained against the cords. "At this rate, lads, we'll hail the Turks in record time."

The men danced the hornpipe below the mains'le, laughing and singing roughly.

A quarter hour later, Nick was ordering the sails trimmed. They wouldn't bear the growing force of the wind. Then in another quarter, he commanded them taken up altogether, leaving the ship's masts bare. The sea mounded up around them and sails only gave the storm a firmer grip on the *Susan B*.

By the sounding of the next bell, Nick was faced with the grim knowledge that he should have listened to Mr. Higgs.

Eve tried to stay on the bunk, but the violent roll of the ship tossed her to the floor. She pressed her cheek to the smooth teak, deciding she was better off right there. She hadn't been sick on the *Molly Harper*, but she'd already cast up the bread and cheese into the captain's chamber pot in the corner.

Waves slapped the stern windows with such force, she expected the sea to rush in at any moment. Sometimes, it seemed the *Susan Bell* stood on end, dancing on the waves like a dolphin on its tail. The ship teetered on each crest. Then her nose would slam down and race headlong into the next trough.

Eve closed the thick interior shutters over the windows. She had no hope of the wood keeping the sea out if the heavy glass gave, but at least she wouldn't have to watch it coming. The next roll sent her sprawling back on the floor.

There was a sharp rap on the door, the bolt slid and the door opened a crack.

"Miss Upshall?" It was Peregrine Higgs. "Cap'n ordered me to see to you."

"I'm here," she said weakly as Mr. Higgs came into the cabin, trailing a stream of water off his oilcloth coat. He snuffed out the oil lantern swinging from the low beam. They were thrown into almost total darkness, the only light a sickly greenish phosphorescence creeping in around the shutters.

"Cap'n has ordered all non-essential lamps extinguished," he explained as he knelt beside her. He pulled a blanket off the bunk and wrapped it around her. "Very wise of you. You'll be safer on the floor."

Safer than what, she wondered. The vessel groaned around them like a woman in labor.

"The *Susan Bell* is as sturdy a ship as a man could wish. And the pumps are staying well ahead of the water in the bilge," he said, his voice clear and comforting.

Eve wondered at his calm speech, his stutter gone, in the midst of calamity. During the wreck of the *Molly Harper*, the sailors swore and cried out in fear. If peril gave a man a chance to show his true mettle, she decided Mr. Higgs was made of solid gold.

"There'll be no supper, I fear," he said. "Cook's sick as a green lubber."

"None needed." Her belly roiled afresh at the thought of food.

"We need only wait till the storm blows itself out."

"So the crew is safe?" The *Molly Harper* had lost a seaman over the side even before the ship struck that reef.

"Aye, Captain ordered everyone below and every hatch battened, tight as a tick."

"Then where's Nicholas?" she asked, forgetting that she shouldn't call Nick by his Christian name before his first mate.

Peregrine was silent for a few heartbeats.

"He's lashed himself to the wheel."

Chapter Seventeen

Eve hadn't spoken to God since her flogging. Oh, she might have launched a quick prayer when she first saw that shark, but everything had happened so quickly that hardly counted. She attended church services when the occasion demanded because it was the "done thing." Even before that evil day when she was humiliated and marked, she'd always relied on herself instead of seeking divine intervention. It seemed weak to expect help from on high when she was perfectly capable of helping herself.

And after her conviction, she hadn't had anything to say to a Deity who would allow an innocent young woman to undergo the pain and humiliation of the lash.

She had plenty to say to God now.

After Mr. Higgs left her in the dark and bolted her in, there was nothing she could do but hunker on the floor and pray.

She prayed for the men manning the bilge pumps. Each time the ship rolled, Eve prayed that the *Susan Bell* wouldn't keep rolling right over till she was keel to the sky. She prayed for her own soul, admitting she wasn't as innocent as she liked to believe.

But most of all, she prayed for the man lashed to the wheel.

She pleaded for Nick's life there in the darkness. Yes, it was his pigheadedness that had put them in this horrible position, but it was also his strength and courage that might see them out of it.

She poured out her fears. She begged for mercy for Nicholas, hoping Someone was listening in the dark. She didn't see how God might even take note of her since she could hardly hear herself over the roar of the sea and the wind and the awful growls of the ship's timber.

She feared the *Susan Bell* might splinter into kindling at any moment.

When the waves washed over her shuttered windows, she held her breath, wondering if Nicholas did the same. Or was his body draped lifelessly over the wheel?

A dozen different images of Nicholas Scott danced before her sightless eyes—brooding, lusty, laughing, furious, courtly, dangerous, brave to the point of recklessness—all mocking her, all inviting her to sample his delicious brand of madness.

All trying mightily now to save her life and that of every other soul on board.

"Spare him, Lord," she murmured as weakness gripped her, pulling her into numbness. She curled into a tight little ball, her knees against her chest. Time expanded and contracted around her till she could only measure it in the next swell, the next breath, the next heartbeat pounding in her ears.

"Save his life," she whispered, her throat raw from pleading. "Save Nicholas Scott because . . . because . . . I love him."

Then as if someone closed her eyelids for her, in spite of the wind and waves, she sank into the blackness of exhaustion, like a pebble dropped into a well.

Someone was shouting. The sound stabbed at her ears, but she could make no sense of the words. Eve tried to open her eyes, but they were crusted shut. She pushed herself into a sitting position and swiped the matter from her lids.

The deck beneath her swayed gently. The sun knifed through the cracks around the shutters, sending shards of light into the cabin.

Feet pounded in the companionway outside her door. Someone threw the bolt and kicked the door open.

"Easy, lads," Higgs was saying as several sailors tried to squeeze through the opening at the same time, bearing a heavy burden. "Mind his head, now."

Nicholas! Eve lurched to her feet. "What's happened, Mr. Higgs?"

"We've come safe through the storm," he said wearily.

"Thanks to the cap'n," Tatem put in.

"Aye, all night and for most of a day, he kept us from broadsiding in a trough," Higgs said with a frown. "But before we could leave the pumps and relieve him, he must have taken a good clout on the head. We tried to make everything fast before we came below, but I must have missed something."

"A storm'll stir up plenty o' things from the deep," Tatem said. "Why, it mighta even been a mermaid what whacked the cap'n on the bean with her tail."

"Stow that racket. You'll scare the superstitious among the crew," Higgs ordered. "My money's on a loose pulley or a bit of the gunwale that ripped free. In any case, Cap'n Scott's been pinched off like a candle."

"Here," Eve said as she pulled back the top sheet on the bunk, so the men could deposit Nicholas there. His eyes were closed and his skin was the unhealthy color of day-old suet. Her heart froze. She couldn't seem to inhale. "Does he yet live?"

"Aye, miss," Tatem said. "Though I had to check twice to make sure."

Her heart skipped in her chest once more.

"It'd take more than a dent on the noggin to do for the likes o' Cap'n Scott." Tatem's voice was even rougher than usual. "But he's in pretty rough shape. Don't suppose a lady like you has much skill in the way of nursing?"

"You underestimate me, Mr. Tatem," she said, hoping she sounded more competent than she felt. These men had slaved all through the storm to keep her safe from the sea, and their work was not yet done. She suspected the *Susan Bell* had sustained considerable damage and it would take all hands to set her to rights. The least Eve could do was tend their captain. "Bring me a pitcher of hot water and a handful of rags. Clean rags, if you please."

"Come, lads. You heard her." Tatem tugged his forelock almost in a salute and led the seamen out of the cabin. "We've plenty to do. Lady Nick has this matter well in hand, I'm thinking."

"Lady Nick?" she repeated.

Higgs unshuttered the windows and light flooded the cabin. "You must excuse them, miss," Higgs said, blinking slowly. Dark splotches showed under his sleepless eyes like deep bruises. "They're naught but simple sailors. Lord Nick has chosen you, so to their way of thinking, you must be his lady. Lady Nick."

"Hmm." There were worse fates, she was certain. "Well, help me get him out of these wet things."

"Aye," Higgs said, tugging off Nick's boots. "Hold up this blanket while I take care of his trousers and trews."

Eve smiled and obeyed him without a word, averting her gaze. She was grateful for Peregrine's calm, competent presence. She'd already seen every bit of Nicholas, but Higgs seemed to want everything done with decency.

Nicholas wouldn't care one whit and in fact, would be amused by having her undress him.

After Higgs smoothed the sheets over his captain's waist, Eve lowered the blanket and helped support Nick into a sitting position while Higgs removed his shirt.

"Oh!" She put a hand to her lips. There was a little blood on the pillow.

Ashen-faced, Higgs parted Nick's hair to reveal a gash and a goose-egg-sized lump at the base of his skull. "I didn't see this before. What shall we do for him?"

Eve had seen two men with similar injuries during her stay at Newgate Prison. One came round on his own after a bit, complaining of an empty belly and a blinding headache.

The other never woke up.

"I can bathe off the salt," she said, noticing the tiny grains trapped in the dark hairs on his arms and chest. "And then, Mr. Higgs, we wait and hope."

Higgs cleared his throat. "I watched a physician perform trepanation on a gentleman with an injury like this once. He said it relieved the pressure and allowed the body to heal. Without his intervention, the patient had no hope. We've no surgeon on board, but with your help, I believe I could—"

"Absolutely not!" Eve said, aghast. "No one is going to cut open his skull."

Tatem returned with the pitcher and rags, and then disappeared to continue his duties. Eve poured some of the steaming water into a basin and wet the rags.

"I can manage now, Mr. Higgs," she said in a gentler tone. "You need some rest."

"Yes, miss," he said. "I expect you've the right of it." Then his young face hardened and he straightened to his full height. He seemed to have grown a couple inches in just the short time she'd known him. "With the cap'n down, I'm in command now. An injury like this can only be left so long and then it's too late. We'll give him till tomorrow morning at eight bells, and then I'll do the trepanation. With or without your help."

Higgs turned and strode out of the cabin.

Eve looked down at Nick, watching his chest rise and fall in shallow breaths.

"You've taught that young man so well, he's even starting to act like you—pigheaded, cocksure and devil-take-the-hindermost," she said quietly. "And if you don't want him to do something you may both regret deeply, you need to wake up before eight bells."

She found a small jar of soap and washed his face. In the deep relaxation of this unnatural sleep, all the frown lines had fled from his brow. Nicholas looked much younger, except for the couple days' worth of beard growth stubbling his chin. Eve considered shaving him, but decided against it. She didn't want to be holding a blade to his throat, in case he should wake suddenly.

She lathered a rag and washed his arms and chest. His hands were swollen and splintered and there was a deep bruise on his shoulder. Eve had seen the heavy leather harness wheel men strapped on to keep the wheel from pulling from their grip and spinning out of control in foul weather. The leather had dug a deep channel in his flesh.

She found a sewing kit on one of his shelves and used a needle to work the splinters out of his fingers and palms. When she swabbed his wounds with the contents of his silver flask, he didn't even flinch. A sure sign he was totally insensate.

She turned back the bottom of the sheet and washed his feet and legs. When she tucked the blankets around him again, his face was still deathly pale.

She propped open the stern windows for a breath of

air. The rap of hammers and the rasp of saws wafted in along with the fresh salty tang.

"The rest of your crew is working and here you are lazing about like a slugabed." She hoped her voice might make him stir. He didn't twitch an eyelash.

She took a clean cloth and turned his face toward the bulkhead so she could bathe the gash on the back of his head. The blood had matted his hair, but she scrubbed it clean. He didn't respond when she dabbed the spot with whiskey. The one bright spot was that the knot just below the gash hadn't grown any larger.

Nick had a little brown mole right at his hairline behind his ear. She bent and placed a soft kiss on the small imperfection. Then she propped him onto his side so she could soap his broad back and his backside to remove the last of the salt residue. Afterward, she let him roll back into the indentation in the feather tick.

There was only one part of him she hadn't cleaned.

"And this is no time to be a prude," she told herself. It wasn't as if she hadn't already seen Nick's cock and balls. But when she drew back the sheet and looked at him there, she knew this time was different.

His balls lay in a relaxed mound with his cock draped over them. Quiescent. Soft. Vulnerable. A wave of tenderness washed over her.

I love this man, she thought in wonderment. She covered him protectively with both hands.

And his cock resurrected itself under her palm.

"Praise be!" Eve giggled as she soaped up that part of him to remove the coating of brine, lest it gald him. Under her ministrations, he grew and swelled to an impressive size. "It appears that part of you will definitely live, Nicholas Scott."

She looked at his face, hoping to see him peeping at

her from under his dark lashes, but he didn't move. Not a twitch. Not a smirk. Not a suggestive raised eyebrow.

Her smile faded. She toweled him off and drew the sheet up to his chin.

It was time to talk to God in earnest again.

And she didn't think she ought to bargain with the King of Heaven while Nick's cock was in her hand.

Chapter Eighteen

Twilight descended on the *Susan B.* Through the open cabin windows, Eve heard rough voices and coarse jokes interspersed with the sound of carpenter's tools. The men were still working by lamplight, trying to repair the damage from the storm. She didn't dare leave the cabin to see for herself what a pounding the good ship had taken.

It was hard enough to deal with the beating the storm had given Nick.

Cook recovered from his seasickness long enough to put together a light supper. Mr. Tatem brought her some piping hot broth and bread, which she hardly touched. She tried dipping the corner of a cloth in the broth and putting it to Nick's lips, but he didn't respond.

Rhythmic chanting told her the men were hoisting a sail. In another moment, she felt the ship quicken and surge forward, borne on the wind over the waves.

The *Susan Bell* was on the mend.

The same couldn't be said for her captain.

As daylight faded completely and Eve lit the overhead lamp, she tried to convince herself that his color was better. That the unhealthy pallor was really just the result of poor light.

"You're quite brave, you know," she said. Emotion threatened to close her throat. She ruffled a hand through his hair, smoothing it against his pillow. "Quite brave and quite foolish. If only you'd listened to . . . oh, Nicholas."

She covered her mouth with her hand to muffle the sob. He should only hear pleasant sounds, not weeping and wailing.

If he could hear at all.

She rifled through his shelf of books and settled finally on a slim pamphlet. She squinted as she tried to puzzle out the words.

" '*Case of the . . . Officers of Excise,*' " she finally managed. " 'By Thomas Paine.' "

She flipped several pages. Since it promised to be deadly dull, it didn't matter where she started. She was only reading so Nick could hear her voice.

" 'To the wealthy and humane it is a matter worthy of concern that their af . . . affluence should become the mis . . . fortune of others.' "

She knew she read badly, halting time and again to decipher the sounds of the letters. But she reasoned if Nick could only hear her and know she was there, surely he'd make an effort to come back to her. She turned a few more pages, looking for an easy passage.

" 'There is a striking dif-fer-ence between . . . dis-honesty arising from want of food and want of prin . . . principle.' "

This was safer than trying to talk to Nick. While she found herself in agreement with the philosophical ramblings of Thomas Paine, the effort of reading kept her from feeling, either for the plight of the poorly paid excise men or for herself.

She stopped between sentences to see if Nicholas showed any response. The only movement was the slow rise and fall of the hands folded on his chest.

Finally, she put the book away and turned down the lamp. She stood at the windows, hugging herself as if she might fly apart. Moonlight shimmered on the black sea, leaving a long silver trail behind the ship.

Eve positioned the chair beside Nick's bunk so she could rest a hand on his chest. His heartbeat was slow, but strong, and his ribs seemed to expand with deeper breaths.

"That's a good sign," she said, more to reassure herself than him. His skin was warm, but not feverish.

She tried to find a comfortable way to rest in the straight-backed chair, but each time she started to slip into sleep, her head nodded and she jerked back to wakefulness.

She'd do Nick no good if she was giddy with exhaustion. Her decision made, she stood and unlaced her bodice.

"Wake up, Nicholas," she said softly. "I'm getting undressed."

Nothing.

She reached under her skirt and removed her panniers and petticoat. She toed off her slippers, ungartered her stockings and pulled them off. Then she eased out of her gown and stood in just her chemise.

For a moment, she remembered what glory it was to have Nick's naked body flush against hers, skin on skin.

"No, I want to wake him. Not kill him with overexcitement," she said as she propped the chair beneath the door's latch. If Nicholas wasn't awake by eight bells, she still intended to fight Mr. Higgs over the threatened trepanning. A quack had performed that barbaric procedure on her father after a horse kicked him in the head, but he died anyway. And in far more agony than if he'd been left alone to die in peace.

"But you are not going to die, Nicholas Scott," she ordered as she pulled back the sheet and eased into the narrow bunk with him. She sidled close, arranging his arm around her so she could rest her head in the crook of his shoulder. She reached up and turned his face toward her. "You are going to live to steal my maiden-head, do you hear me? If you don't, I'll never forgive you."

She couldn't be sure if she imagined it, but she was almost certain one corner of his mouth twitched.

"Miss Upshall!" Peregrine Higgs raised his voice and banged his fist against the door to the captain's cabin. "Open at once."

"I can't," came the answer. "I'm not yet fully dressed."

What the devil was she doing undressed? "How fares the captain?"

There was no answer, so Higgs pounded again. "Miss Upshall, there seems to be some obstruction here. Please open the door."

"Of course there's an obstruction. I put it there. Now unless Mr. Tatem is here with a bit of breakfast, please go away."

"Captain Scott!" he called out. "Are you awake, sir?"

"Of course, he's not awake." Miss Upshall's voice sounded closer now. If he put his eye to the crack around the door, he expected he'd see her glaring back at him. "It's far too early."

"Eight bells have sounded, miss. And we had an agreement."

"No, we did not," she answered with false honey in her tone. "You made a reckless suggestion which I utterly rejected."

Several sailors were working near the opening of the companionway. Plying their long, curved needles and sinewy thread, they pretended to be intent on mending a ripped sail, but Peregrine knew their ears were cocked to this exchange.

If he couldn't control a single woman, how could he lead these men?

"This discussion is over, Mr. Higgs."

"No, it is not."

Dammit, did she think she was the only one who cared about the captain? The success rate for trepanation, according to the doctor he'd observed, was directly proportional to the length of time between the injury and treatment. He might have already waited too long hoping the captain would come around on his own.

"If you do not open this door immediately, Miss Upshall, I'll call the ship's carpenter and have it taken down with a crowbar."

"But I told you, I'm not decent."

"Then I suggest you hurry with your toilet, miss." Peregrine turned and bellowed up the companionway in a voice that rivaled Captain Scott's at his belligerent best. "Mr. Rowley! Report to the captain's cabin! Make that double time and bring your sledgehammer!"

"Belay that order, Mr. Higgs!" a male voice rasped from the cabin.

"Captain?" Higgs pressed his ear to the door.

"Well, it's not the bloody king of France," came the muffled response. "Open the door, woman, and let the lad in before he tears my ship apart."

There was a scrape of wood on the other side of the door and it opened slowly. Miss Upshall was knotting the laces at her waist in a hurried bow, but took time to wave him in.

Captain Scott was propped up on his elbows. He still looked like death on a leeward shore. The whites of one eye were bloodred, but his eyes were both focused on Peregrine's face. He could see. His speech was clear. He'd mend.

"Mr. Higgs, don't you think the *Susan Bell*'s seen enough rough treatment without you staving in her hatches?"

"Aye, sir," he said with a grin.

"Then report, Mr. Higgs," the captain demanded.

Peregrine snapped to attention. "The bilge is holding no more than three feet of water. Pumping crews assure me that level falls by the hour. The men are repairing sail as we speak. Mr. Rowley says we'll have to wait till we raise the Turks before he can replace the foremast," he said, eyes straight ahead. "But the main mast is sound and bearing full canvas. I make our position two hundred miles south by southwest of Bermuda and our speed a solid five knots."

"And the crew?"

"All present and accounted for."

The captain let himself sink back on his pillow and closed his eyes. Miss Upshall pressed a wet cloth to his forehead.

"Actually, the number of souls aboard is more than we figured," Higgs said. *May as well tell the captain now. He's bound to find out eventually.* "We have a stowaway. Reggie Turnscrew."

The captain chuckled. "I'll wager he's thought better of that already. That was a wicked blow."

Peregrine smiled. "The boy's still pretty green about the gills. I didn't think anyone that small could cast up that much."

"We'll let the storm be his punishment, Mr. Higgs. Lord knows, it was mine." The captain draped an arm over his eyes. "Has he found his sea legs, then?"

"Aye, he's been making himself useful, between trips to the rail."

"Good," the captain said. "Put him in the galley to help Cook and tell him to be careful not to slice off something important. Is there anything else?"

There was, but Higgs figured it would keep till the captain was recovered. "No, sir."

"Carry on, Mr. Higgs."

As Higgs closed the cabin door behind him, he caught a glimpse of his captain and Miss Upshall just looking at each other. He felt his ears heat. It was a look of such soul nakedness, Higgs was as embarrassed as if he'd caught them doing the deed.

Chapter Nineteen

All through the long night of the storm, Nick had sensed Eve's presence there at the wheel with him. When he braced for each wave that crashed over him, she'd been by his side. When he strained to steer the ship's prow into the waves so that she wouldn't go belly up on the next swell, her face shimmered before his eyes and gave him strength to keep fighting.

Now she was here before him in truth. Gazing back at him with her heart in her red-rimmed eyes.

He should look away. He'd nearly killed her with his willfulness. He'd nearly doomed them all with his stubborn recklessness. He didn't deserve to have her now.

But by God, he'd take her.

"Eve—"

"Hush now," she said, dipping the cloth into the basin and returning it to his forehead, suddenly all business. "You need to rest."

"Christ, my head's pounding like a smith's hammer."

"That's to be expected," she said. "You took a nasty blow."

On the edges of his mind, he vaguely remembered the foremast snapping like a twig. The whole timber went flying past him like a giant's javelin, its rigging whistling along behind it. He'd turned and ducked, but one of the heavy pulleys whiplashed back and smacked him a glancing blow.

He put a hand to the base of his skull and fingered the tender lump. Not so glancing, after all. He'd seen stars wheeling, but somehow, he'd managed to stay upright and continue to fight the wind and waves. Then as dawn broke and the storm blew itself out, he felt himself sinking. Darkness crept into the edges of his vision till it tunneled completely. No amount of treading would keep his head above that black water.

"Good thing you woke when you did," Eve said, her voice hoarse. "Mr. Higgs was coming to perform a trepanation on you."

"Was he, now?" Nicholas started to laugh, but it made him light-headed. "I didn't know our Higgs fancies himself a surgeon."

"He was desperate," Eve said. "He thought it was the right thing to do."

"But you wouldn't let him?"

She arched a brow at him and a little of the old vinegar crept into her tone. "I think, sir, that you have need of every bit of the pudding in your brainpan."

"Ah, woman. Your tender concern touches my heart." He tapped his breastbone, but even that slight movement came at a price. Blood thundered in his head.

"Higgs was afraid for you," she said, her eyes welling. "*I* was afraid for you." Her chin quivered. Then her face crumpled. Finally, she threw herself across his chest and buried her face in the crook of his neck. "You wicked, wicked man! How could you do something so monumentally stupid?"

She swatted his shoulder right on the deep bruise. He had to bite his tongue to keep from groaning aloud. Even though she seemed spitting mad at him, at least she was in his arms. He didn't want to do anything to make her think better of it.

"Higgs tried to tell you the storm was too close, but would you listen?"

He decided the question was rhetorical and gathered her closer, stroking her back in what he hoped were soothing circles. Never mind the throbbing in his head.

"And then strapping yourself to the wheel! Of all the idiotic—"

"Someone had to—"

"Well, of course, someone had to because you just had to have your own way." She raised her head and palmed his cheeks. "Oh, Nicholas, I was sick with worry for you."

"You were?" If he'd known doing something incredibly stupid would work this well, he'd have done it much sooner. He just would have picked something that didn't endanger his ship and crew.

And her.

"I was very worried," she said softly and leaned down to kiss him. Her butter-smooth lips were a balm on his sea-blistered ones. A lock of her hair tickled against his cheek.

He wanted to kiss her back. He wanted to fist her hair and hold her mouth there for him to plunder as long as he wished, but when he ordered his hand, it rebelled. Lifting his arm was suddenly too much effort. It fell back to his side.

He was too weak to ravish a woman who was his for the taking.

God, it seemed, had a perverse sense of humor.

Eve didn't seem to mind his lethargy. She continued to kiss him till he grew dizzy. Then she pulled back and searched his face, peering down at him with a frown.

"You look terrible."

"There must be honey under your tongue. You say the sweetest things." He cocked a brow at her and winced. Every twitch was agony. Even his hair hurt.

"You can't let your crew see you like this," she announced. "The first thing we need to do is to give you a good shave."

He managed a small, painful grin. "Am I to trust you with a blade?"

"You don't have any choice in the matter, sir."

He wanted to touch her and this time, his hand responded as he willed it to. He managed to grasp her forearm. "Eve, stay a moment. Last night, I think I woke once or twice."

A curtain drew down behind her eyes.

"It seemed to me," he said slowly, "that someone was sharing my bunk."

Those blessed moments when he surfaced and felt a soft breast pressed against his chest, a slim leg carelessly hooked over his, were like a bit of heaven till the blinding pain in his head dragged him back down.

"Did you sleep beside me?" he asked.

She drew her lips into a tight line and then nodded.

"I thought so. I'm still so very tired," he said. "But I wonder if you'd do it again, while I'm awake enough to enjoy it this time."

She fidgeted with the skirt of her gown, balling it in her hands. She'd crumple it even more than it already was if she kept that up.

"You really need to eat something instead," she said.

"Later. My head won't let me touch a bite just now. Please, Eve," he said softly. "I know you must be done in, too. Only for a little while."

She hesitated a few heartbeats and then started to join him.

"Last night, you weren't wearing your gown. Were you?"

"For a man who was dead to the world, you were awfully observant."

He shrugged and then wished he hadn't. His shoulders hurt like hell.

"This is a narrow bunk," he said. "I'm only thinking there'll be more room for the two of us to sleep without all that extra fabric."

She eyed him skeptically. "That's all you're thinking?"

"No," he admitted with a wolfish grin, "but until this headache goes away and the cabin stops spinning, thinking is all I can manage."

"If it will help you sleep, I suppose there's no harm," she said primly as she picked up the chair and braced it against the door. "In case Mr. Higgs comes back unexpectedly," she explained as she began to loosen her laces.

Nick watched her with complete absorption as she removed her boned gown. Light from the stern windows was diffused through her thin chemise. He was treated to the shadows of her legs all the way up to the promised land between them. Her breasts were swinging free as she bent to scoop up the gown, fold it neatly and deposit it on the chair.

As she walked back toward him, his body roused to her. But since the slightest movement resulted in pain roughly equal to plunging an ice pick in his ear, he knew he'd just have to suffer.

But what delicious suffering! When she climbed under the sheet and molded her sweet body alongside his, his cock thrummed with excitement. He felt the hard buttons of her nipples through the cotton chemise and his body throbbed at the evidence of her arousal. If she were already his mistress, he'd take her hand and guide it to his shaft.

The mere thought of her touch made his balls tighten.

"We'll just settle this arm like so," she said, arranging him to suit her. His left arm was around her and she placed his hand at the dip of her waist. On the outside of the sheet, more's the pity.

She nestled her head on his shoulder. "Comfy?"

Like a man on a rack.

"Fine," he managed. He inhaled deeply. Her hair still smelled faintly of jasmine and the rest of her smelled of brisk sea air and warm woman.

Her breathing was deep and even as she relaxed into him. She must be worn slick after the storm and nursing him, he reasoned. He let his hand drift down to her hip, but the movement cost him. His cock, however, cheered the move with an aching twitch.

"What are you doing?" she asked, suddenly tense.

"Just trying to get comfortable," he said, drawing a deep breath. Her body melted back into his and he knew almost to the moment when she relented and let herself drift into an exhausted slumber. Her breath blew in small puffs against his chest hairs.

Nick ignored the directive from his cock and closed his eyes. The *Susan Bell* was safe. All his crew had survived. He was lying beside the delicious Eve Upshall with naught but a thin bit of cloth separating them.

It was enough. For now.

Her hand brushed against his swollen cock. It roared with aching life.

"What are you trying to do to me, wench?" he demanded. Had she forgotten so soon about the painful lump on his head?

"What do you want me to do to you?" Eve asked in sultry tones. She threw back the sheet and ran her gaze over his nakedness from head to toe. Then she walked her fingers down his chest, past his navel and circled his groin in maddeningly light touches. "Oh, that's right. Your big head's pounding so, you can hardly move your little one."

He'd known all along that the woman had a cruel side.

"*Of course, it's not so little now, is it?*" she said as she drew her finger from base to tip.

That was more like it.

"*How about . . .*" She leaned down and kissed his belly. "*If I . . .*" Her hair brushed lightly over his cock like thousands of slender fingers. "*Do the moving for you?*"

She grasped the length of him while she moved up to kiss his mouth, swallowing his response and offering her tongue in exchange. She ran her hot palm over his cock in rhythm with her tongue thrusts.

His muscles contracted in concert. His head felt suddenly just fine.

Then she reached down and gathered his balls in her palm, tugging the sac gently. She ran a fingernail along the faint strip of darker skin that marked the centerline of his scrotum, abrading his flesh. The distinction between pain and pleasure blurred.

Eve finally pulled back, peering down at him with a feline smile. "*Perhaps you'd like something else in your mouth besides my tongue?*"

"*You're reading my mind, wench. Have a care, lest I denounce you for a witch.*"

She loosed a low throaty laugh and stooped to grasp the hem of the chemise. In one smooth movement, she bared herself to him. Her breasts were alabaster globes topped with deep rose nipples. She cupped them, thrumming her thumbs across her own stiff peaks. Then she arched her back, presenting them to him as if they were offerings to a heathen god and he was empowered to accept them on the wicked deity's behalf.

She climbed astride his prone form, pressing the auburn curls that covered her sex to his chest. She was wet enough to leave a faint trail of fragrant musk as she slid down his body.

"*Is this what you want?*" She lowered her breasts toward his lips.

"*Aye, lass.*" His mouth watered and he tried to raise his head *to claim a nipple but he suddenly discovered he was bound to the bunk with a leather strap across his forehead. His hands were similarly tied.*

She sat upright, taking her luscious breasts beyond his reach. She stretched her arms overhead, lifting those orbs farther from him. He longed to run his tongue along the crease beneath them.

"Eve." He could say no more without begging.

"Oh, all right," she said, sounding more like Magdalen by the moment. "Here."

She leaned forward and gave him a teat to suck. It was like nectar on his tongue. She began rocking herself against him and moving down his body once more.

She stopped when the head of his cock met her soft opening. He strained to fill her, but she held herself out of reach.

A little fluid leaked from his tip. His balls drew up in a tight bunch, poised for release.

Then she relented and moved down, settling her naked rump on his groin. She sat upright, grinding herself down on him. He wanted to reach for her breasts, to thumb her little nub of pleasure, but he was restrained. He couldn't touch her.

"Never mind, Nick," she said. "I'll do it for you."

The tip of him protruded between her legs and she massaged his most sensitive spot with her thumb. He broke out in a cold sweat, biting his lip to keep from spilling his seed onto his own belly. She leaned forward and kissed him hard, shifting her body so the tip of him entered her.

"You'll do as I say next time, won't you, Nicholas?"

"No . . . yes . . . I don't know," he said, straining to tear loose from his bonds, but they wouldn't give. "Release me, you b—"

He was incoherent with need and he'd almost called her a bitch to boot. That'd fix things!

She sat up and rocked herself over the length of him, luxuri-

ating in her own arousal. His hips rose to meet her. She reached
between her legs to spread herself. Her fingers circled and she
arched her back in pleasure.

Nick groaned.

She relented and took him in hand, guiding him into her
warm, wet velvet. She touched herself as she moved, pushing
herself toward the pinnacle, throwing her head back, her long
black hair flying.

Her first spasm began.

Long black hair. Wait. Eve's hair was deep auburn.

He realized in fury that it wasn't Eve perched on his cock.

It was Magdalen Frith.

"No!" Nick shouted as he jerked awake.

His cock went off like a cannon anyway. He could no
more stop the reverberations than he could stop himself from bleeding if he was sliced with a saber. His
whole body shuddered with the force of his wet dream
emission.

Eve scrambled out of the bed. "What is it, Nick? Are
you hurt?"

"No." He clutched the sheet up over his chest. Maybe
she hadn't seen. "It's nothing."

He squeezed his eyes closed. His head still pounded,
but it hurt more to look into her startled face.

"I think I could eat something now," he said. Anything to get her out of the cabin for a bit.

"Of course," she said, skittering to the chair by the
door to retrieve her gown.

He kept his gaze fastened on the beams overhead
while she dressed. He'd looked at her too much. And
dreamt of looking at her far more.

Until they settled things between them in truth, he
was done sneaking peeks at her. Done undressing her

with his eyes instead of his hands. Done sharing a bunk without sharing themselves.

"I'll be back directly," she said as she pinned her long hair into a neat auburn twist. Then she moved the chair from the door. "Maybe you'll feel better after a shave, too."

She disappeared down the companionway.

No, only a good hard swive would make him feel better. And it had to be with Eve Upshall. He was either going to bed this woman or he was going to maroon himself on the first deserted isle they came to and order his crew to leave him with a single ball for his pistol.

But first, he had to crawl out of the bunk and clean off his belly.

Preferably without his head tumbling from his shoulders.

Chapter Twenty

The trouble might have been that Eve had very little experience with nursing. But honestly, Nicholas Scott was not an easy patient.

He was moody. She never knew whether he'd present her a courteous face or a snarling one.

He seemed determined to exhaust himself every day. He pushed himself further than he ought, striding the decks making sure the operation of the *Susan Bell* was humming along, putting his own back into whatever heavy labor presented itself, especially if she warned against it.

He was short with everyone, even Mr. Higgs. And when had Peregrine Higgs ever done anything but support him, even when he not-so-secretly disagreed with Nicholas?

And most puzzling of all, after sweet-talking her into doffing her gown and climbing into his bed, he'd insisted Eve take the bunk for her own. He had strung up a hammock for himself from the low beams of his cabin ceiling.

But he didn't like to lounge in it when he wasn't sleeping. So he sprawled on a blanket on the hard cabin floor this evening, one arm behind his head, the other propping his copy of *The Arabian Nights* on his chest. Eve sat in the chair, mending a ripped bit of lace on her petticoat, but she stole glances at him every other stitch.

He shifted uncomfortably, raising both knees.

"You may have the bunk, you know," she said.

He tossed a scowl in her direction and rolled onto his side, laying the book on the floor before him and propping himself on one elbow, his back to the curved stern.

"Or I could move to the bunk and you may have the chair," she suggested.

"I'm fine." He stared at the book with absorption but she noticed he hadn't turned a page in the last quarter hour.

"Don't you like your book?"

"I like it fine." He tossed her a pointed look and flipped a page noisily.

"Is your head hurting again? Maybe I should make a new poultice for—"

"My head's *fine*." He ran a hand over his head without a wince to demonstrate his recovery. "I just need a little quiet."

She turned her lips inward for a moment. Then she tied a knot in the thread, bit it off with her teeth and jabbed the needle back into the pincushion. "Perhaps I should take a turn on deck and leave you to yourself then."

"No!" he said with such force she flinched. He dragged a hand over his face. "No, Eve. Don't go."

"Then tell me what vexes you so?"

One corner of his mouth turned up and he shook his head as if in bewilderment. "You."

Her chest ached. "Then you shouldn't care if I leave." She rose and made for the door.

He beat her to it.

"No, Eve, that's not what I meant." He gripped her by the shoulders with both hands. "Ever since I met you, you've turned my life upside down. And I'm about to burst out of my own skin if I don't make love to you."

"I see." She blinked hard. "Because you've been without for some time and I'm the only available female for hundreds of miles?"

"Of course not."

When she'd first met him, she'd suspected he was the sort to mount any woman who caught his eye, but now she saw only sincerity in his eyes. "Then why?"

"I don't know. I mean, I'm not sure what to name it." He cupped her cheek. "All I know is, I can't stand being in the same space with you without holding you in my arms. I want to take off every stitch of your clothes and have you take off mine." He drew his fingers down her neck and across her collarbone. Pleasure shimmered after them.

"I want to lie down beside you, Eve. I want to touch every bit of your skin." His thumbs traced her jaw, then brushed her parted lips. "I want to know you. All of you. Not in a rush. Not afraid you'll ask me to stop at the next moment."

She didn't feel like stopping him now.

"And I want you to know me," he said in the same hushed tone people reserved for church or the grave of a loved one or some other profoundly solemn occasion.

It was no declaration of love. But neither was it a rake's false promise. Looking into his dark eyes, she sensed no guile. He wanted her.

Eve had already realized she loved him.

Perhaps that was enough.

She didn't trust her voice to speak. Instead she took his hand and brought it to the neatly tied bow at her waist. On cue, he tugged it free, not in a heated rush, but slowly, drawing out the torment. She took a deep breath and felt the boning in her bodice give.

"I'll be gentle, Eve," he said, his tone husky. "As much as I can."

She watched his face as he loosened her laces enough

for her to pull the bodice open. She slid her arms free and wiggled the bodice down over her hips until she stood before him in just her chemise, stockings and slippers.

Nick ran a finger along the lacy top of the chemise. Her nipples tightened at the nearness of his hand. He skimmed over them and placed his hand on her abdomen just south of her belly button.

Eve closed her eyes as Nick rucked up the hem of the chemise and touched her intimately. She parted her legs shoulder-width to give his hand room to delve in and find that she was already wet and slick and aching. His fingertip circled her sensitive spot, teasing and petting, whipping her into a hard little nub.

She needed this as much as he. She wanted to say a thousand things to him, but all she could do was feel.

"Hot and wanting," he whispered. "You're a goddess, Eve."

No, just a woman who loves you, Nicholas. She was thinking the words so hard, it seemed inconceivable that he couldn't hear them.

He bent his head and his mouth found her breasts, tugging at her nipples through the cotton chemise.

"Oh, yes," she moaned and untied the ribbon at the center of her neckline. The chemise parted. He pushed it off her shoulders with one hand. The other was still busy playing a lover's game with her mound. He took her nipple in his mouth. His lips on her bare skin were both torment and delight. She groaned with need as the chemise dropped off her arms; it would have pooled at her feet except for his hand between her legs holding it up.

He straightened to plant fevered kisses on her neck, her jaw, the corner of her mouth, her closed eyelids. She whimpered.

"Make that noise again and I'll rip off the rest without caring if I tear the fabric. Then I'll spread your legs and swive the very breath out of you," he promised.

"I may hold you to that."

He scooped her off her feet and carried her to the bunk, heedless of his head injury. He dropped her on the waiting linens and then flopped down beside her.

They melded together in a tangle of arms and legs, kissing, stroking, pushing away troublesome articles of clothing. Without breaking their kiss more often than absolutely necessary, she managed to pull his shirt over his head and tug off his breeches and trews. His skin was smooth and warm, stretched taut over hard muscles. He rocked against her thigh and she could feel the blood, pulsing strong through his primed cock.

"Wait, wait." She came up for air from one of his soul-stirring kisses. "We were going to go slow."

"Slow?" His chest heaved.

"Aye, slow." She sat up. Looking down the fine length of his body to his swollen cock, she nearly forgot the rest of what she'd intended to say. She was surprised to find she was panting shallowly.

He traced a circle around one of her taut nipples, watching intently as it drew even tighter. "It's been . . ." he drew a shuddering breath ". . . long enough for me. It's hard to wait." He met her gaze. "But I know you're a virgin. I want to make this good for you, so never say Nicholas Scott doesn't keep his promises. I'll go slow."

He pulled her down for another kiss. He wedged his knees between her thighs, pushing them open. She didn't fight him.

" 'Twill be all right," he said as he positioned himself. Just the tip of him entered her.

She throbbed, a deep, low drumbeat between her legs, but she narrowly resisted the urge to squirm down and take him in. She felt so *empty*, so longing to be filled.

He drew a ragged breath. "Now, listen. This is very, very important. Whatever you do, Eve, don't move till I tell you. Can you do that?"

He raised himself on his elbows to look down at her, his face taut with need.

"Why do I have to be still?" She pulled him down and peppered his face with kisses. When she reached his ear, she suckled his lobe.

Nicholas groaned. His eyes rolled back in his head and his balls tightened. He had to regain control over himself. He bit his lip. He didn't want to spill his seed all over her like a callow youth. Her hands fluttered over his back like a pair of butterflies.

Eve, oh, Evie.

Her name wove through his brain like a half-remembered song. He wasn't able to find the end of it and it kept repeating in rhythm with his impending release. He tried recalculating the last reading from the sextant in his head to distract himself.

He buried his nose in her hair and clutched her tight. There'd be one chance, only one, to earn her trust. He raised himself on his elbows to look down at her again.

His cock strained toward her. Her warmth, her wetness, the pliant womanliness of her sent blood surging through him. Her body would raise the dead, he decided.

"I'm not doing this very well, am I?" she said softly.

She must have sensed him drawing away to regain control.

"I think you're wonderful."

He bent to kiss her again, but she turned her head.

Her mouth formed a hard line across her face, her lips turned inward as if to hide from him.

"In Newgate Prison, I was witness to plenty of carnal acts. It was always as fast as the women could make it, because they couldn't bear for it to go on a moment longer than necessary," she said softly, trembling a little beneath him. "The women gave themselves to anyone who'd offer them a bit of food."

"But you didn't."

"I was only there a few weeks. I guess I wasn't hungry enough," she said. "I didn't want my first time to be part of some . . . trade. I want it to be . . . a gift."

"A treasured gift. It is my honor to be your first." *And last*, he promised himself. "If you'll let me, I'll pleasure you before I take my own satisfaction. My gift to you."

A smile lifted one corner of her mouth and he dipped to kiss her there, at the juncture of moist intimacy and smooth skin.

"I'm willing to let you try," she said, her gaze darting away, suddenly shy. "You saw me in the bath. I'm no good at this. What if I . . . just can't?"

"Then it will be my fault," he said.

He took her mouth, delving and seeking. She opened to him, accepting his exploration, playing her tongue against his in a warm, wet joust.

She moaned into his mouth.

He pulled back. "Like that, do you?"

"Come back here." She reached up and pulled his head down for another kiss.

He slipped a hand between them and found her breast. She was so soft, so "kneadable," all except her hard little nipple. He had to taste it again. She made mewling sounds that tugged at his cock.

Then he kissed his way up her throat, pausing to suck at the point of her pulse. She was so sweet, he could savor the smooth skin of her neck for hours, but he moved on, past her thin clavicle, back to the soft mounds of her breasts. He drew circles with his lips. He feathered his warm breath across them. By the time he finally took her tight little bud in his mouth, she was writhing beneath him.

He sucked. He set his teeth around her taut nipple and bit down just enough to make her whimper. Her fingers twined in his hair, kneading his scalp, heedless of the barely healed gash and receding lump.

"What should I . . . what do you want . . . me to do?" she asked raggedly.

He came up for air, surfacing like a pearl diver, dragging in a sweet lungful of her arousal.

"I don't want you to do anything," he said as he eased down and nuzzled her navel. "I just want you to feel."

She raised her arms above her head in a gesture of surrender, one forearm draped across her eyes, her artless way of shielding herself from him. Later, he didn't intend to let her hide, but this time, it might be easier for her. With a smile, he worked his way down and laid his head on one of her thighs.

From this vantage point, he could scan the hills and valleys of the kingdom of Eve. From the trembling point of her upthrust chin to the rose-tipped peaks of her breasts, the indentations of her ribs and the shallow goblet of her navel, she was all that was lovely. And farther down, the tender skin of her inner thigh, the curling hairs, the hidden folds and glistening entrance to her deepest secrets, her little nub, erect and quivering, were all waiting for him.

This was the kingdom he intended to rule, the

throne he must mount and keep. Not to subjugate her, but to serve her. To serve her well. To reveal her to herself in ways she'd not yet discovered.

It was time.

"Not yet."

Eve clenched her teeth and fisted the sheets. After all her worries about whether or not she was even capable, he'd told her *not* to let herself come.

Easy for him to say. She wasn't tormenting *him* beyond bearing.

"Almost, Eve. Only a little longer."

She was trying, but he was making things damn difficult. Her pubic hairs swayed in the hot breeze of his breath. His fingers had driven her to aching fury and now she supposed he thought this was a respite.

Then another sensation tickled along her thigh. His tongue. Warm. Wet. Just a little rough. He teased the crease of skin at her joint.

He took one of her throbbing folds between his lips. Then the tip of his tongue slid into her cleft, slippery and slick, in slow deliberate strokes, tormenting her with her own need. He circled her little nub of pleasure.

Her breath caught. She forced herself to inhale.

Both his hands cupped her bottom and he lifted her to his mouth. She didn't resist.

His lips closed over her and he suckled, ever so gently.

Ache. Throb. Want.

"Not yet," came his muffled voice.

She was hollow as a gourd. Longing stretched her out on its rack.

His tongue probed into her, a soft wet invasion. He pressed his teeth against her spot and suddenly, Eve unraveled.

Deep inside her, the insanity began, spasms of bliss. Her body bucked in tandem with the contractions over which she had absolutely no control.

"Stop. Oh, stop," she pleaded.

He showed her no mercy, driving her to a higher peak. She was dizzy and disoriented, but her insides continued to pump. Joy flooded her veins. Her limbs were no longer her own.

She felt lighter, as if she might rise from the sweat-damp sheets and float above them. Then the madness subsided and she settled back into herself.

She looked down along her body to where his dark head lay between her legs. Was she imagining it? No, her skin actually glowed a little. Then the radiance faded and her heart slowed its pounding.

But the flush of pleasure remained, wrapping her in its silken cords. She drew in deep breaths, reveling in his sharp masculine tang.

Nicholas moved up to lie beside her, his head on her pillow. He slid one long arm under her and draped the other over her, splaying his fingers possessively over her belly.

"Still think you're not good at this?" he whispered into her ear.

Her belly jiggled. "No, I think it's safe to say, I'm . . . oh my! That was . . . extraordinary." She turned her head to look at him. "You know a great deal about women, Nicholas."

"I know a great deal about you, Eve."

"You know," she said as she raised herself on her elbow to look down at him, "that's not really fair. Now that you know what I like, you're at a distinct advantage. When do I get to learn what you like?"

His smile was dazzling. "I thought you'd never ask."

Chapter Twenty-one

"You'll have to show me," she said, feeling almost desperate to return some small measure of the pleasure he'd given her.

"To begin with, you've already given me much of what I want. I love to touch you." He ran his thumb along her breastbone, then around each of her breasts. Her nipples rose once more. "And taste you."

While he sucked, his hands continued to skim over her breasts, her ribs, the curve of her waist. Delight shimmered over her, but she planted both her hands on his chest and shoved.

"But when do I get to touch?" she asked, her gaze darting southward, while heat bloomed in her cheeks. "And taste?"

"Right now, my saucy little wench," he said with obvious delight. He rolled onto his back and shifted her on top of him. Then he reached down to his discarded shirt on the floor and pulled a handkerchief from his sleeve. He folded his arms under his head, keeping the little cloth balled in one fist.

Eve tossed him a questioning glance.

"We'll need it for later," he said, "but for now, feel free to touch and taste anything you like."

"Anything?"

He lifted a brow. "Especially anything."

Eve swore under her breath and grinned at him. "You are quite full of yourself, aren't you?"

One corner of his mouth twitched up. "No, just looking forward to having *you* full of myself."

"I am, too." She slid off him and ran a hand down his flat belly and cupped his genitals. His gut clenched and his breath hissed over his teeth.

"Did I hurt you?" She drew her hand back as if from a fire.

He caught her hand and placed it over his erect cock again. "If you did, you have permission to hurt me again."

His grin was so broad, she felt her own mouth curling up to match it.

"I've heard it does hurt." Then her smile faded. "Will it . . . will you hurt me?"

He ran a hand behind her nape and pulled her down for a soft kiss.

"Aye, lass, it'll hurt," he said after he released her. He met her gaze in silence for a few moments. "But only this once. After that, 'twill be pleasure alone that's shared between us."

And what of love? Shall we share that, too? she longed to ask. This man had saved her from the sea and completely reordered his life for her and her friends. He'd quite literally swept her off her feet and endangered his ship and crew to keep her from leaving him. Wasn't that love?

How important was it to hear the words? Wretchedly important, but she still had hope she might.

"Then let us begin again." She leaned over, nipped his earlobe and was rewarded by the hitch in his breath. "So that's how I'll know if I please you."

"How?"

She pressed her mouth to his chest and ran her tongue around his hard brown nipples, reveling in the salty taste of his skin. She felt his breath quicken.

"That," she said. "The change in your breathing."

"Oh, aye. How do you think I knew what to do with you? I watched and listened. You told me every step of the way whether you liked something or not with your little moans and wee kitten noises."

"Wee kitten noises?" She ran a hand down his chest, over his flat belly and found him erect and straining. She trailed a single finger along his length and watched in fascination as his cock rose to meet her stroke. Then she grasped him firmly and he made a low groan. She arched her brows at him and slanted him a sidelong gaze. "At least, I don't sound like a bull."

She leaned down and gave his cock a playful lick. A small pearl of liquid formed at the tip.

"Have a care, Eve." He sat up and caught her in his arms. "Later I'll be able to bear more teasing, but if I let you do more of that now, you'll have me bellowing like a bull at stud."

"My every intention, sir."

His laugh warmed her to her toes. They sank back down onto the blanket in a hailstorm of kisses.

"When?" Eve asked, her tone tight, as though she forced the word out through clenched teeth.

"Not yet." Nick nuzzled between her legs, drunk on her scent, desperate to draw this first loving out, desperate to sink into her sweet flesh and find release.

"Please," she whimpered.

No, Eve. Only a little longer. Let us drain this cup to the dregs.

"I want to be sure you're as ready as possible," he said. "I'll hurt you less that way."

"I don't care if it hurts." She arched herself into his mouth. He devoured her for a moment, only pulling back when he thought he detected the slightest pulse of a contraction in the soft lips of her sex.

His balls tightened in response to her need.

Without even realizing he'd moved, he found himself knocking at her gate, poised to slide into her wet velvet. His cock screamed at him.

It was time.

He pushed in with a slow stroke, stopping at the barrier of her purity. He lifted himself on his elbows and cupped her cheeks.

He lowered his mouth to hers to distract her and gave his hips a hard thrust. He swallowed her cry, and her body tensed beneath him.

"No more pain," he promised as she molded around him in a warm, wet embrace. His balls drew up into a tense mound. He held himself motionless, willing the urgency to subside so he could revel in the joy that was Eve a little longer. Only a little. His heart pounded in his cock.

"No more pain," she whispered.

He began to move.

She was tight and wet and the sweetest little morsel he'd ever had. She moved with him, tilting her hips to take him in all the way. He quickened his pace.

When he looked down at her, at the soft gape of her mouth, the way her brow furrowed in distress, he knew he couldn't keep her much longer balanced between want and release. He had to let her come.

He covered her mouth with his and flicked his tongue in, loving her with his tongue and his cock in tandem. She moved beneath him, urging him in deeper with little noises of desperation that threatened to shred his control.

A little longer. She was so warm and tight.

She turned her head away. "I can't stop—"

He felt it start.

Nicholas arched his back, driving in as deep as he could. Her inner walls contracted around him. Bliss, sharp as a blade, sliced through him, rending him soul and marrow.

Her whole body convulsed under him. Pleasure whipped around him, through him, radiating from his groin out to his fingertips. Eve flared beneath him into a fiery glow, like a being aflame.

Then he began pulsing. He pulled out and covered his cock with the handkerchief just in time to catch the hot spurts of his seed.

Alone at the end. As usual.

Nick wouldn't chance getting her with child. He was used to making sure his mistresses didn't increase. It was part of the unspoken bargain. They each took pleasure and Nick made certain no one paid for it with her life in childbed.

But after all their bedplay, all their heart-stopping lovemaking, it felt like a cheat to pull out of that final joining with Eve.

For both of them, if her puzzled frown was any sign of what might be dancing in that pretty head of hers.

When her breathing slowed to normal, she sat up.

"Why did you do that?" she asked.

"Why do you think?" His tone was surlier than he intended. She had been a virgin, but a knowledgeable one in some ways. Was it possible she could be ignorant of what caused a woman to bear?

"You didn't want to give me a child," she said.

"No, I didn't, and you're welcome."

"Get off, you oaf," she said, shoving him out of her way and onto the floor. He landed on his bare arse with a thud. By the time he found his feet, she'd donned her chemise and was tugging on her stockings.

So much for after-play.

"What's wrong with you?" he demanded.

"How can you ask that, you barnacle-crusted toad?"
She wiggled into her gown and cinched the laces at her
bodice tight. "You take my maidenhead and then you
won't chance getting me with child. What? Are you
afraid I'll force you into marriage?"

Marriage? Where had that come from? There'd been no
talk of marriage between them.

"Eve, why are you making this more complicated than
it is?" What they had was extraordinary. Why muck
things up with talk of marriage? He dragged a hand
through his hair. "Besides, you should know by now that
no one can ever *force* me into anything."

Her slipper came flying through the air, but he
caught it before it could bean him squarely on the nose.

"No, of course not," she said. "Because you're bloody
Lord Nick, master of all you survey."

"Damn right, I am."

"Well, you're not the master of me." She grabbed the
slipper from him and balanced stork-legged while she
stuffed her foot into it. "And you're well enough not to
need a nurse anymore."

She turned and started to open the door. Nick
shoved it closed and held it fast with one hand above
her head.

"Let me go," she said, her voice brittle as French glass.

"Not until we've settled things," he said.

She turned and leaned her back against the door,
crossed her arms over her chest and glared up at him.
"And just what do you think we need to settle?"

"You'll want a stipend, I should think."

"A stipend?"

"That's how it's usually done. A line of credit at the

milliner and modiste, of course. Jewelry, if you care for it. I've a mind to see you in a long rope of pearls." *And nothing else.* "You might want some provision for a pension, but I've never been anything but generous to my mistresses." He leaned down to kiss her, but she turned her face away at the last moment, leaving him to plant his lips in her hair. "Besides, I don't intend for you and I to have a parting."

That should please her.

"Oh, you don't?"

"No, Eve, I don't." He suspected now would be the time to speak of love, if he had any talent in that quarter, but he had ever been a man of action, not flowery sentiment. "We can draw up a contract if you like, but my word has always been good."

"Your word," she said softly, relaxing her stance. "You'd really give me your word?"

"Aye, my word." He smiled down at her.

She returned his smile. And then she grasped his shoulders and rammed her knee into his unprotected groin. He bent double, cupping his genitals with both hands.

"That, Captain Scott, is *my* word."

She was out the door before he could stop her.

The way his gut roiled, he wasn't sure he wanted to. He wallowed on the floor in agony for a few moments. Then he dragged himself back to the bunk and climbed in, drawing his knees up with a low groan.

The little minx had tried to unman him.

And he was forced to inhale her lingering scent on his pillow. Sweet, soft, opening to him like a lily to the sun.

And now she was gone.

Emptiness closed over him like a coffin lid.

He searched for anger and was strangely surprised to

find none. He was more puzzled than anything else and so hollowed out, he didn't think he'd ever be full again.

Eve's absence hurt him even worse than his aching balls.

Chapter Twenty-two

Rage carried Eve as far as the door leading out of the companionway and onto the open deck. She saw only Mr. Tatem on the poop manning the wheel. While the rest of the *Susan Bell*'s crew slept, she was sure there was at least one other soul about serving as officer of the watch.

She strode to the rail and then marched forward, trying to put as much distance as she could between herself and Nicholas. Even though her knee to his groin had incapacitated him, as she'd learned in Newgate it would do to any man if delivered with enough force, she knew the effects were short-lived. Eventually, his strength would return and he'd be furious.

She only hoped he took the time to throw his clothes back on before he came looking for her. She didn't want to see his glorious naked body again.

Ever.

Liar, her aching heart named her.

When she reached the pointed prow, she grasped the rail with both hands and stared ahead into the darkness. The deck rose and fell gently beneath her feet. She drew in a deep lungful of rain-washed air.

And smelled Nicholas on herself. There was no mistaking his sharp, masculine tang.

The clouds had fled in the wake of the storm and stars shimmered overhead, winking down at their reflections in the black water. If Nick only loved her, they'd be looking at the stars together now.

Rage gave way to despair. Eve's chin quivered.

She broadened her stance to keep her balance as the swells came harder beneath the ship. Her inner thighs were still slick and wet. She laid her head down on the rail and let the tears come.

He only treats me as a whore because I played one. What had she been thinking?

She hadn't.

She'd let her body make her choices, trusting Nicholas Scott, of all people, to do right by her.

"The man wouldn't know what's right if it bit him on the arse," she whispered down to the *Susan B*'s buxom figurehead.

And neither did she, evidently. But how could she deny her heart? She loved him, blast the man!

Maybe a knee to the groin wasn't the best way to show it, but how else could she have gotten his attention?

"A stipend!" she said with disgust. As if she'd entered into a matter of commerce with him. A damned service arrangement!

Despair dissolved into shame.

He thought he could buy the use of her body on an ongoing basis, when she thought she'd offered him her heart. She put her hand to her mouth to muffle her sobs.

"Miss Upshall." Mr. Higgs's voice interrupted her misery. "What are you doing here?"

She straightened and swiped her eyes. "I needed a change of air."

Eve had hoped to avoid the officer of the watch by hiding in the forwardmost part of the ship. She didn't know many of the sailors since she'd been cooped up in Nick's cabin for most of the voyage. On the *Molly Harper*, she and her friends had been warned not to wander about the ship alone; seamen were not known for gentlemanly behavior and couldn't be trusted. But as it was Mr. Higgs who found her here, she felt no trepidation at being caught on the deck alone. Higgs was comfortable as an old frock.

"You've been crying," he pointed out as if she wasn't aware of it. "Is something the matter with the captain? Is he worse?"

Worse than what? she almost asked. *A kick to the head? A knife to the heart?*

"No, Mr. Higgs, the captain is fine."

Well, he would be after the swelling in his balls went down, but Higgs didn't need to know those particulars. She blew her nose on the hanky he offered her, thankful that Peregrine Higgs was enough of a gentleman not to press any further for the reason behind her tears.

Why couldn't she have fallen in love with someone so dependable? So steady as Higgs. Why in heaven did she have to lose her heart and her maidenhead to the bloody Lord of Devil Isle himself?

"You're sure the captain is well?" Mr. Higgs asked.

As well as a demon in mortal form can be.

"Aye, he's well enough. In fact, the captain is so fully recovered, he no longer requires my nursing. Is there another cabin where I may stay?" she asked. "I can no longer remain in his without damage to my reputation."

The hammock Nick had strung up for himself kept up the illusion that her presence in his cabin was merely for the sake of his health. His crew seemed to have forgotten that he'd carried her on board under protest and kept her in his locked cabin even before the storm.

As usual, whatever *Lord Nick* did was right.

Even if she became his mistress publicly, he'd suffer no censure for it. Only Eve's name would suffer.

It wasn't fair, but it was as much the way of the world as the eastern sunrise.

"The *Susan Bell* isn't equipped for passengers, miss," Higgs said, frowning. "All the crew sleeps in hammocks strung belowdecks."

"No officer's quarters?" she asked hopefully.

Higgs shook his head. "We're a trim ship with no wasted space. A cargo ship, you see."

An idea popped into her head. "A smuggler's ship, perhaps?"

Higgs shrugged. "On occasion, the old girl has been known to bear a few items not listed on the manifest."

"Then you must have a smuggler's hold," she reasoned. Who knew a few weeks in Newgate Prison would have taught her so much about criminal activity of all sorts? "Someplace the excise men wouldn't think to look, even if they boarded you."

Higgs smiled. "You are too clever by half, Miss Upshall. Aye, we have a secret hold, but it's not fit for the likes of you."

"Let me be the judge of that, will you, Mr. Higgs?" She sniffed once more into the hanky. "May I see it?"

Higgs frowned. "I ought to ask the captain first. Not even everyone on the crew knows where the secret hold is located. The fewer who know a secret, the likelier it'll be kept, you see."

She tried flashing her most winning smile at him. "I can keep my own counsel, Mr. Higgs. Your secret will be safe with me."

"All the same, that's a decision for the captain." Higgs straightened to military bearing and Eve wondered what sort of service Higgs had seen in the past. "If you'll wait here, I'll make inquiry for you."

"No, Mr. Higgs," she said. "Please don't trouble him."

"No trouble. I'm only glad you alerted me to this change in his condition so we can alter matters."

Without another word, Higgs turned on his heel and

strode away. Taking with him her one chance to hide on board the ship.

Higgs could barely contain his fury. He'd served Nicholas Scott with a willing heart for better than ten years, but his patience was finally spent. He tolerated Nick's eccentricities because he was the best seaman Peregrine had ever met. But since the captain had abducted Miss Upshall and put his crew and ship into needless harm, Nick had tumbled from the pedestal on which Higgs had enshrined him.

Now he'd made Miss Upshall cry.

It was time to have it out with Nick—first mate to captain.

And if that didn't work, man to man.

When Peregrine rapped on the cabin door, the captain called out for him to enter in a voice like thunder. Higgs screwed his courage and shoved open the portal.

The captain was seated on his bunk, his long legs dangling over the side. A sheet was draped over his lap, but otherwise, he was clearly naked.

"Report, Mr. Higgs."

"What have you been doing to Miss Upshall?" The words flew out of Peregrine's mouth before he thought better of them.

The captain's brows lowered in a frown. "Nothing that need concern you."

Higgs fisted his hands at his sides. "If you've abused her, it concerns me."

"If I've abused her?" Cap'n Scott laughed mirthlessly and shifted on the bunk with a wince. "You've got things backward, lad. I'm afraid the boot's quite on the other leg."

"Then why did I find her in tears?" Higgs straightened to his full height, which was difficult since some of the ceiling beams were low. "And I ceased being a lad some time ago."

The captain arched a brow at him. "Aye, so you did. Tears, hmm. What did she tell you?"

"That you're well enough so she no longer needs to remain in your cabin to tend you." Privately, Higgs thought the captain's color was a little off. He looked ready to cast up his accounts, but surely Miss Upshall knew best. After all, she'd been right to keep Higgs from attempting that trepanation. "She wishes to see if the secret hold will do for her during the remainder of the voyage."

"And how in thunder did she learn about that hold?" he bellowed.

Higgs swallowed hard. Captain Scott had intimidated better men than he. But none as determined to champion a lady's cause as Peregrine Higgs.

"She guessed we might have done a bit of smuggling over the years," he admitted. "And I confirmed that we had such a spot. All she wants is a bit of privacy. It seems a simple enough request. If you'd seen her weeping . . ."

"Are you daft, man? Women use tears like the Royal Navy uses nine pounders." Nicholas dragged a hand over his face. "They soften you up and then when you least expect it, it's 'prepare to be boarded.' And let me tell you, Higgs, brigands and privateers may parley, but women give no quarter."

"Permission to speak freely, sir."

"What the devil have you been doing?" the captain asked with indignation. Then he shrugged and waved a hand. "Permission granted."

"I've sailed under your colors for more seasons than I can remember and I've always supported you." Higgs set his face. Now that he'd started, he couldn't stop. "But you've gone too far this time."

The captain narrowed his eyes. "Explain yourself."

"When you rescued the women overboard the *Molly Harper,* every man jack of us was proud to serve under you. When you took the ladies into your home and treated them with proper respect, we saw you for what we all believed you truly are, sir, a gentleman at heart."

"You, of all people, should know better than that, Higgs." The captain's eyes flashed a warning, but Higgs pressed on.

"Then you brought Miss Upshall on board against her will. You put to sea and sailed ahead of a storm when any prudent seaman would have stayed in port," Higgs said. "To say your judgment has been cloudy of late is to be charitable indeed."

"Is that all?"

"No. I'll not have you bringing Miss Upshall to tears again," Higgs said, squaring his shoulders.

"You'll not have it?" The captain rose, still clutching the sheet around his middle. "Blast it all, Higgs, what right have you to interfere? Never say you fancy her!"

"No, nothing like that," Higgs said. His heart was still in the keeping of the delicious Miss Sally Munroe, whether that lady knew it or not. "But it's not only my right to interfere. It's my duty."

"Your duty?"

"Miss Upshall is not like Magdalen Frith and the others, sir. She is a lady. I mean to see she is treated like one. She deserves the privacy of her own cabin on board."

"What if I say she'll remain with me anyway?"

Higgs shifted his weight. "Then sir, I would have to challenge you, though it gives me no pleasure to do so."

Nicholas Scott threw his head back and laughed, though there was no joy in the sound. Then he sank back onto the bunk.

"So, it's come to this. I swear, that woman's worse than a nor'easter. Who'd have thought anything could drive a wedge between you and me?"

Higgs knew what he meant. When Higgs first went to sea as cabin boy, Nicholas Scott took him under his wing. He was like the older brother Higgs never had. He didn't let Higgs's speech impediment keep him from promotion, and gradually Higgs lost the stammer completely each time they set sail. Everything Peregrine knew about the sea, the captain had taught him. He devoutly believed there was no greater sailing man on the seven seas than Nicholas Scott.

But Peregrine had no desire to learn what the captain knew about women. When a petticoat was involved, Nicholas Scott sowed nothing but grief all around. His disastrous marriage had been tempestuous, at best. His riotous affairs were like skimming a vessel over a shallow shoal. Eventually the bottom of the hull would always be ripped out.

And Higgs wanted to spare Miss Upshall, if he could. At least until he could make sure she was with the captain of her own accord. After that, he could wash his hands of the situation with a clear conscience.

"Very well, Higgs," the captain said wearily. "Miss Upshall will have her private quarters. Where is she?"

"I left her near the bowsprit."

"Go back and make sure she stays there, till I come for her."

"Aye, Cap'n." Higgs straightened smartly and turned to the door. He stopped with his hand on the knob. "There's one more thing, sir."

"What is it?"

"At the end of this voyage, I'm resigning as your first officer." Higgs didn't dare tear his gaze from the brass doorknob. "It gives me no pleasure to do it, but I think it for the best."

"A man must make his own decisions," the captain said slowly. "Do as you will."

Higgs closed the door behind him softly. The captain had finally called him a man.

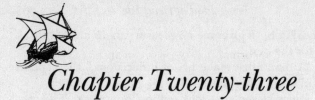

Chapter Twenty-three

Nick dressed with care, making sure every button was fastened, every seam on his breeches straight. His balls still ached, but the pain had subsided to a manageable discomfort. The nausea had passed. He pulled his hair back into a queue and bound it with a leather thong. Finally, he cocked his tricorne on his head at a rakish angle.

After all, a gentleman had to be at his best to do a lady the honor she "deserved." Satisfied, he took a final look around the cabin. He'd made the bunk and tidied the small space. There was fresh water in the ewer and a clean towel hanging from the peg.

She'd have no cause for complaint now.

He made his way to the prow where Higgs and Eve were involved in a heated, but whispered conversation. He listened for a few seconds, but couldn't make out any of the words. She sounded upset and off balance. Every few seconds, she knocked her fist on the rail.

Miss Upshall was discomfited. That was something at least.

"Ah, there you are," he said as he came around a large coil of rope. "Thank you, Mr. Higgs. Relieve Mr. Tatem at the wheel, if you please. I'll stand the rest of your watch. That'll be all."

Higgs saluted smartly and turned on his heel as if the great divide that now yawned between them was but a figment of Nick's imagination.

"But, Captain—" Eve began.

"Nicholas," he corrected. "I rather think it's too late to return to formalities between you and me, Eve. Don't you agree?"

She turned and rested both forearms on the gunwale. "Nevertheless, I would prefer that we observe them."

"Oh, aye, I've heard a great deal about your preferences this night." He settled against the rail beside her, turned so he could watch the moonlight silver her features. "In this instance, I fear you'll just have to bear the disappointment. I shall continue to call you Eve and I insist you call me Nicholas."

"It wouldn't be appropriate."

"It would be inappropriate not to. For good or ill, we are no longer mere acquaintances whom bad luck and the sea have tossed together." He noticed her hands were trembling. "My dear Eve, we are 'intimates' and the sooner you come to terms with it, the better off you'll be."

"You mean the better off you'll be." She clutched her hands together to still them. "After all, it would mean you have a mistress to swive whenever you've a mind to."

He made a tsking sound, though her earthy tongue amused more than shocked him.

"Did I say anything more about you becoming my mistress?" He covered her hands with one of his. They were icy cold. She pulled them away and crossed her arms beneath her breasts. "No, I just pointed out the obvious. You can't unring a bell. You can't undo a deed."

"And it's much easier for a man to take advantage of a woman he's already ruined and insist she become his mistress," she hissed at him. "What a very convenient philosophy."

"No, it's more an acknowledgment of the facts." He

grinned down at her. "We have been lovers, Eve. No amount of formal language can change that. But evidently you're still thinking about becoming my mistress since you keep bringing it up."

She whipped back her arm to strike him, but he caught her hand and held it fast.

"I think there's been enough violence done between us this night, don't you?" he asked softly, his gaze never wavering from hers. The fire went out of her eyes and she bit her lower lip.

"I'm sorry if I hurt you," she said, tears trembling on her lower lashes.

"And I you."

Where did that come from?

Apologies were for weaklings. All he'd done was offer to provide her with a life of luxury and shared pleasure at his side. Why was he apologizing for that?

He cleared his throat. "I believe you want your own accommodations."

"Mr. Higgs mentioned your smuggler's hold as a possibility."

"And I should have the turncoat flogged for it," he said with a snort.

Her eyes flared wide and he could have kicked his own arse.

"No! Please, Mr. Higgs didn't do anything wrong. It was my fault. I—"

He grasped her shoulders. *Christ, why did I mention flogging to her of all people?* "Steady on, Eve. I'm not such a monster as that. Mr. Higgs is in no danger from me." He loosened his grip but didn't release her. "And neither are you. If you'll come with me, I have a private cabin prepared for you."

She blinked in surprise. "Where?"

"If I'm not in it with you, what does it matter?" He offered her his arm. "My absence seems to be your main requirement, after all."

She hooked a hand around his elbow. "You make it sound as if I'm being unreasonable."

Aren't you? he wanted to ask, but he bit back his frustration.

He'd never had a woman refuse him. None of them had even led him much of a chase. It was enough for him to crook a little finger and they'd come running. And once he bedded them, they always seemed ready for more of his brand of bedplay. Eve had certainly enjoyed it if her body-bucking climax was any measure. He couldn't decide if he was bewildered or hurt by her aversion to him now.

"I think you'll find this arrangement to your liking," he said, trying to keep his tone even as he walked her across the open deck.

She cast him a sidelong glance. "I don't know. I wasn't terribly receptive to your last offer of an 'arrangement.' My opinion has not altered since our last conversation. I will not be your kept woman."

"There you go, bringing up being my mistress again," he said with a wry grin. "Have I said aught more about the proposition?"

"No," she admitted with a frown. "But you were thinking about it."

He chuckled. "You're right. However, no man may be held accountable for his thoughts, Eve." His smile faded, as he chased those libidinous ideas. "No matter how pleasurable, how forbidden those thoughts may be."

Nicholas stopped and gazed down at her. Lust flared in him again. Her lips parted slightly and he remembered how she'd looked when she came beneath him, slack-mouthed, passion-spent and gasping. He could still taste her salty-sweet slit.

"Nicholas . . ." Her lids drooped and he sensed she, too, was reliving their lovemaking. It felt so right between them, this fiery connection, this instant surge of heat.

If she were any other woman, he'd scoop her up then and there and carry her back to his bed. He'd take her hard and fast and make her body remember she wanted him, even if her lips claimed she didn't.

He'd prove her a liar.

But she wasn't any other woman. She was Eve. And he wanted more than a good hard swive from her. Much more.

He just wasn't sure how to get it. Or even what "it" was. *Love?*

He batted that notion away. His last bout with love had ended with heartache all around. Love was loss. Love was pain. It was pure folly to even consider taking to those murky waters again.

And yet, here was Eve Upshall standing before him, doe-eyed and ripe for the taking.

But not if the price was love.

He cupped her cheek. "No woman may be held accountable for her thoughts either." Her skin was like satin under his hand and he sensed her leaning slightly into his touch. "Unless she wants to act on them of her own free will."

That broke the spell. Eve turned her eyes away. "Please take me to my new accommodations."

"You'll find them rather like your old ones," he said as he led her back down the companionway.

"No, Nick." She stopped dead in the narrow space. "I'll not share a cabin with you."

"I'm not expecting you to." He opened the cabin door

and waved her in. "Please accept my quarters as your own for the duration of our voyage." When she didn't budge, he propped the door open and strode in by himself. He unhooked his hammock from the low ceiling beams. "I'll string my bed with the men belowdecks for now."

"You would do this for me?" she said softly.

Christ, he'd battled a shark for her, hadn't he? When would the woman learn he'd do anything for her? But he only said, "Aye, lass. It's a small matter."

"Not to me." Eve stepped back into the cabin. The space still held the musk of their lovemaking, but she didn't seem to notice. "Thank you, Nicholas."

She stood on tiptoe and planted a quick kiss on his cheek. Her tremulous smile warmed him clear to his toes.

Nick beat a hasty retreat. He sensed he'd won a strategic victory of some sort. Staying any longer might tempt him beyond bearing and he didn't want to give back the slight advantage he'd gained.

Once he closed the cabin door behind him, he sagged against it, shaking his head. He'd never been so off balance. His life had always been about setting goals and achieving them. Since it was clear Eve wouldn't be his mistress, he wasn't even sure what outcome to hope for in this romantic skirmish.

He only knew that he had made her happy.

And even though he'd spend the rest of the voyage swinging in a hammock alongside his sweaty, farting, snoring crew, he was strangely happy, too.

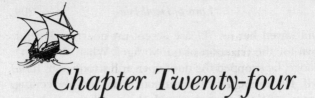

Chapter Twenty-four

The trip from St. Georges to the Turks should have taken them five days, owing to a favorable current. Since the storm blew the *Susan Bell* well out of that invisible path in the sea, it took nine days instead.

Eve stood at the gunwale and peered into the distance. The color of the sea had lightened from deep indigo to delicate turquoise, so she knew the ocean floor was rushing up to meet the *Susan B*'s hull. She raised a hand to shield her eyes from the glare of sun on the water. At the edge of the earth, she saw faint blue and white smudges.

"Is that Turks?" she asked Nick, who was standing beside her with his spyglass at one eye while he scanned the horizon.

"Aye, lass." He handed her the glass so she could see a hint of palm trees rising from the blur of land. "'Tis the second point on our little triangle."

"Triangle?" Eve frowned, trying to pick out anything that resembled one on the distant shore.

"Our trade triangle."

Nick had removed himself from his cabin, but his instruments and charts were still stored there. Eve had been privy to his navigational calculations and was amazed by his mathematical abilities. When she expressed her admiration, he merely said, "It's all just lines and angles, basic geometry really."

Now she realized he often thought in the shapes of navigation as well.

"Bermuda and Turks," she said. "And the third corner of your triangle is . . . ?"

"Charleston," he admitted, then hurried on. "Think of it as a triangle with all sides the same length. We have more cedar than we need in Bermuda, but there's no lumber to speak of on Turks or Caicos. Those little islands are dotted with natural *salinas* where seawater collects through the rocks and leaves behind a thick brine. The Colonies are always desperate for more salt. We need foodstuffs from the Colonies and so the triangle is complete."

"And you profit at every corner of the triangle," she said, but all she was thinking was *Charleston*. He was going to take her to Charleston, after all. And by rights, she should be thrilled, but for some unaccountable reason, her belly spiraled downward.

"Aye, lass, but don't sound so doubtful about it. There's no harm in profit," he said with a grin. "After all, it's my ship and crew taking the risks. It's only fair we should reap some benefits."

He hadn't even tried to reap anything from her for the last few days. Eve sighed and mentally cursed herself. She should be grateful he stayed away. It saved her from having to shove him aside if he was still intent on making her his mistress instead of offering marriage as a gentleman should.

But in the meantime, she noticed him intently at every turn. The crisp dark hairs peeping from the deep vee in his shirt, the way his eyes met hers at unguarded moments, his strong hands on the ship's wheel—they all made her squirm inside her clothes. Even keeping his distance, the man had the power to seduce.

"Look sharp, lads," Nick called out. He gave the order to drop some of the ship's canvas in order to slow their approach. "The sandbars shift from time to time and we don't want to end up like those poor bastards."

He pointed down into the crystalline water to the wavering remnants of a ship whose back was broken over the coral on the steeply rising ocean floor. A long barracuda floated over the sunken prow.

"The islanders scavenge every wreck they can, but this one's pretty deep," Nick said. "Went down in the last hurricane, I'll wager."

Eve watched the wreck passing beneath them until it fell astern. When she looked up, the islands were drawing nearer. She could tell that, like Bermuda, Turks and Caicos was a cluster of little dots of land all alone in the vast blue. The *Susan Bell* skirted along the eastern edge of the archipelago.

"Prepare to drop anchor," Nick ordered.

"We're not going in to port?" Eve asked as the men scurried to do Nick's bidding.

"There is no port," he explained. "No deep harbor. The *Susan B* is shallow on the draft, but even she'd have her belly scraped if we dared too much farther. So we anchor outside the reef and use the jolly boat. Will you be pleased to go ashore, Eve?"

"Oh, yes," she said gratefully. She was mortally tired of having the world heaving beneath her feet. "I assume there's a decent inn."

Nick grinned. "You assume wrong. Grand Turk is but a notch or two above a pirate's hole, but I'll see you suitably protected from the rain. I've a business partner on the island I usually stay with, but I warn you, the ratio of men to women is decidedly lopsided here. You'll have to share a chamber with me if you decide to venture ashore, for your own protection."

"And who'll protect me from you?"

"I will," he said softly.

"That's not very reassuring."

"Stay or go as you please, Eve. It's of no consequence to me either way, but if you are going, I need to know now." His knuckles whitened as he grasped the gunwale. "Choose."

She looked up into his deeply tanned face. His dark eyes searched hers, but otherwise he was perfectly still. She didn't even think he drew a breath.

"I'd like to go," she said.

His lips twitched, but otherwise she had no idea if he was pleased or disappointed. He touched the brim of his tricorne briefly and left her side to supervise the anchoring of his ship at a safe distance from the white shore.

Eve looked back at the island, where clumps of palms swayed. Tangles of blooms overlooked the long stretch of sand. A breeze brought the scent of hibiscus and oleander wafting toward them. If ever there was a setting for seduction, this was it.

"What am I doing?" she murmured.

But for the life of her, she wouldn't undo it. Nicholas didn't seem to want her to come ashore, especially. Did he have a brown-skinned girl waiting for him on this island?

The mere thought of Nick with another woman disturbed her. For good or ill, she loved him and she couldn't bear to lose him.

But if he didn't love her, she couldn't very well keep him either. Eve remembered her first day at St. Georges and the gorgeous dark-haired woman who whipped her horse past them as they drove up to Nick's home for the first time.

That'd be Magdalen Frith. Lord Nick's regular lady, Reggie Turnscrew had told them.

At the time, Eve was too concerned over what would meet them at the top of the hill to spare any thought for the woman barreling down it. Now she wondered about Miss Frith.

And all the others who had undoubtedly preceded her.

If Eve relented and became Nick's mistress, how long would it be before he tired of her and sent her packing down that long, winding cart path? Wouldn't losing him be all the more bitter after having had him?

"Miss Upshall? The cap'n sends his compliments and asks will you be pleased to board the jolly boat?" Mr. Higgs's voice pulled her from her dark musings.

Eve followed Higgs to the opposite side of the ship, where the landing party was climbing over the gunwale to the boat bobbing alongside. Nick was already at the tiller of the small craft.

"I can't clamber down like that," Eve said. Not only would she likely lose her footing or catch her hem in the rope ladders, but all the men in the jolly boat would be treated to a view up her broad skirts.

"Of course not, miss," Higgs said. "That's why the captain asked us to set up the hoist. We use it to load cargo when we're riding at anchor like this, but it'll do fine to lower you to the jolly boat."

Seaman Tatem brought out a woven cane chair and lashed it to the end of the boom. Eve settled into it and tucked her skirts tight, both around and between her legs. The crew heaved her up and over the gunwale. Then they lowered her gently down to the waiting boat while Nick shouted directions.

Nicholas was there to grab the swaying chair with a grin on his face. "That wasn't so bad, was it?"

"No, it was fun, actually," she admitted. "Much better than having you strap a rope around me and haul me up like you did that first night."

"Not from this vantage point," he said with a rakish grin as he helped her onto the seat beside him. "I much preferred the other view."

Higgs and the remaining crew hauled the cane seat back up. Then Nicholas raised his voice. "Cast off, lads. Now put your backs into it."

Eight pairs of oars moved in concert as the jolly boat pulled away from the *Susan B* and rocked over the waves toward shore.

Once the hull scraped the beach, the first pair of seaman leaped into the spray and hauled on the prow, dragging the boat forward. The next set of oarsmen followed suit. Finally Nick stepped into the curling surf up to his knees, holding out his arms to Eve.

"Only one way to land without wetting your feet," he said as he scooped her up and carried her past the sand to the sparse salt grass.

"Nicholas Scott, as I live and breathe," came a booming baritone from behind a tall clump of date palms. "I always tell Maia you'll die at the hands of a jealous husband. I can only assume none have caught you yet."

Eve turned to see a large man in tattered knee britches and a buttonless waistcoat lumbering toward them. He wore no shirt and his bare arms and chest were as dark as some of Nick's African crewmen, but his long, English face and startling blue eyes proclaimed him a displaced son of London.

"I see Maia's cooking is still as fine as ever, Hugh," Nick said as he set Eve lightly on her feet. "You've gained two stone over the winter if you've gained an ounce."

The man patted his protruding brown belly. "My woman likes a man with meat on his bones and who am I to argue?"

His eyes flicked over Eve with amused interest.

"Hallo, luv." He removed a greasy and battered tricorne to reveal a bald, freckled pate. The man sketched the memory of a courtly leg to her. "Hugh Constable's the name. Who might you be and what in the name of the briny deep is a high-in-the-instep miss like yourself doing with a no-good, smuggling son of a blowfish like our Nicholas Scott?"

Eve decided she liked this odd fellow very much. "I'm Eve Upshall and I ask myself the same question with regularity, Mr. Constable."

The man threw back his head and laughed. "Call me Hugh," he said as he crammed his disreputable hat back on his head. "We're too poor here on Grand Turk to afford niceties like last names."

"Don't let him fool you, Eve," Nick said. "Hugh is the richest man on the island."

"Which is a little like being the only one-eyed man in a kingdom of blind fellows." Hugh winked at her. "But we rub together well enough here."

Hugh clapped a ham-sized hand on Nick's shoulder. "Come on up to the house and we'll raise a pint or two."

Nick gave instructions for Tatem and a pair of rowers to ferry the jolly boat back to the ship to fetch the next group of sailors bound for shore. Only a skeleton crew would stay on board the *Susan B* and the men rotated that duty so all had a chance to feel dry land beneath their feet at some point during their stay on the island.

Hugh led Eve and Nick up to a cart path where his mule-drawn gig waited. There was only room for Eve on the seat beside Hugh, so Nick stood on the rear of the equipage and clung to the handrail. They set off with a clatter of wheels down the road, which was little more than two sandy tracks overgrown with salt grass.

Off to her left, Eve saw workers knee-deep in shallow

ponds, skimming white brine with wooden rakes. They passed several leaning, ramshackle huts that had never seen a coat of paint.

"Don't mind our living arrangements, Eve," Hugh said. "Not much point in building a palace if the next hurricane will knock it down again. Usually all that's needed is a place to get out of the rain or the baking sun."

Eve shook her head. "And when a hurricane comes, where do people turn for shelter?"

"Some go to the caves. There are a few about the island. But most of my people come to Go Lightly—that's my house." He pointed to the low-slung home rambling ahead of them on a bluff overlooking the endless ocean. "Limestone walls, you see. Go Lightly might lose a roof sometimes, but those walls are hell for stout."

As they drew nearer, Eve realized Go Lightly wasn't one structure, but several, built close together around a central court with palm-covered walkways connecting each separate room.

"Right-o, here we are then," Hugh said as he tugged the mule to a halt before the largest of the stone structures.

A woman with cinnamon-colored skin appeared at the open door dressed in a vibrant, off-one-shoulder garment that appeared to be merely draped around her buxom form. Her kinky hair was shorn close to her head, accentuating her strong features. A dusting of white hair graced her temples.

A wide smile split her dark face as she recognized her visitor and moved toward them with the grace of a she-panther. She was as bright and exotic and sensually earthy as the flowering shrubs lining her walkway.

"Ni-cho-las Scott, you black-eyed devil-child," she called out in a sultry voice that caressed and stretched each syllable of his name. "It's too long since my eyes have seen your handsome face, bwoy."

"Maia, you gorgeous creature." Nick hugged her and kissed both her round cheeks. "When are you going to leave this old sod and run away with me?"

Eve blinked in surprise. Maia was not the sort of brown-skinned girl she'd envisioned waiting for Nicholas on Grand Turk.

Maia swatted his shoulder with her pink-palmed hand and laughed. "Shame on you, young cub. It makes no never mind about Hugh. He's used to menfolk trying to steal me away, but don't you try to turn my head in front of your lady."

Maia turned to Eve and smiled. "Here on the island, when the sea casts up a newcomer, we see a friend. Welcome to Go Lightly. Don't just stand there looking handsome as the devil, Nicholas. Introduce me."

Nick did the honors and Eve was charmed by the guileless island woman.

"You'll want to rest a bit after your journey. Come, children," Maia said as she led them to the next little stone room in Go Lightly.

A string bed draped with mosquito netting was set between open windows that allowed the fresh breeze in but not the hot sun. Colorful rag rugs dotted the clean-swept, broad-planked floor. Maia opened a small wardrobe where a couple of bright garments like hers hung on pegs.

"English ladies wear too many clothes for the island. If you want, you help yourself to these, Eve," Maia offered. "Hugh says the white folk on Bermuda pretend they are still in England, but you'll find no such foolishness here. No one will shame you for not wearing sticks under your skirt."

Eve laughed. Sticks under her skirt was a fair assessment of her panniers and hoops. "Thank you, Maia. I'll think about it."

"Oh, child, the world be too fine and too full of marvels to waste time thinking so hard about something so unimportant as what you put on your body. Sometimes, you just got to *be*." She patted Eve's cheek and then winked at Nick. "Got a pot of conch shell soup boilin' whenever you're ready. I'm thinkin' it's your favorite."

"Whatever you make is my favorite, Maia. You know that."

"That honey-tongue of yours gonna get you in trouble one of these days." Maia left them with a roll of her magnificent hips.

"My goodness," Eve said. "Mr. Constable certainly has a wonderful housekeeper."

"Maia isn't Hugh's housekeeper. She's his wife," Nick said. "Or she would be if they could find a preacher who'd speak the words over them. They've been together since Hugh came out here to manage his family's holding twenty years ago. You wouldn't know it to look at him now, but he was once the second son of a lord."

Eve fingered the twisted driftwood footboard of the bed. "What did his family say about Maia?"

"They cut him off, of course."

"Poor Hugh," Eve said softly. "He can never go home."

"Poor Hugh?" Nick shook his head. "The lucky bugger doesn't know or care what day it is. He doesn't have to conform to anyone's wishes but his own. And he has the love of a beautiful woman who thinks the sun rises and sets on his bald head. Believe me, Hugh Constable *is* home."

Chapter Twenty-five

Nick left Eve to her privacy in the guest chamber and rejoined his friends in the main room of their unusual home. The interior limestone walls were crusted with bits of shells and Maia had decorated the space in her unusual island way, complete with a hammock strung from the ceiling beams. Nick tumbled into it and let Hugh put a horn of date palm wine into his hand.

They talked about the progress of the current salt crop and the rate of trade for Nick's cargo of cedar, then moved on to the doings of the island's "Belongers," those who'd been there since birth or in Hugh's case, those who had no other place to call home. No matter how long it had been since he'd last visited, Nick always felt as though he and his comfortable friends had stepped right back into the same conversation they'd left.

"Your lady, she be lovely, Nick," Maia said as she settled onto a pile of pillows on the cool floor. "Be her heart as sweet as her face?"

"Sweet? Eve?" Nick asked incredulously. "She's acid-tongued, prone to violence, passionate, mule-headed and single-minded, but never sweet."

"Sounds like a man in love," Hugh said as he lowered his bulk to join Maia. "Your Eve Upshall must be quite a woman."

"She's not mine," he said sourly. "She won't have me."

"Smart, too," Maia said with a laugh.

"She's here with you, ain't she?" Hugh said. "That says something, lad."

"It says I forcibly carried her aboard the *Susan Bell* and locked her in my cabin," Nick admitted with a wince.

"Nicholas, don't take it so to heart." Maia made a tsk-ing sound. "Just because a woman say no the first time you ask her will she marry you, it don't mean she won't come 'round to it by and by."

"I didn't ask her to marry me."

"Then what—" Maia's dark eyes went round. "Oh, Nicky, you bad bwoy. You try to make a fancy gal out of a lady and it no work every time it be tried."

"Aye, I offered to make her my mistress." He swung his legs over the side of the hammock. "What's wrong with that? I'd treat her well. She'd not want for anything. It's surely no insult. And besides, it's not really so different from what you two—"

Nick stopped himself, realizing his friends might take offense.

Hugh's face went an unhealthy shade of purple.

"Forget I said that," Nick said quickly. It was as close to an apology as he ever uttered. Not because he feared Hugh's rage. Those were little squalls quickly spent, but because he genuinely liked Hugh and Maia and hated that he'd offended them without meaning to. "It was stupid of me."

"It also be wrong," Maia said. "Hugh and me, we be married, even if no one else say so. Our hearts know. You make to give this girl money and fine things so she take you to her bed. Why you surprised you fail? Anybody with eyes can see she want your heart."

Was there even anything left of it after Hannah? Nick didn't know. And if there was, he wasn't sure he wanted to risk it again.

And yet he couldn't deny his feelings for Eve, even if he resisted naming them.

Nick rose and put his empty drinking horn down on the table. "I'm going swimming."

"Take a spear with you," Hugh called after him as Nick stomped out.

Maia dug her elbow into his ribs.

"What?" Hugh demanded. "The boy's clearly frustrated. It'll do him good to kill something, and I wouldn't mind a fresh sole for supper."

"It do him more good to get un-frustrated," Maia said as she ran a hand over the front of her husband's breeches. "Don't you think?"

"Ah, as always, you are as wise as you are beautiful, my love." Hugh cradled the back of her head and pulled her down for a long, satisfying kiss. "Have I told you lately how happy you make me?"

"Not since breakfast."

She slipped her sarong down and bared a brown breast for him. Hugh bent to take her mauve nipple in his mouth while she teased him through the twill of his breeches.

"My, my, you be a very happy man," Maia said as her husband's body roused to her.

Hugh laughed. "And you know how to keep me that way. I know you'll ease *my* frustration, love, but how can we help the lad?"

Maia looked out her window and caught a glimpse of Eve coming out of the guest chamber wearing a red and gold sarong. Maia frowned. The girl's shoulders were hunched and she looked uncomfortable in her own skin. Even though the dress was much different from her English getup, her head should be high. She should carry herself like a princess. Like a woman who is loved.

And if Nick didn't love this Eve Upshall, Maia would

give him no peace till he started using the sense God gave him.

"We can't help him, but I know someone who can." Maia rose from their couch of pillows. "I be right back, old man. Keep thinking happy thoughts."

The sun caressed Eve's arms and the breeze slipped indecently through the slit along the side of the one-shouldered loose garment. She felt as if she were standing naked in the little courtyard. The thin silk brushed her nipples and her breasts hung free beneath the soft fabric. Usually her panniers kept the yards of muslin in her broad skirts from coming anywhere near her legs. This sinful garment brushed against her thighs and teased the small hairs at the apex of her legs when the wind was right.

Her slippers had looked ridiculous with the sarong, so for the first time since she was a child, Eve was going barefoot outside. She'd almost forgotten the pleasure of cool grass under her feet, the long green blades slipping between her toes.

Now she understood why English womanhood insisted on whalebone and wires, on yards of itchy wool and stiff lace. If a woman let her body actually *feel* her clothes on her bare skin, why, she might do anything.

"How lovely you be, my friend."

Eve turned toward the sound of Maia's voice. The woman was heading toward her, her bare feet crunching the smooth pebbles of the footpath.

"Come sit in my garden."

Eve joined Maia on the bench under the shade of a mimosa. It was shedding its little petals. They fell like pink snow around the women. Maia had planted a number of flowers Eve didn't recognize and a small patch of spices and herbs she did—rosemary, thyme, lavender and lamb's ears.

"You have a beautiful home," Eve said. It was unlike anything she'd ever seen or imagined, but it fit the island perfectly.

"It keep the rain from our heads," Maia said as she turned on the bench to face Eve. "On the island, we know we see each other again soon, so we speak truth to each other. It be easier that way. So even though we two be new to each other, I speak truth to you, Eve Upshall."

Eve concealed her surprise. In England, Maia's directness would be considered terribly forward and gauche, but here, it made perfect sense.

"Very well. What truth do you have to tell me?"

"Somebody hurt you."

"What do you mean?"

"Your scars," Maia said. "I saw a little welt when you turned to look at my herbs. Those fancy English clothes hide 'em, but in an island dress, you be what you be. Someone cut you, didn't they?"

Eve lowered her eyes and nodded. "I was flogged."

Maia cupped her chin and made Eve meet her dark gaze. "So was I." She swiveled to show Eve the long stripes on her brown shoulder. "But don't you look down, girl. The shame be not on us. It be on the man with the whip."

Eve saw no hint of cringing in those black eyes. Neither did she find any bitterness.

"How did you get over it?"

"Love," Maia said simply. "Hugh take me away from the man with the whip and love me so good, there be no room for anything else. Nicholas could do the same for you, I'm thinking."

Eve folded her hands on her lap and unconsciously

stroked a thumb across her own knuckles. *If he were capable of love.*

"You love our Nick?"

Eve's breath hissed over her teeth. "Is it that obvious?" If Maia knew, surely Nick did, too.

Maia nodded. "Like a daisy to the sun, your eyes follow every place him go. How not?" Maia went on as if Eve had agreed with her aloud. "He be handsome and young and rich and hardworking. And I 'spect he has a fine willy on him—"

"Maia!"

"Rest yourself, child. I don't know for a fact. I just saying it makes sense him be sporting a good one when you think on the parts of him folk can see any day of the week," Maia said, fanning herself languidly. "Stand to reason him willy be something special, too."

Oh, aye, he has an exceeding fine willy, Eve might have told Maia if she were a forthright islander. But her mother had tried to raise her to be a lady in Kent. And a lady was never supposed to entertain thoughts of willies, much less discuss their merits with a virtual stranger. Eve felt her cheeks heat. If she closed her eyes, she could see Nick striding along in the glorious altogether, his exceeding fine willy leading the way.

"Bet that bwoy knows how to use it, too."

It was time to change the subject.

"I know one has to be careful about sea bathing, but I wonder if there's someplace close where I might swim safely," Eve said, wondering why the breeze seemed to have died. Her whole body was achy and covered with a thin layer of perspiration.

"Oah, yes," Maia said and pointed to a pebbled path leading between two of the limestone structures that made up her house. "Just walk that path down to the little beach. The water be cool and clear. There be a good reef so you can't be pulled out in a riptide and the big fellows with teeth can't be getting in."

"It sounds like heaven. Thank you, Maia." Eve stood and hurried down the path.

Maia sat in the shade until Hugh came out to join her.

"Well?"

"She be going swimming."

"Where Nick is swimming?"

"Mm-hmm." Maia nodded and grinned wickedly at him. "And best of all, the girl has a willy on her mind."

"I hope she's not the only one," Hugh said, waving his tricorne to stir the breeze.

"Don't worry, old man." Maia leaned over and kissed his sweat-salty cheek. Then she stood and walked toward the stone structure that held their bedchamber. She turned around and waggled her finger at her husband. "She not be the only one 'round here with a willy on her mind."

Chapter Twenty-six

Nick didn't move a muscle. He held the spear aloft in the waist-deep water. Small waves tickled his ribs as they passed on their way to the shore. There was a goodly sized grouper working its way toward him. Its side fins trilling the water, the fish nosed along the outcropping of coral to Nick's left. It took no more notice of him than the sea horses clinging to the red fan coral or the little school of clown fish darting in and out of the anemones.

The grouper was looking for a hidey-hole to snug its tail into. Then it would wait to make a lunge and grab when something it wanted to eat swam by.

Nick grinned. He was doing the same thing. Except by standing still, he'd hidden in plain sight.

He angled the tip of the spear into the water and the sunlight made the shaft appear as if it were broken into two. He bit the tip of his tongue in concentration. That was the tricky thing about spearing from above. The angles changed. But if he was swimming beneath the surface, he'd have already disturbed the grouper enough to send it whipping back to the blue depths beyond the barrier reef.

Maybe he was looking at his problem with Eve from the wrong perspective, too. Instead of trying to dive into bed with her at every opportunity, he'd given her plenty of her own company for the past few days. But she hadn't moved in his direction until he dangled the prospect of dry land before her.

Maia thought he should offer Eve marriage, but what man in his right mind takes a second bite of poisoned fruit?

She wouldn't accept his carte blanche, so short of a proposal, what was left? A declaration of love?

Suppose he did actually love Eve? Wouldn't telling her so leave him even more at her mercy? He'd never said the words to Hannah, though she ought to have known how he felt from all the things he did for her.

If he admitted to love, he'd expose a weakness to one who could cut him deepest.

She'd certainly shown little regard for his physical well-being. Why should he think she'd be any more concerned about the welfare of his heart?

He jabbed his spear point toward the grouper. And missed. The fish disappeared with a quick flip of its tail, leaving nothing but a puff of sand rising from the ocean bed behind it.

Nick loosed a low curse.

"Was something else supposed to happen just then?" Eve's voice called to him.

He turned to find her seated on the beach just beyond the wet packed sand, next to the pile of his clothes, which she was neatly folding. He'd left them in a perfectly good heap. Why did a woman always feel the need to come behind a man and rearrange him to her liking?

"I was trying to catch your dinner," he said moodily.

"Maia already has that delicious-smelling conch soup." Eve leaned back on her elbows and tipped her face to the sun. "I doubt she needs your contribution."

"But what if I want to—" he caught himself before she could pull him into another circular argument. The woman had a gift for them. "I can't talk any more. It scares away the fish."

She was an eyeful in that red sarong, but he forced himself to look back down at the wavering reef.

Several minutes passed and she said nothing. Had she gone back to the house in a huff? He sneaked a glance back at the beach.

She was still sitting there, forearms propped on her raised knees, watching him.

He was ignoring her and she still seemed genuinely interested. Maybe feigned indifference was the key to a woman's heart.

No, he didn't want her heart, he told himself. He wanted her wit in his parlor and her body in his bed. He wanted to shower her with expensive baubles and swive her silly whenever he had a mind to. He wanted an uncomplicated agreement that benefited them both.

Eve Upshall was a clever woman. Why could she not grasp that perfectly sensible concept?

He couldn't seem to focus on fishing another moment longer.

Perhaps if they could just have a civil conversation about the matter, he'd be able to bring her around to his way of thinking. Aye, that was the ticket. The last time he'd broached the subject badly, when they were both still reeling from the most pleasurable lovemaking he'd ever known. He'd assumed too much then. He wouldn't make the same mistake now.

He balanced the spear on his shoulder and began walking toward the shallows.

He's magnificent, Eve thought when he turned back toward her. Sun-kissed skin glistening, his dark hair whipped by the wind, he was like a sea god rising from the waves. Eve ached to kiss her way from his brown nipples to the thin trail of dark hairs that started at his navel and spread downward. She watched until his cock came into view and then she carefully averted her gaze.

Exceeding fine willy indeed.

She stared at the scrub bushes at the far end of the beach, but she could still hear the swish of his footfalls on the hard-packed sand. When a shadow fell across her, she knew he was near.

"Something interesting over there in the bushes?" he asked.

She heard him shake the sand from his clothing and wondered which piece he was putting on first.

"If you must know," she said, "I'm just trying to give you a bit of modesty since it's obvious you have none of your own."

"Guilty as charged." He laughed. "In a strange way, we balance each other. For a woman who was convicted of public lewdness, you have a good deal more modesty than one would expect."

She whipped her head around, not caring if she caught him naked now. "Who told you that?"

He cursed his careless tongue as he finished hitching up his breeches and fastened the buttons on the flap front. "Damn, I didn't mean to say that."

"Who?"

He shook his head. "It doesn't matter. I know you weren't guilty, but is the tale true? Is that why you were flogged?"

She stared at the curl of surf running along the sand. "Aye, it's true."

He settled beside her, stretching out his long legs and propping himself on one elbow. "Tell me."

She shook her head. "It's a long story."

"I'm not going anywhere. I've been wondering how a girl whose father had a 'Sir' before his name learned to swear as well as you, so be sure to throw that part in, too."

She rolled her eyes at him and sighed. "Very well. My parents died in the summer of my eighth year, just a couple months apart. Unfortunately, my father left a good deal of debt. The estate was sold to satisfy it, and I had no other family but my mother's brother."

"And he didn't help you?"

"He couldn't be found in time," she said. "He's in Virginia, as far as I know."

Nicholas nodded. "And the distance made waiting for a response impossible. Go on."

"So I was taken to an orphanage in London." She didn't want to wallow in memories of that squalid place. Within a fortnight, Eve had gone from being her father's princess to just another faceless brat. It was a bitter time. "But I was healthy and presentable and in short order, I was taken in by the Tuttles."

"Fostered out?"

"Aye, they needed another pair of hands to help run their tavern, and I was sturdy and quick enough to be of use to them." She'd toiled from sunrise to well after midnight seven days a week, hauling water and coal, scrubbing floors and serving mugs of dark ale. "I picked up my . . . unique vocabulary from tavern patrons."

"And the ability to look out for yourself," he added with a gleam of respect in his dark eyes.

"Aye, I had to," she said. "At first, Mrs. Tuttle was kind when she had half a moment. The poor woman worked from sunup to sundown because her husband was a bit of an idler and someone had to see there was bread on the table. But as I grew, her tongue grew sharper as well. Mr. Tuttle had no use for me as a child. But once I was older, he was rather too keen on me."

"I see."

"One day he caught me in the back room and tried to kiss me. Before I could wiggle away from him, Mrs. Tuttle came in." Eve swallowed hard, fighting back revulsion for the pair of them. Memories of her real mother had faded with time, but her memory of the woman who'd raised her was as fresh and ugly as a day-old bruise. "She's the one who accused me."

He took one of her hands, but didn't say anything.

"She told the magistrate I'd been baring my breasts to her husband and some of the tavern patrons. She must have offered free drink to them, because a couple of the louts appeared in court to support her story."

"And no one stood by you," he said softly as he traced a thumb over her knuckles. "I wish I'd been there."

She wished he had, too. "You know what happened after that."

"Aye," he said, still playing the back of her hand with lazy strokes that soothed and pleasured her warm skin. "And now what are we going to do about the rest?"

"The rest?"

"The rest of your life? I can't believe you really want to marry a planter in the Carolinas sight unseen," he said.

"No, I never did." She sighed. Then she lifted her other hand and shielded her eyes from the glare as she gazed out on the gentle aqua sea. If only the answer to her future was out there to see as plainly. "I intended to separate myself from Lieutenant Rathbun once we made port and then try to find my uncle." Her gaze darted toward him to gauge his reaction. "You must think me terrible to repay his kindness like that."

Nick shook his head. "I don't think your Lieutenant Rathbun is especially kind. And I seriously doubt he was taking you and your friends to moneyed planters either. Trying to find your uncle sounds like a smart plan."

Her heart sank to her belly. It sounded as if Nick was surrendering to her stated intentions. Just when she'd almost decided she didn't want him to.

"But it's always wise to consider other options," he said casually.

"Such as?"

"Stay with me, Eve."

She met his dark-eyed gaze. "As what?"

He frowned. "You're making this far more complicated than it needs to be. We'd be together. That's the important thing. I want you. Can you deny you want me, too?"

"That is beside the point," she said, pulling her hand away. "I will not be your mistress."

"You're muddying the issue with that word." He searched her face as though seeking out a point of vulnerability. "If you were with me, I could protect you. As long as I draw breath, I swear no one will ever hurt you again."

Except you. Still, she was tired of feeling so alone, unable to depend on another soul. The temptation to lean on his strength was fierce, but her carefully crafted reputation was all she could call her own. Besides, the protection of his body was not the same as the protection of his name. "I wouldn't be able to show my face in public."

"Nonsense," he said. "St. Georges is not London. No one would dare look cross-eyed at you or they'd answer to me."

"They probably wouldn't show disrespect to my face, but I'd hear the sniggers behind my back."

Nick's jaw tightened. "Why is what others say so important to you?"

"You've never been falsely accused and convicted on the basis of what someone says about you. If you had, you wouldn't ask that."

She fought the burn of anger in her belly. Life was different for a man. His public life wouldn't change one jot if she became his mistress. He had no idea the kind of direct cuts she'd face every time she entered a shop or tried to attend church. If he had the slightest inkling how difficult it would be for her, he surely wouldn't ask her to become his tart.

He put a hand to her cheek. "Eve, I . . . care about you."

It was no declaration of love, but it was something. Her eyes teared up. "Then show me you care by not asking me to become less than I am."

He snorted. "How does letting me care for you and provide for you make you less? I'll treat you like a queen. I'm very generous. Ask anyone."

"Shall I ask Magdalen Frith?"

"This is not the same thing."

She nodded sadly. "Oh, yes it is." *The man's generous with everything but his heart and love is the only currency I'll accept.* "Why is it you cannot speak of marriage?"

"Because it doesn't mean a damn thing." His eyes hardened before he looked away. "If a man and woman care for each other, marriage will not increase their affection. If they don't, a few words said by a vicar won't make a speck of difference."

A horrible possibility rose in her mind. "Are you . . . already married, Nicholas?"

His silence made her belly flutter.

Nick dragged a hand over his face. "No, but I was. Once."

He stared out at the curling surf and spoke in monotones of a failed marriage, an unfaithful wife and her untimely death.

Eve's heart constricted for his pain over the dead Hannah. So this was the cause of the deep sadness she'd sensed in him. She bore her scars on her back, but Nick carried his in his soul. If he'd been given a choice, he'd probably have chosen a flogging. She put a tentative hand on his arm. He covered it with his other hand immediately and gave her fingers a squeeze.

"I'm sad for you," she whispered.

"Don't make me out a martyr, Eve. There is no innocent party in this sorry tale." He cast a darting glance at her, as if trying to gauge her reaction. "I've no talent for being a husband."

"But you're confident of your talent as a lover." She blurted out the words before she thought. Memories of their lovemaking washed over her like a seventh wave.

He arched a brow. "You know firsthand, Eve. You tell me. Didn't I give you pleasure?"

More than she could hold. She broke their gaze, but thoughts of his blessed hands, his skillful tongue, his body joining with hers made her feel feverish.

"We seem to have reached an impasse," he said finally. "And baring one's soul is weary work. It's deucedly hot today. As long as we're here, do you want to swim?"

Eve fisted her hair and lifted it from the back of her neck. "Not as long as you're here to watch me strip and walk to the water."

"It's not as if I haven't already seen you without a stitch," he pointed out.

She shot him a pointed glare. "Reminding me of my past lapses in judgment is not the best way to endear yourself to me."

"What if I don't look? I could avert my eyes as you did when I came out of the water."

"Not likely." She wouldn't admit she'd waited until she'd been favored with a quick look at his impressive attributes before she turned her gaze away.

"What if I promise?" he insisted.

She slanted her eyes at him.

"Have I promised you aught and not delivered?" He cocked his head.

"No," she admitted.

"Then it's settled." He swung his legs off to the side. "I will stare fixedly at my big toe for the count of 20. That should give you ample time to reach the water."

"But—"

"One . . . two . . ."

A hot bead of perspiration slid down her spine. The water looked like a slice of heaven. As he said "three," Eve leaped to her feet and pulled the simple garment over her head. She folded it quickly and was off like a rabbit by the time he reached "ten."

The dry sand was fire under her soles, but the wet sand nearer the shore cooled her feet. She didn't stop running when she hit the waves, droplets flying all around her. Once she was thigh deep, she grabbed a breath and plunged in all the way. The water took her into its refreshing embrace.

She swam naked under the smiling sun. The magistrate who'd sentenced her for public lewdness would not be a bit surprised.

But Eve didn't feel lewd. She felt free. And more unabashedly joyful than at any time in her life since the loss of her parents. She surfaced and drew in a big gulp of air before diving back down.

Brine stung her eyes, but the silent underwater world was a riot of color too gorgeous to miss. Sunlight danced along the ocean floor. Fish of every conceivable hue darted out of her path over patchwork beds of different types of coral. It was all so unnecessarily beautiful, she thanked God for her eyes.

Then a large body whooshed past her, leaving a trail of bubbles in his wake.

Nicholas! She clawed to the surface.

He bobbed up an arm's length from her.

"What are you doing here?" she demanded. "You promised."

"I promised not to watch you strip and walk to the water, and I didn't," he said with a grin. "I made no promise about what might come after."

She sent a splash toward him and started to swim to shore. He caught up to her, wrapping his arms around her. They rolled in the surf like a pair of otters. Then his feet touched bottom and he stood, holding her flush against him. His heart pounded against her breasts.

"Eve, why is it so hard for you to admit you want to be with me?" He bent his head and kissed her, a salty wet kiss. His lips beckoned, enticed her to soften under them. So different from that first hard quick kiss when he was about to face a shark for her, though he didn't even know her name at the time.

Wave after wave washed by them. Nick swayed with the surf, but continued to make love to her mouth. Her lips parted and he slid his tongue in. One of his hands stroked down to cup her bottom and press her against him.

The familiar ache between her legs started up again.

He released her mouth and rested his forehead against hers.

"Wanting to be with you isn't the problem," she began, but stopped when he put a finger to her lips.

"Then let's not borrow one," he said. "We're on an island. If we don't bring it with us, it's not here. Let's agree not to bring anything. Just this once, can't we pretend that now is all that matters? There is nothing else."

She looked up and fell into his dark eyes. The sadness in him had faded a bit, but she ached to erase it completely. Her whole body throbbed with longing. Her breath grew short. His body fit so seamlessly along hers, it was as if they were already one person. She wrapped her arms around his neck and her legs around his waist.

"You're right," she whispered. "There is nothing else."

Chapter Twenty-seven

"For as long as we're on this island, there is nothing else," Eve said when she pulled away from his kiss and drew a shuddering breath. "Once we leave, we're back in the real world once again. This is just for now."

He nodded slowly. "It's not as much as I hoped for, but I'll take it."

She tipped her face up to him for an open-mouthed kiss, while his hands and the ocean played over her body. Her nipples were hard and aching against his broad chest. She kissed her way down his neck, savoring the salty-sweetness of his skin. He groaned when she took his earlobe between her lips and sucked.

Hearing his need magnified her own. The emptiness between her legs made her whole body throb. As a lady, she knew she should resist when his hand found her crotch and teased her little folds. But as a woman, she couldn't do it.

Grand Turk was an island of fantasy. The rules simply didn't apply here.

When his fingers ran over her delicate secrets, they slid easily. She was slick and wanting. He lifted and centered her before his body. The tip of him entered her and she tried to move down to take him in, but she was too buoyant. She nearly growled with frustration.

"Is the lady in distress?"

"Yes, dammit," she blurted out before she thought.

He laughed, the little lines of sadness on his brow smoothing. "Then allow me to come to your aid."

She wanted to come to his, too. She wanted to wipe away every trace of sorrow from him.

With infinite slowness, he slid his cock in up to the hilt. He held her still, his gaze burning into hers. The island faded from her peripheral vision. The ocean caressing them seemed suddenly distant. All that mattered was this man, this joining, this heart of his thudding against her chest.

He kissed the tip of her nose. "I'll always come to your aid."

"I know." She kissed his neck, his square jaw, then his chin. He was promising more than relief from the needs of her body, though she reveled in the hard thickness of him filling up her empty place. He was promising her the protection of his glorious body.

But not the protection of his name.

She shoved the thought aside. As long as they bided on the island, such concerns didn't exist.

"Come here." Eve pulled his head down for a deep long kiss.

The little minx. Nick's eyes rolled back in his head before he shut them. She was undulating on him, riding his cock as if he were her stallion. She was so tight. Her wet velvet sucked around him with each thrust. The muscles in her thighs flexed and relaxed. She'd hooked her ankles behind his back and one of her heels rested at the top of his buttocks, kneading his spine just above the crevice.

He didn't need to hold her up. The water and her legs wrapped around him did that. So his hands were free to touch every bit of her glorious skin. His eyes popped open at that thought.

"Lie back," he suggested and eased her hands away from his neck. "I want to look at you."

She didn't fight him when he spread her arms wide. She gave the top half of her body to the ocean's arms. He grasped her hips to steady her and keep the rhythm they'd built going. She closed her eyes and let the water bear her up, her pink nipples pointing sunward, her breasts and long hair moving with each wave, as if she was part of the colorful reef spread out around them.

A mermaid of his own.

He drove into her again and again. Her brows drew together and her mouth went slack. Nick knew that look of anguished ecstasy. She was close. He thrust deep and held himself still while one hand found her little nub of pleasure and stroked.

She cried out and convulsed as the first contraction of her release pounded around his cock. Nick bit the inside of his cheek to keep from spilling himself into her. He knew he should pull out to be safe, but he wanted to feel her joy, to revel in her losing herself to him completely.

Her orgasm continued, caressing his erection in frenzied pulses. It pulled him closer to the edge of climax. His balls drew tight, but he still couldn't bear to leave her. He ached not to be alone when he came, but he knew he should withdraw.

Only a little longer, he promised himself, drawing her close and holding her tight so he could feel her whole body tremble with the force of her release.

Her gaze met his and she rocked her pelvis, grinding against him. "Come with me," she begged. "Oh, please."

A ragged cry tore from his throat. It was as if he were a loaded pistol and she'd pulled his trigger. He couldn't stop, couldn't hold back another heartbeat. His seed spurted into her in hot pulses as he arched his back to drive in as deeply as possible. She moved against him, drawing out his release.

Nick growled with pleasure as Eve's narrow tunnel spasmed around him. Then guilt washed over him even though he was powerless to stop himself. After Hannah, he never let himself come inside a woman without the protection of a French letter. If he didn't have one of the sheep bladder condoms, he always withdrew, separating from his partner at the moment of deepest intimacy. It never failed to make him feel bitterly alone.

He looked into Eve's eyes as he gave the last of himself to her keeping. She wasn't upset. She was smiling at him, her heart shining in those unusual aqua eyes. Accepting him. All of him.

But what if she should quicken? The horrific image of Hannah dying in the birthing chamber sliced into his brain. Christ, he'd put Eve in mortal danger through his carelessness.

"I'm sorry—"

"I'm not," she said with a finger to his lips.

Then she kissed him again and all hint of loneliness fled.

Eve lost track of the days. She and Nicholas swived each other like wildcats at every opportunity in their little guest house. They discovered every inch of each other's skin, lavishing the beloved flesh with hands and lips and tongues. One night, Nick grabbed up a blanket and carried her back to the secluded beach. They made tender love while the surf broke at their feet and the stars wheeled overhead.

Then the day came when the *Susan Bell*'s hold was filled with cakes of white salt. Nick sent for Higgs to come to his business partner's house. Eve served them both drinks made from the local rum distillers and then started to leave them in privacy.

"Stay, Eve," Nick said. "Our plans concern you as well."

She settled in the swinging indoor hammock to listen to their discussion.

"You intend to resign as my first officer and I respect your choice. I've been thinking for some time now that you're ready for your own command," Nick told Peregrine. "I want you to take the *Susan B* on to Charleston."

"You'd trust me with your ship?" A shocked smile split Mr. Higgs's face, then faded as quickly as it came. "But, Cap'n, what about you and Miss Upshall?"

Eve took silent note that Mr. Higgs was on dry land and was not stammering. Something had changed.

"Last time we were here, I ordered a smaller sloop built hoping you'd captain it for me. I wanted it to be a surprise, you see. Instead we'll use it for our return to Bermuda," Nick said. "They tell me it'll be ready in a week. Leave me five or six crewmen and the boy Reggie and we'll make out fine."

"What do you say to this arrangement, Miss Upshall?" Mr. Higgs asked, stone-faced. "Would you rather take passage on the *Susan Bell* to Charleston? That was your original destination."

It had been so long since Eve had given serious thought to finding her uncle in the Colonies, the idea was jarring to her. She realized Nick was creating an excuse for them to remain a while longer on Grand Turk. Their lovemaking in recent days had been tinged with the urgency of those who know their time is short.

"I have no objection to remaining here a bit longer," she said, biting back a secret smile she reserved only for Nick. "Besides, if I arrive in Charleston's port without a female companion, my reputation will be in tatters."

Such things didn't count on Grand Turk. She was beginning to forget why they mattered so desperately elsewhere.

"Which is why I've arranged for a lady's maid for you when we return to St. Georges," Nick said with a grin.

So that was why he'd wanted her to be privy to this conversation, she realized. He'd managed to extend their idyllic interlude and protect her reputation when it ended. If only he'd just offer her marriage, there'd be no need for their time together to end at all.

But a man who intends to marry a girl has a care for her good standing. Perhaps this servant and solicitude was prelude to a proposal.

"Plenty of people saw you carry me on board the *Susan Bell*," she pointed out.

"People have the memory of a gnat when it comes to such things," Nick said. "They'll be more interested in the fact that we survived that storm and returned in a new schooner. If you return in the company of a servant, they'll assume you left with one."

Higgs nodded slowly. "That's true."

"You know the agent we deal with in Charleston as well as I," Nick said to his first mate. "Make the trade as usual and when you return to St. Georges, the schooner will be waiting for you to captain her." Nick narrowed his gaze at Higgs. "If you're still willing to sail under my colors."

Higgs thought a moment, then extended his hand. "Aye, Nicholas. We have an accord."

It was the first time Eve had heard Mr. Higgs address his captain as equals. It seemed right.

"Good," Nick said as they shook on their new partnership. "I expect you'll sail with the tide this afternoon."

"Aye, the *Susan B*'s ready to go. Don't worry. I'll take good care of her." Higgs made a neat leg to Eve and saw himself out.

Nick joined Eve in the hammock, his long body snugged up close with a leg casually hooked over hers.

"That was cleverly done," she said.

"I'm glad you approve." He ran two fingers over the tops of her breasts and then toyed with a nipple. "Taking the new ship back to St. Georges buys us more time."

She covered his hand to still it. She didn't need the distraction of her body's reaction to him just now. "There is another way to accomplish that."

His sensual smile flattened. "Eve, you know I care for you. More than I wanted to."

"But you won't marry me."

"I've already proved I'm no good as a husband," he said. "I haven't changed my mind about marriage."

"And I haven't changed mine about becoming your mistress," she fired back at him, stiffening in his arms.

He feathered his lips along her jaw and trailed soft kisses in a line to her ear. "It may have escaped your notice, but you already are my mistress."

She rolled out of the hammock, unbalancing the load and sending him to the floor. "No, I'm your lover. But that's a situation we both knew would change. It may as well start now."

Eve stomped out without a backward glance.

It was just as well that she barred her door that night. Her woman's curse arrived and she wouldn't have been able to welcome him to her bed in any case. It was so late, she'd begun to suspect she might have conceived. She was both disappointed and relieved she hadn't.

There was nothing she'd like better than to bear Nick's child. But if he wouldn't marry her for herself, she didn't want to force his hand with a bastard who needed a name.

He knocked again the next night, but she refused to admit him.

He didn't even try the night after that.

Her new maid arrived, a silent island girl with a dark bruise on her jaw. She was clearly anxious to leave Grand Turk and wanted to please, but since she was fearful of speaking, she was very little company. Eve had no relief from her depressing thoughts.

She should have taken Mr. Higgs up on his offer of transport to Charleston. But she couldn't bear to leave Nicholas entirely. Surely the man would come to his senses eventually.

When the day came for the new schooner to sail back to St. Georges, he sent Reggie to collect her. She said a tearful good-bye to their hosts, Maia and Hugh, apologizing for Nick's absence at their leave-taking.

"Best you hurry, miss," the boy said. "Cap'n says he'd as soon leave ye as take ye—oh! I shouldn't oughta have said that. You won't tell him, will ye?"

"No, Reggie," she said. "He won't hear it from me."

Chapter Twenty-eight

Peregrine Higgs paced the dock at St. Georges. He'd sighted an unfamiliar sail from the northernmost window of Whispering Hill skirting around the island's reefs with the ease of familiarity. Even though he hadn't recognized the ship, he recognized the skill of her captain. It had to be Nicholas Scott. Higgs had bolted to the stable, hitched up the wagon and drove hell-for-leather down to meet the ship.

Not that the captain would thank Higgs for his trouble.

Nicholas Scott was going to be royally pissed to find Peregrine waiting for him. Especially since the *Susan Bell* was not safely berthed at the St. Georges wharf.

Well, the captain would just have to come to terms with this rude new development. The world was full of shabby surprises.

Like the fact that Miss Sally Munroe was now Mrs. Archibald Snickering.

Higgs could see it pained Miss Smythe to tell him, but she twisted her hanky and managed to choke out the tale. At first, it boiled his gullet that Miss Munroe hadn't even given him a chance. But once he got over the initial surprise, he found very little real anguish in his heart considering the way he'd mooned around over her.

Truth to tell, it bothered Higgs a lot less to lose the incomparable Miss Munroe than he'd expected, but the fact that Miss Smythe seemed sad for him tugged at his heart.

Higgs handled disappointment well. Captain Scott would have to take a page from his first mate's book. If Higgs could just keep him from gutting someone first.

Like me, Higgs thought as the schooner made its way through the channel and into the harbor.

He spread his legs to shoulder-width and clasped his hands behind his back as the schooner sidled up to the wharf. She was a pretty piece, a bit wider of beam and shorter in length than the *Susan B*, but a fine craft all the same.

And but for this rotten luck, she might have been mine to sail.

"Higgs!" Nicholas Scott bellowed from the wheel of the schooner. "What in blue blazes are you doing here? We didn't expect you to beat us back to Bermuda."

The captain left the rest of the mooring to Mr. Tatem and stomped down the gangplank toward Peregrine. Higgs resisted the urge to take a step back when Nicholas stopped before him. He had counted on the captain being in a good mood after an extra fortnight with the lovely Miss Upshall. A squall must be brewing on that front if the captain's black scowl was any measure.

"I don't see my ship anywhere, Mr. Higgs," he said, his face taut, his voice brittle. His restraint might have been because Miss Upshall and her new maid were disembarking behind him and the captain was on his best behavior before the ladies.

Higgs didn't think it would last.

"The *Susan Bell* is . . . detained," he said, grateful that his stammer hadn't returned.

The captain's eyes burned in their sockets. "And yet I see you standing here bold as brass. Report, Mr. Higgs."

"Not now. Not here. There are too many ears about."

"Was it Bostock?" Nicholas asked in a tone of suppressed menace. "Oath or no, if he's commandeered the *Susan B*, I'll have the man's guts for garters."

"No, it wasn't Bostock. The difficulties are . . . political." Peregrine drew a deep breath. "Saint George Tucker has returned to the island. He'll explain everything."

"Saint's back, hmm?" Nicholas frowned at the pavement, clearly churning over the possibilities. "Tell him to come around for supper tonight. We'll get to the bottom of this at the house then."

Tatem and a couple of the lads finished loading up the last of the baggage in the back of the wagon and handed Miss Upshall up to sit beside the driver. Her maid clambered into the back of the wagon with the luggage and pulled her bonnet down to shield her face. Nick climbed into the driver's seat.

"I'll expect more details when you get back to the house," Nick said as he grasped the reins. "Tell Saint if he's responsible for 'detaining' my ship, he'd better have a damn good reason for it."

"But wait," Higgs said. "I didn't bring an extra horse. How will I get home?"

"Mr. Higgs," the captain said evenly. "If you can manage to return to Bermuda without my ship, I expect you can find your way up a hill without a horse."

He snapped the reins and the wagon rattled away.

A stiff wind whistled by and Higgs shoved his tricorne down tighter on his head. The Tuckers were one of the oldest families on the island and their home on Water Street wasn't far from the wharf. Saint George Tucker had left Bermuda at the age of nineteen, a bit of a bounder. His father, Colonel Henry Tucker wanted him to study law. Whether Saint heeded his father no one knew. He'd left to seek his fortune in Virginia without so much as a backward glance at his home island.

Until now.

Higgs would find the prodigal at his father's house and he'd be able to deliver his message.

But he doubted Colonel Tucker had killed the fatted calf.

"There's something afoot," Nicholas said to Eve as soon as they left the town behind. He sniffed the air as if the change was something he could scent. "I need you to do something for me."

"What is it?"

"I'll be having dinner guests this evening." All Nick wanted was to get Eve alone and settle things between them. Her silent aloofness was driving him batty. Working his way back into her good graces was going to be hard enough without Saint on the island stirring up trouble. "I need for you to be my hostess tonight. Will you arrange things with Santorini?"

Eve nodded.

"Dinner should be a fairly sumptuous meal. Plan on a dozen guests."

If he knew anything about Saint, it was that the man would have plenty of cohorts. Distracting, dividing and defeating him was the order of the day. If Nick could deal with Tucker's schemes in one evening, so much the better.

"A dozen dinner guests tonight? That doesn't give me much time," she protested.

"Santorini would walk through fire for you." He didn't add that he would, too. "You'll come up with something."

"What's this all about?"

"I don't know. Higgs wouldn't say much on the docks," he said. "But if it's important enough to drag Saint George Tucker back to Bermuda, it doesn't bode well."

"Why?"

"Because he's a radical. Always has been. I suspect he's gotten mixed up with that bunch in Boston who're preaching independence or I'll eat my hat." Nick shook his head. Politics were only important when they interfered with trade enough to make his smuggling profitable. "And to make matters worse, the bastard's holding my ship somewhere."

She looked at him sharply. The two of them might have suffered a rift, but he was sure Eve knew full well how losing the *Susan Bell* would affect him.

"And if you host this Saint person for a lavish dinner for all to see, no one can accuse you of joining him secretly in whatever you think he may be planning," she said, following his logic as flawlessly as if he'd spoken his reasons aloud. "Be careful, Nick."

"Always."

The dinner was spectacular. Santorini delivered a fish-laden white soup, followed by honey-glazed chicken, lamb shanks, braised beef and duck a l'orange. Eve sat at the far end of the long table, amusing Nick's guests with tales of London that he suspected were products of her own lively imagination, but she kept the conversation light and sparkling.

Eve was so lovely, so gracious, Nick found himself wondering why he resisted asking her to be his wife. He was sparing her, he reminded himself. He was a sorry excuse for a husband and not likely to improve with age. Still, the thought crossed his mind more than once as he watched her glide effortlessly through the evening.

Miss Smythe rose to the festive occasion and allowed herself to be persuaded to play the clavichord for his guests after the meal.

No one acknowledged the stench of sedition swirling beneath the surface.

As they pushed back their chairs to move to Nick's parlor for the after-dinner music, Saint Tucker said casually, "I understand your Thoroughbred mare has recently foaled. Don't suppose I could see the colt."

Now it comes. "Certainly," Nick said. "If the rest of you will excuse us."

Nick walked in silence toward the stable beside his former friend. Saint was younger than he by half a dozen years, and much more dandified. But between them they'd closed down some of the better taverns on the island more than once. When Tucker's politics turned against the Crown, Nick had severed their friendship.

Treason was bad for business.

Studying law in the Colonies had evidently been good for Saint. His waistcoat was of rich velvet and his silver shoe buckles gleamed. His horsehair wig was in the first stare of fashion, but prosperity had not changed his politics.

"It's come to this, Nick," Saint said as he leaned over the stall to stroke the colt's soft nose. "King Geordie won't listen to our demands. He's left us with no choice."

"A man always has a choice."

Saint bared his teeth in a half smile. "And here's yours, Nick."

He handed him a letter.

Nick broke the seal and read the missive by the yellow lantern light. It was couched in flowery language and self-justifying rants, but the gist of it was that the Colonies would no longer trade foodstuffs for salt. They wanted the gunpowder stored in the British magazine on the island.

Nothing less.

The letter was signed by someone styling himself "General George Washington."

"So you're determined on armed rebellion." Nick refolded the letter and handed it back to Saint. It meant a sure trip to the gallows to be in possession of such a document.

"Our cause is just," Tucker said.

"Is starving an island full of people just?" Nick demanded. "You were born here, Saint. You know we can't grow enough to feed ourselves. The land won't support farming. We must trade for food."

"Nick, we need that powder."

"Then take your petition to the governor."

"You know better. That old fool won't do anything against the Crown's interests."

"Imagine that."

"Besides, he's only a puppet, not a man of parts, like you and I," Saint said. "Everyone on the island knows who the lord of the place really is. If one wants something done, one must see Lord Nick."

"I won't do this." Nick turned and started to walk away.

"Suit yourself," Saint called after him. "But the consequences are on your head. How long will it be, do you think, before people start boiling their shoes?"

Long before winter storms turned the Atlantic into a bitter froth. No help would come from England. The Crown's resources were stretched thin enough trying to support the troops sent to discipline the Americans. Devil Isle was on its own. Without a chance to lay up stores from the Colonies, every family on Bermuda would stand around a grave before spring. They'd bury their sick, their elderly and their young.

Rage burned in Nick's chest. He couldn't let that happen. No amount of loyalty to his king justified a dead child.

"Damn you, man." He rounded on Saint and snatched him up by his shiny lapels. "Midnight. Fourteenth of

August. Anchor a ship, a whaler if possible, in Tobacco Bay. You'll have your cursed powder."

Nick released him, sending him sprawling on the straw-covered floor, and stomped away.

"America will be grateful," Saint called after him. "We'll remember those who help us fight against tyranny and unjust taxation."

This wasn't about taxation. It wasn't about the divine right of kings. It was about starving children.

"I'd better see the *Susan Bell* tied up at the dock on the fifteenth and her hold had better be full of beef."

"You won't regret this," Saint promised.

Nick shook his head. "I regret it already."

As Saint George Tucker picked himself up and dusted himself off, Reggie Turnscrew peered down at him from the overhead loft. The bleedin' sod had made Lord Nick angry. That was enough to make Reggie want to pelt him with horse apples, but none were to hand.

The worst of it were that Lord Nick had to agree to something he didn't want to do. Something about powder, which he knew Lord Nick didn't use. No fancy folderol for the likes of him. Wigs were for fops and dandies, so Reggie didn't see why giving up powder should upset Lord Nick.

Maybe it was the bit about boiling shoes what had the captain so flummoxed. Lord knows, Reggie's stomach had knocked against his backbone more than once and it were a serious state of affairs.

Not that he'd had cause for complaint since he took service with Lord Nick. Far from it. Reggie went to bed with his belly stretched tight and full every night.

And it sounded like the captain was taking steps to ensure that happy state continued. But they were steps he weren't too keen on, that much were certain.

Reggie lay back in the straw. Powder and whaleboats at midnight and boiled shoes. It was more of a riddle than he could figure.

This was just the sort of puzzle Miss Eve might be able to untangle. He watched through the open stable door until that Saint fellow was halfway back to the big house. Then scrambled down from the loft and hotfooted it 'round to scale the fence enclosing Miss Eve's private garden. She used to like sitting in the moonlight before they all sailed off to the Turks.

Reggie had sat in the scratchy crotch of a big cedar and watched her several evenings. With any luck at all, she'd take a turn around her garden before she retired and Reggie would get his chance to put the riddle of what he'd overheard to her.

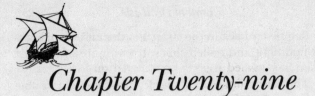

Chapter Twenty-nine

Higgs watched Penelope Smythe's fingers fly over the black and white keys of the captain's clavichord. It was probably out of tune, not that Peregrine had an ear for such things, but he'd never heard anyone play the instrument with more depth of feeling. Or with such lovely white hands. He hadn't expected Penny to display such talent.

And he hadn't expected to start thinking of her as Penny either.

She glanced at him from under her lashes between movements in the charming little sonatina, as if to gauge his interest. He was interested all right. It was almost as if he'd never fallen under the spell of Sally Munroe.

Too bad there were other fish to fry this night.

The captain slipped back into the room and settled into a chair behind him. Saint Tucker followed a few moments later.

The message was delivered. Higgs fidgeted in his seat, wondering what the captain had decided to do.

Damn, he wished he hadn't stumbled onto that patrol ship with the *Susan B.* Evening fog had gathered off the Carolina coast, but Higgs had seen a chance to make a run for port. Instead, he'd run into the Colonists' blockade. It might have happened to the captain as well and Nicholas admitted as much when Higgs told him the particulars.

How could he have known the Continental Congress had just thrown up an embargo against British ships?

And Bermudian vessels counted since they flew the Union Jack.

He just wished it hadn't happened on his very first voyage as captain. Nicholas Scott might have decided to fight instead of heaving to when the Americans declared their intention to board him. But the *Susan Bell* was outgunned by the big colonial frigate and though Higgs might have outrun her, he didn't want to risk the captain's ship.

When had the colonials developed a navy? True, the frigate was probably just a merchant vessel refitted to carry an impressive battery of guns, but both sides of the Atlantic had done a good deal of saber-rattling without much substance up till now. This new militarism proved that tensions ran higher than usual between the Crown and its distant subjects.

War was on the wind. And Bermuda was caught in the middle.

Higgs wondered uneasily which side Nicholas would come down on. No man considered treason lightly. The penalty was too severe.

The sonatina ended and the assembled guests clapped politely. Higgs clapped enthusiastically.

And when the captain announced his intention to offer port and cigars to his guests, Miss Upshall and Penny made their good nights and started to withdraw.

Faint heart ne'er won fair maid.

Instead of sitting back down with the rest of the men, Higgs followed the ladies out of the parlor. He'd worry about what the captain had decided to do about the American's offer later.

"Miss Smythe," he said. It was a minor miracle that his stammer hadn't returned since making port this time. In fact, now that he thought on it, he hadn't stuttered once around Miss Smythe. Sailors were a superstitious lot. Higgs usually made fun of his mates over their hokum, but now, he began to wonder if Penelope Smythe wasn't his own private good luck charm. "I'm not a smoker myself. I wonder if you'd like to take a turn around the garden with me before you retire."

Her smile was a bright dawn with not a cloud in sight.

Silence finally reigned in the big house. The last of the dinner party guests was gone. Now all Eve heard was the wind soughing through the palm tree outside the door in her private garden. The breeze whispered a conversation she didn't understand, punctuated by the loud tick of the long case clock in the distant foyer.

Penelope had come to her chamber earlier, gushing and starry-eyed.

"Mr. Higgs kissed me, Eve. Right on the mouth."

"In that case, don't you think you ought to call him something other than Mr. Higgs?" Eve suggested with an indulgent smile.

"I suppose you're right. Peregrine." Penny tested the name on her tongue. "It's a beautiful name, but fierce as well. A peregrine is a falcon, after all. Don't you think it's the best sort of name a man could have?"

Eve agreed that it was a name to charm the angels, and it had certainly worked its magic on Penn, but she was distracted by her need to speak to Nicholas. She let Penny rattle on for another half hour, an astounding occurrence for one so naturally shy, and then pled a headache so she could dress for bed and be alone.

She put an ear to her door, listening for Nick's tread on the heart of pine. When she heard him coming, she nipped over to the chair before her fireplace and picked up the book she was plowing through. It wouldn't do to let him think she'd been waiting for him.

The footsteps halted outside her door.

Good. The man had better stop and speak to her this night. Not that she needed his word to know her dinner party was a sparkling success. She didn't want to talk about the party at all.

She wanted to know about the treasonous conversation Reggie Turnscrew had overheard in the stable. Before Penny's visit, Reggie had surprised Eve by shinnying over her garden wall with a twisted tale spewing out his mouth as fast as he could tell it. From what she could piece together from Reggie's account, Saint George Tucker was up to something dangerous. Surely Nick wouldn't be so addlepated as to join in whatever madness Mr. Tucker was planning, but according to the stable lad, it sounded as if he had agreed.

The floorboards outside her door squeaked and Nick moved on.

Eve swore under her breath. He must have seen the light shining beneath her door. He knew she was still awake and yet he walked on.

They hadn't spent any time alone since she'd finally and irrevocably refused to become his mistress. When he'd asked her to serve as hostess at the dinner party, she'd hoped it meant he was warming up to the idea of making her his wife. After all, she was performing a wife's duty in the eyes of all their guests.

But he didn't knock at her door.

So be it. She'd go to him.

When she reached his door, she turned the latch and strode in without knocking. Nicholas was just peeling off his shirt, his broad back kissed by the yellow light of his bedside hurricane lamp.

"What have you agreed to do for Saint George Tucker?"

He turned slowly to face her. "I'm considering selling him that colt if he comes up to my asking price."

"No, you're not." She folded her arms beneath her breasts, painfully aware that his gaze had fallen to them. "You're doing something that's like to get you hanged."

"Who'd you hear that from?"

"Never mind," Eve said, unwilling to name Reggie. Nick wouldn't appreciate the little wretch's sharp eyes and wagging tongue. Eve had sworn Reggie to silence, but Nick might have other ideas. "I know about the powder."

His gaze jerked back to her face and he closed the distance between them in a couple of long strides. "What do you know about it?"

Reggie's details were sketchy. The boy thought Nick and his guest had argued about rice powder—"the kind them dandies wear"—but Eve suspected powder of a more dangerous kind.

"Tell me." Nick grasped her shoulders and gave her a slight shake.

She lifted her chin. "I know you're being forced to do something you shouldn't."

"Eve, you know me." He chuckled softly. "I follow no law but my own will. Do you really think I can be forced to do anything I don't want to do?"

"If the stakes are high enough, anyone can be manipulated."

"You give me hope, wench. You really do." Anyone else might have been fooled by his careless laugh, but his smile didn't reach his eyes. "I still want you. Obviously, I simply haven't offered you the right stakes."

"No, you haven't, you stupid oaf."

"Charming, as always," he said with a shake of his head. "How can I resist? Suppose I offered you marriage . . ."

"But you haven't and now you're trying to change the

subject." She shook off his grasp and poked his naked chest with her forefinger. If he thought he could dazzle her into distraction with a ham-handed proposal, he was sadly mistaken. Besides, she wanted more than his name. She wanted his heart. And even if he asked her to marry him, she promised herself she'd say no unless he offered his love as well. "I'm not leaving until you tell me what you're planning to do."

Nick stared at her for a moment, then stalked over to his bed and sat on the end of it. "I'm going to commit treason."

Eve followed and sank onto the bed beside him. "Tell me."

She listened wild-eyed while he repeated the colonials' demands. Gunpowder for food. Nothing else would do.

"It should be fairly easy," he said. "The magazine is lightly guarded and—"

"But if you're caught . . . oh, Nicholas!" The penalty for treason was still the same as when Henry the Eighth sat on the British throne.

Hanging, drawing and quartering.

"I won't get caught."

"But . . ." Her voice failed. The thought of his beautiful, strong body destroyed so utterly made her lightheaded.

"Your concern is touching, love." He cupped her cheek and drew a thumb across her parted lips.

Love. If only he meant it. Well, she *did* mean it, even if she couldn't say it. And she wasn't going to let him risk himself without a fight.

"Nick, you don't understand." She took his hand between both of hers. "It's a fearful thing to fall into the hands of the law. You don't know what it means to lose control of your body. They'll take you and they'll do horrible things and they'll . . . break you." Her voice hitched in a sob. It was almost as if the lash was descending afresh on her back. "You won't be able to stop them, and I won't be able to bear it."

A shudder wracked her whole frame. Nick drew her into his arms and she went willingly. He was so warm, and she could feel his heart galloping beneath her palm. She tipped her mouth up to him and he covered her lips with his.

"If there is any other way around this, Eve, I will take it," he said. "But I can see no other course but the one before me."

She nodded woodenly. Of course, he couldn't let the islanders starve. She understood that. But he was running a horrible risk.

"I solemnly promise you," he said, kissing her fingertips between each word, "that I will not be caught. You and I have unconcluded business. Do you think I'd leave you when we still have a fight to finish?"

She was weary of fighting him. "Perhaps we can declare a truce."

He laid her back on his bed and untied the drawstring at the neckline of her night shift. "For the next week, you and I are no longer at war." He bent his head and claimed a tight nipple, sucking her through the thin cotton. "Until then, you make your bed with me and pleasure is our only law."

She arched her breast into his mouth. "And hostilities may resume between us once you square things with the Americans?"

He pinned her beneath him and she felt his belly jiggle with a laugh. "Or perhaps we'll decide to make the truce permanent."

"Perhaps." She surrendered to his touch and willed herself not to think beyond her next breath.

Chapter Thirty

Nicholas peered through his spyglass at the dark horizon. Over the silver-tipped waves, white sails showed at the farthest edge of his vision.

"That'll be the *Lady Catherine* out of Virginia and the *Charleston and Savanna Pacquet*, of South Carolina," Saint said at his elbow.

And between them on a tight leash, rode Nick's own *Susan Bell*, whose hull was full to bursting with the promised foodstuffs. The ships were cruising beyond the range of the governor's scout vessels. They'd have the wind of any patrol boat that took an interest in them.

"If something goes awry, the Americans will turn tail and head for home," Nick said grimly.

"Nothing will go awry." Saint clapped him on the shoulder. "And we won't turn tail. History is written by the winners, Nick. When all this is over and America is free of the Crown, we'll remember what you do here tonight."

"What's this 'we'?" Nick demanded. "You were born a Bermudian, Saint."

"But I'm an American by choice," he said softly. "I know this is difficult for you. It's hard for me, too."

Nick snorted. "Not hard enough."

"It's a sober thing to take up arms against one's sovereign," Saint said. "But freedom is worth a man's life, even a man's honor. Once you're determined to pursue it, there's no road back."

"None that doesn't end in a noose," Nick said, lifting the glass to his eye again. "Here come the whaleboats. I make half a dozen of them."

He handed the spyglass to Saint. The American ships lowered smaller boats to creep into the shallow bay. The flotilla had just passed the first ring of reefs.

Nick looked at the men who waited for his word. Along with Higgs, he had called on the small group who'd returned to Bermuda in the schooner from Grand Turk since the bulk of his crew was still on board the *Susan Bell*. Saint had brought a few trusted men as well, including, surprisingly enough, his father, Colonel Henry Tucker.

From the scowl on the elder Tucker's face, Nick suspected the old man's involvement was more about salvaging his shipping rights with the Americans than any sympathy with the rebels' cause.

And if things went badly this night, Nick had as good as signed each man's death warrant.

"Let's get started."

Nick led the party back up the short hill to where the magazine was positioned in a lonely part of the island. The moon overhead was only a few days past full. There was plenty of light to see that no guards were in sight.

"Thanks be to God for incompetent governors," Nick muttered. "Tatem, Dunscombe, you two will serve as lookouts. If you see anyone, sing out like a teal. The rest of you, with me."

The magazine was made of limestone blocks, several feet thick, and the door could not be jimmied from without.

"Give me a boost to the roof, Cap'n," Higgs suggested. "We'll pull off some tiles and you can lower me down."

Nick laced his fingers and Higgs stepped into them. Nick lifted him with a grunt. Higgs grabbed at the roof ledge and scrabbled his way on up, swinging his long legs wildly. Nick signaled to Saint to boost him up after Higgs.

Once they were both up, Nick and Peregrine worked several roof tiles loose and peered into the blackness of the magazine. A whiff of sulfur rose to meet their nostrils.

"Wish me luck," Higgs said as he let his legs dangle into the opening.

"Steady on, lad." Nick stopped him with a hand to his shoulder. "If I don't bring you back in your present configuration, Miss Smythe will never forgive me. I'm the one who's going in. You're getting off this roof and pulling the men back to a safe distance."

A single spark was all it would take for the magazine to go up like a Roman candle.

"You might need me," Peregrine said with a grin and disappeared down the hole.

Nick leaned over the opening, trying to see. "Blast and damn, Higgs. This is no time to disobey a direct order."

"You can order me flogged later," came the disrespectful reply.

"I think you're in the main chamber. Pick your feet up. You don't want a spark," Nick hissed at him, then turned to direct the others on the ground. "Get back, all of you. We'll signal when the door is open."

Then Nick lowered himself into the blackness. When he dropped the few feet to the stone floor, the slap of his boots striking the pavers sounded unnaturally loud. He didn't move for a moment, waiting for his vision to sharpen in the darkness. The single shaft of moonlight flooded the chamber with shades of gray. Nick made out barrels stacked around the room more than shoulder high.

"The door's over here," Higgs whispered.

"That'll only be the interior door," Nick said. "We need some more light."

The inner door opened with the lifting of the latch. Nick led the way through the portal and into the narrow corridor that ringed the cache of powder. Once they left the central chamber, all trace of moonlight fled and they plunged into tarry blackness.

The magazine was designed as a box within a box, both sets of walls fashioned of limestone blocks and each a couple feet thick. Nick ran his fingers along the inner wall, searching for a lantern recess. Once he found one, he pulled out his flint and tinder.

"Let's hope the governor's men are better at keeping this passage clean of powder than they are at guarding it," Nick said as he trimmed the wick and lit the lamp by feel alone.

Yellow light flooded the narrow white-washed space. A thin pane of vellum stretched across the back of the recess. It allowed lamplight to penetrate the inner chamber without the risk of open flame.

"I'll light the other lamps," Nick said. "Get to work on the outer door, Pere."

"Aye, Cap'n." Higgs moved back down the corridor, whistling through his teeth, heedless of the fact that one moment's inattention might blow them both to the stars.

Damn, if the scamp isn't enjoying this. That flirtation with Miss Smythe was turning the staid and reasonable Higgs into a daredevil.

And about time, Nick thought with a grin.

By the time Nick had all the lanterns lit, Higgs had pried open the door and the first barrels of powder were being carefully rolled down the hill to Tobacco Bay. Nick relieved Higgs and took up his station in the powder room, handing the barrels out to waiting hands. There was no need to risk more than one person in that volatile chamber at a time.

The workers were silent; the only sound was the scrape of boots at the threshold. Then came the occasional thud of a wooden barrel against a rock or bared tree root. And lastly, the eternal breath of the sea rushing over them.

Nick kept a tally in his head, starting the count afresh once he'd handed out the hundredth barrel.

Perhaps this is going to work.

The low warning cry of a teal made Nick freeze. The lookouts were signaling.

"We're done here," Nick said as he carried out the barrel he was holding and shoved it into Saint's arms. He pulled the door to the magazine closed behind him.

"But there are half a dozen barrels left," Saint complained.

"If what the colonials already have stowed in the whaleboats isn't enough to satisfy them, I'd be pleased to take it back," Nick said, fingering the loaded pistol he'd shoved into his belt.

"No, no," Saint said. "This will do."

"Good. Higgs, go with them and bring the *Susan B* home. The rest of you are dismissed."

Nick's crew scattered like leaves before a gale.

He drew his pistol and loped toward the lookouts, bent double to make himself a smaller target in case the governor's guard was abroad with their muskets.

When he reached his lookouts, he found Tatem and Dunscombe standing over something, shoving each other back and forth, nearly ready to come to blows.

"You coulda just cracked his noggin," Tatem was saying in a furious whisper.

"He's a damn Frog," Dunscombe growled. "What's it to you?"

"Report, Mr. Tatem," Nick said softly as he joined them. A body lay at Dunscombe's feet. The dead man was wearing a French officer's uniform.

"This feller were nosin' about, Cap'n," Tatem began.

"And I didn't bloody well like the look of him, not by half," Dunscombe interrupted.

"So you killed him." Nick turned the man over with his foot. The Frenchman's throat had been slit, his blood blackening the white cravat elegantly tied at his neck. The epaulets at his shoulders marked him as a man of rank.

"Aye, Cap'n. I figgered we didn't need the likes of him tellin' what he knows about our business." Dunscombe folded his beefy arms over his chest.

"This Frenchman is an officer. Likely on parole," Nicholas said. The British navy frequently dropped enemy combatants on Bermuda. Once they gave their word they wouldn't engage in further hostilities against England, the soldiers and sailors were given free run of the island. "Someone's bound to miss him. See to it no one finds his body. With luck, the authorities will believe he broke his parole and took ship."

"Aye, Cap'n," Dunscombe said with a snaggletoothed grin. "I knows just where to stash him."

"Mr. Tatem, give him a hand."

"See, what did I say?" Dunscombe lifted the feet of the dead man and nodded to Tatem to grasp him under the armpits. "Killin' a Frog weren't no cause for complaint."

Nick snatched Dunscombe up by his greasy collar. The Frenchman's legs dragged bonelessly on the ground.

"Mr. Dunscombe, you have killed a man tonight. Not a frog. And by stealth, too, from the looks of it." Nick gave Dunscombe a jaw-rattling shake. "Think, you dunderhead. That Frenchman wasn't likely to report stolen powder. He'd have been more likely to roll the barrels to the beach with us since it would hurt the Crown."

Truth to tell, the paroled officer was probably scouting the area for a possible French raid on the unguarded magazine.

Damn the governor's incompetence! Weakness was a prayer to the devil. It always invited attack. If the powder had been well guarded in the first place, the Americans might not have blackmailed the Bermudians for it.

Nicholas glared down at the dead man. *Damn you, too, for being in the wrong place.*

"Once this night's work is done, come round to collect your pay, Dunscombe. You no longer have a berth on my ship."

Nick stalked away, trying to dust the black powder from his hands. He had betrayed his sovereign, stolen from his own military and a man had died because of Nick's decision to place the welfare of the island above his king.

He didn't think it was possible to feel any dirtier.

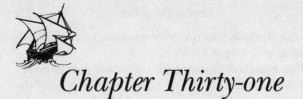

Chapter Thirty-one

Eve rose to add more water to the big kettle. Its intermittent whistle kept her from drifting off to sleep. When Nicholas returned home, he'd want a bath.

And she would wait for him with water on the boil.

Nick was in danger and she couldn't rest till she knew he was safe. She was an unmarried woman waiting in a man's chamber, preparing his bath. There was no disguising what that made her. But she almost didn't care what sort of name the world would hang about her neck anymore.

All that mattered was Nick coming home safe.

When she heard his tread in the hall, she rose to her feet and skittered to open the door. He was stopped, head bowed, outside the door to her chamber, one arm against the doorjamb, bracing himself upright.

"Nicholas." She ran down the hall to him.

When she would have hugged him close, he held her away.

"Keep clear of me, Eve. I just wanted to let you know I've returned." His voice had a ragged edge. "I'm covered with powder." His words sank to a whisper. "You'll only dirty yourself with me."

"Then let's get you clean," she whispered back. She caught up his hand. It was grimy, but she refused to release it. He let her lead him down the corridor to his chamber, where the hip bath waited.

He stood still while she peeled off his garments one by one, but his dark eyes followed her every move.

"These will be the very devil to get clean," she murmured, glancing at his clothes.

"Burn them."

She nodded. That made sense. She thought she could salvage his breeches and shirt, but once the theft came to light, this much powder on a man's jacket would be incriminating. She'd see to burning it first thing in the morning.

"All went well?" she asked as she ran her gaze over him, checking for wounds. He seemed unscathed.

"A man was killed."

Eve gasped. "Who?"

"No one you know."

He sank into the waiting bathwater even though it was cold. Eve wrapped a hot pad around the kettle handle and grasped it with both hands.

"Spread your knees," she said.

When he obeyed her, she poured in the steaming water, taking care not to hit him with it. The thought that Nick might have killed someone that night flitted through her mind. She didn't see any blood on him or his clothes.

"Was it one of the colonials?" she asked softly.

"I don't want to talk about it."

Perhaps it was best if she didn't know. She pressed her lips tight and knelt beside the bath. It was enough that he was safe. He'd tell her more when he needed to.

She picked up the jar of soap and a cloth and began sudsing one hand, taking care to scrub away every trace of blackness. Once his skin glowed with cleanliness, she turned to his other hand.

He watched her in wonderment. She had every reason to be upset with him. It was a minor miracle that she was even still in his house, much less in his chamber.

Why could he not give her what she wanted?

He felt the love he knew she craved, but he couldn't speak the words. It should be a simple matter.

I love you, Eve Upshall.

They'd danced on the end of his tongue any number of times. Never more tantalizingly than right now. But he knew why he wouldn't say them.

He didn't *deserve* to speak those words.

"Lean forward and I'll wash your back," she said matter-of-factly, as if this were a service she performed for him with regularity. A wifely duty.

As her hands ran over his skin, the tension drained from his muscles. She scooped up a dipper of water and poured it over his head, careful to shield his eyes with her hand. Then she washed his hair, kneading his scalp.

Her love washed over him with every touch. Forgiveness. Peace.

The temptation to accept it was too great for him to bear. When she knelt down beside the tub to scrub his chest, he noticed her gown was wet. Her breasts showed through the thin material as clearly as if she was naked. Her nipples were clearly visible beneath the muslin. He reached over and circled one with the pad of his thumb.

Her lips parted and her breath caught. She met his gaze and he saw his own face reflected back in her pale eyes. He squeezed her nipple and her eyelids drooped languidly.

"Eve—"

"The water's getting cold." She rose quickly and walked to the fire. The shadows of her long legs beneath her gown made his groin twitch.

He soaped himself quickly and stood. Water sluiced down his body in soapy runnels. "I don't need more hot water."

She turned and stood there with the kettle in both hands. Her gaze swept over him, lingering on his cock.

Just when he thought he couldn't get any harder.

He climbed out of the bath and walked toward her. "Put the kettle down, lass, before you burn someone."

"Of course." She gave herself a slight shake and obeyed him. Her eyebrows drew together and her chin quivered.

"What's wrong?"

"It's just . . . I was so afraid for you." She threw her arms around his neck and kissed him. He was still wet from the bath, but he felt her hot tears against his skin.

"I'm a traitor to the Crown, Eve." He palmed both her cheeks. "I don't deserve a woman's tears."

"Maybe not." She forced her lips into a tremulous smile. "But you have mine."

He kissed her cheek, tasting the salty drops, then her lips. "I won't make you cry again, Eve. I promise."

He dropped to his knees before her and pressed his mouth against her belly through the muslin gown.

"If womankind had tuppence for every time a man promised that, we'd own the Bank of England." A little ginger returned to her tone and she ruffled his wet hair with her fingertips.

He laughed and ran his hands up her legs, lifting the hem of her gown. She went still when he stopped at the triangle of auburn hair between her legs. He leaned forward and pressed a kiss there. Her breath hissed over her teeth.

She'd performed a wifely service for him. He'd perform a lover's service for her.

He cupped her bottom and drew her close. "Spread your legs."

He buried his face in the crisp, curly hairs, inhaling her woman's scent. When he kissed her this time, he slipped his tongue between her soft folds, tasting her musky sweetness. The fragrance and taste of her went straight to his balls and they tensed into a tight bunch.

He willed his body to relax. This was for Eve.

He tongued her slowly, finding between those soft pink lips the little pearl that would pleasure her most. He sucked. He circled with the tip of his tongue.

She gasped. She trembled.

He spread her with both hands and laved her roughly. His cock ached with need.

She was saying something incoherent. Amid her whispered curses, he heard his name over and over.

Her knees threatened to buckle, but he steadied her and held her upright. He wouldn't let her go. Not until he'd broken her with pleasure.

He slipped two fingers inside her as he continued to torment her with his mouth.

"Oh, Nick."

He felt her tense. She was close. He gave her a light nip, just to push her over the edge.

Her whole body shook as her inner walls squeezed his fingers. Her release pounded around him. When the last contraction ended, she collapsed bonelessly into his waiting arms. He cradled her against his chest and cupped her quivering sex with his hand.

He rocked her as she settled, crooning little endearments in her ear. He kneaded her sex softly.

"No, no more," she pleaded when the tip of one of his fingers grazed her sensitive spot. "I can't bear it."

"I'll be the judge of that, love," he whispered, and carried her off to his bed.

Chapter Thirty-two

POWDER STEAL

*Save your country from ruin and the righteous
wrath of our Gracious Sovereign. The Powder
stolen from the magazine late last night cannot
have ventured far as the wind is light.*

A GREAT REWARD
*will be afforded any person who makes a proper
discovery before the magistrate.*
—Archibald Snickering, Esq., Assistant to
The Honorable George James Bruere, Governor

Digory Bock couldn't read, but he knew exactly what
the official proclamation said. The contents of the gov-
ernmental placard were cussed and discussed all over
the island, but no one stepped forward to claim the
"great reward." The islanders had their suspicions
about who might have been bold enough to relieve His
Majesty's troops of the powder. Suspicions that were
confirmed when the *Susan Bell* wallowed up to the wharf
late in the afternoon, riding low in the water. She was
heavy with goods from the Americas.

Fear over the embargo with the Colonies had already
led some to start hoarding, but a deal had evidently
been struck. Trust Lord Nick to act on their behalf.
There were rumors of a missing Frenchman on folk's
lips, but no one cared much about what might have

befallen him. Every larder in Bermuda would be full come the winter storms. The island was grateful.

No one in his right mind would go to the magistrate.

"Not even me," Digory mumbled into his tankard. "Me what has no reason to love Cap'n Scott."

"Pardon me, sir, but did I hear you mention Nicholas Scott?" The dandy at Digory's elbow leaned toward him.

"Who's asking?"

"Lieutenant Fortescue Rathbun, retired." The man swept a sissy bow and straightened his powdered wig.

Digory spat a gob of phlegm on the tavern floor.

"More important," Rathbun said, slapping a coin on the bar. "I'm the man who'll buy your next drink."

Digory nodded for the man to sit. For the price of a drink, he could stand anyone's company, even a perfumed popinjay like this one. The man signaled for another tankard to be brought.

"Now tell me," he said. "What have you against Captain Scott?"

Digory slurped the foam off the dark ale. Didn't the man know it would go bad if a body let it sit too long?

"Well?"

"He cuts me off'n his crew, that's what. And why, I asks ye? Just because I likes me ale." Digory took another pull at the tankard. "Me, what never did him harm. Even now, wouldn't do him no harm."

The stranger chuckled. It was not a pleasant sound. It seemed to Digory that the man was laughing at him. "And how could the likes of you harm 'Lord Nick'?"

"I could harm him plenty. We all could."

"You have piqued my curiosity, indeed," Rathbun said, leaning confidentially on the bar. "As much power as Captain Scott wields around here, I find your assertion highly doubtful."

"Don't you be troubling yourself 'bout my ' 'sertions,' "
Digory said. He suspected a " 'sertion" was something a
molly might take an interest in and he wanted no part
of that sort of unnatural doings. "But I could bring the
cap'n low if I was of a mind to and I'd line me pockets in
the doing of it, too."

Digory glanced meaningfully at the placard he
couldn't read and cocked a hairy brow. The man followed his gaze to the official proclamation.

"Hmm."

The man sounded impressed. Perhaps he'd spring
for another pint.

The man lowered his voice to a whisper. "You're certain Scott was behind this Powder Steal?"

"Sure as shite stinks."

"Then if you have evidence that Nicholas Scott per-
petrated this crime, what's keeping you from reporting
him and claiming the reward?"

"Ah, there's the rub." He had no actual evidence
against the cap'n, only the pinch in his gut to go on.
And besides, Digory was not high in the court's favor.
The judge was still smarting over an altercation involv-
ing Digory and the magistrate's pig.

"And mighty good eating it were, too, though nothing
could be proved, all the *evidence* being missing, ye see,"
he'd told his mates later.

If it came down to Lord Nick's word against his, Digory knew full well whose ear would be pinned to the
stocks.

The man was getting restless. He might not buy any
more drink unless Digory kept him talking. Digory
swilled the last of his pint and wiped his mouth with
the back of his hand.

"I could go to the magistrate, but the folk on the island, they love the cap'n. Lord knows why! Now if I was

to go to the 'ficials . . ." Digory held out his tankard hopefully and the man nodded to the alekeep. Digory waited till the fresh pint was in his hands before he continued. "Well, I wouldn't likely live long enough to spend my 'great reward,' would I? Folk won't stand for anyone speaking against the man who brings them beef for the winter."

"Ah, yes. Your Captain Scott's a veritable Robin Hood," the man said dryly.

"Weren't no hoods robbed," Digory said. Blast, if the man wasn't a bit simple. "It were only the powder what was taken."

The man rolled his eyes and slid off the bar stool. Then he stomped out of the tavern.

Digory lifted his tankard toward the placard. "Here's to ye, Cap'n. Ye may have cut me from the crew, but this day ye saw me safe to two pints what didn't cost me a penny." Digory took a big gulp of the bitter dark liquid and then belched loudly. "God keep ye, Nicholas Scott!"

Rathbun strode across the cobbles. His shoes no longer sported silver buckles. He'd sold them a week ago. Every day spent on this cursed island was costing him money he didn't have to spare.

The fact that Nicholas Scott had stolen the King's powder was an open secret, but he could find no one who would testify against him. He'd tried to approach the magistrate with the information as soon as the rumor reached his ears, but without concrete proof, no one would give Rathbun even a small portion of the promised "great reward."

Somehow, he needed to return to his original plan.

It was elegant in its simplicity. Rathbun only needed to deliver three bona fide English ladies to a certain madam in Charleston and his financial worries were over. Miss Marabelle had agreed to make him a half partner in her brothel as payment upon delivery of said Englishwomen.

According to the proprietress of The Red Lady, she had a wealthy, reclusive client with particular tastes. He was a devotee of the teachings of the Marquis de Sade and planned to re-enact all that Frenchman's cruelest fantasies on the flesh of three Englishwomen whom no one would miss.

His requirements were simple.

They must be wellborn virgins. They must be English. They must be expendable.

And the mysterious gentleman was willing to pay most handsomely to indulge his passions.

Sally Munroe was already beyond Rathbun's reach, married to that simpering bureaucrat Archibald Snickering, but if he could see Nicholas Scott incarcerated, Eve Upshall and Penelope Smythe would be without protection. Two English ladies were better than none. They'd be forced to continue on to the Carolinas with him.

Of course, women who are forced to do something become difficult to handle. When he'd dangled the prospect of marriage to wealthy planters, they'd been amenable enough, but now that they enjoyed the protection of Nicholas Scott, that carrot held no allure. He waffled back to considering the use of force, but Captain Bostock had promised not to support him if the women were unwilling travelers.

Somehow, he had to convince Eve Upshall and Penelope Smythe that they *wanted* to go with him. He sat down on a bench in the shade of a mimosa tree in a little park on busy Water Street to give the matter a think.

Across the street, a carriage rumbled to a stop and the two women in question climbed out just as a brilliantly workable idea formed in his mind.

"Here, Reggie," he overheard Miss Upshall say to their young driver as she dug in her reticule for a coin. "Get yourself some penny candy and pick us up at teatime, if you please."

Not till teatime, eh?

No one would miss them for hours.

When Lieutenant Rathbun first stopped them on the street, Eve was only annoyed. Now her heart hammered in her chest. Rathbun knew Nick was behind the raid on the magazine and he claimed to be able to prove it.

"So you see, as a loyal subject of the Crown, it is my duty to turn over the evidence I've collected to the magistrate," he said.

"What sort of evidence?"

Rathbun put a finger to his mouth. "That's a matter for the court, not you. Suffice it to say that not everyone on this island is in Lord Nick's pocket. I have three credible witnesses who saw him steal the powder and will swear to it."

Three! Only two was enough for her to be sentenced to flogging. She lifted her chin.

"No one would testify against Captain Scott," Eve said, willing it to be so.

"I admit they were afraid to come forward without my protection." He paused to smooth his wig. "But upon my word, they will testify."

"Everyone respects Captain Scott," Penny said. "No one will believe your witnesses."

Hope flared in Eve's heart.

"A man like Scott has as many enemies as friends. This audacious crime has blacked the governor's eye," he said. "They'll believe my witnesses because it's in their interest to settle the matter. Governor Bruere needs to be seen punishing someone swiftly for this act of treason."

The English court had been quick to believe witnesses against her, and Eve was innocent. Nick was guilty. Hope guttered in her heart and fizzled entirely.

"You do remember the penalty for treason, don't you, ladies? Much as I hate to bring up such a ghastly business, I don't doubt St. Georges will be full to bursting on the day when they hang, draw and quarter Nicholas Scott and his whole nefarious crew."

"His crew?" Penelope went white as parchment.

Eve's vision tunneled, but she forced herself to drag in a deep breath.

Rathbun nodded. "You don't think Scott did this evil thing alone, do you? No, his whole scurvy crew will watch their own entrails burn."

Penny sagged but Eve grasped her arm and steadied her. "That will not happen. The islanders won't allow it," Eve said stonily.

"Hmph! So trusting, my dear. The Bermudians may love Nicholas Scott now, but when they realize the wrath of our king will rain down on this island, they'll clamor for his blood," Rathbun said. "Did anyone speak up to stop your flogging?"

She shook her head, unable to trust her voice.

"And they won't stop justice from being done here. And do you know why?"

"I know one thing that will stop you from telling me." She tried to push past him, but he grasped her forearm. "Let me pass."

"Not until you hear me out," he said. "The islanders will see him punished because people love a spectacle. Hanging, drawing and quartering a whole crew is something they can talk about for years. They'll deplore it loudly, of course, but they won't be able to look away. They'll hang on every scream. They'll gawk in horrified fascination as the guts spool out. People love the misery of others. You, of all people, should know that."

She swallowed back the rising gorge. "We are on a public street. Remove your hand from me or I will scream."

"If you scream, you sign his death warrant," he promised. "But, if you come with me to the Carolinas now, both of you, and without a fuss, I will not bring forth my witnesses."

"No, we aren't going with you." Eve had to find Reggie and the carriage. They had to hurry back to Whispering Hill. Nick would know how to deal with this.

"Suit yourself, though I doubt you'll look good in black," he called after them. "Oh, wait! You're not his wife, so you won't even be able to publicly mourn him. Not that mourning a traitor is a healthy idea."

Eve kept walking. Rathbun dogged them.

"I know what you're thinking. You plan to run back to warn him now." His voice seemed eerily disembodied, coming from behind them. "Be assured that the magistrate will send troops to arrest him long before he can see his crew assembled and his ship under sail. He has no way to run. No place to hide. And neither does his crew."

"His crew." Penny stopped in her tracks. "We have to go with him, Eve."

"But—"

"There is no other answer for it," Pen said. "I love Peregrine. I can't let him be . . ." Her face crumpled and she sobbed into her kerchief.

Shaking with fury, Eve turned on Rathbun. "You're bluffing."

"Perhaps," he admitted with a cruel smile. "And perhaps I just spent the morning with Digory Bock, a man your captain thoughtlessly cut from his crew. He and his friends will testify."

Digory Bock. The name sounded familiar to Eve. Yes, that's the one Nick had struck from the ship's roll for drunkenness.

"The stars are aligned against your captain. Someone will be blamed for the theft of that powder. Someone will be made to pay. The common folk may love your 'Lord Nick,' but let me assure you, those who hold an official post don't think much of someone styling themselves with a title they don't really deserve."

"I don't think he has any witnesses, Penny," Eve said, trying to sound more confident than she felt.

"Are you willing to wager his life on it?" he asked. "I assure you I can point the magistrate in Scott's direction and he makes an admirable target. Mr. Bock was quite willing to talk to me." Rathbun narrowed his eyes at her. "The stakes are rather high, aren't they?"

Too high.

"We'll come with you." Eve spat out the words. "But know this. If I get half a chance on the way to Charleston, I'll feed you to the sharks. So sleep lightly, Lieutenant."

"Thank you, Miss Upshall." He dipped in a low, mocking bow. "Forewarned is forearmed."

Chapter Thirty-three

Reggie twisted his cap in his hands. *Oh, Lord, oh Lord. Now I'm in for it.*

"What do you mean they're gone?" Nicholas Scott bellowed. He was like to wear a trough in the floor with all that stomping about.

"They waren't there. I does just like Miss Eve says, I nipped round to the general store and had a couple o' cinnamon sticks. Then I brings the carriage back to Water Street at the time she tells me, but they plumb aren't there." Reggie shifted his weight from one foot to the other. "I checks every store, but no one seen 'em, not even the hatter and if ladies is going to buy anything, they always buys hats."

The captain snatched him up by the collar and brought him nose to nose. "Stick to the point, Reggie."

"Aye, the point." He breathed a sigh of relief when Lord Nick set him down and resumed pacing. Reggie had never seen the cap'n so fit to burst, straining at his moorings like a ship battened down for a gale, he was. "Then I drives down to the wharf to see had me mates seen the ladies. They tells me 'aye,' they seen 'em."

The captain stopped pacing and glared at him. "Go on."

"Me mates says the ladies boarded the ferry with this feller what looks like a dandy, but seems a bit down on his luck. Frayed about the edges, he were."

"Which ferry?"

"The one bound up the country to Ireland Island and Somerset village."

"Bostock makes berth there."

"Aye, that's the name me mates said they heard. The dandy, he pays the ferryman extra to sail 'mediately. He were plannin' to take passage to the Colonies on the *Sea Wolf*, he says, if they could catch it, that is. Cap'n Bostock were sailing today."

Nicholas snatched his spyglass from the desk and strode to the nearest westerly window. "I see the tip of a mast sailing into the sun."

"Be it the *Sea Wolf*?" No one could work for Nicholas Scott long without hearing whispers of his enmity with the master of that unnaturally named vessel. Every proper seaman knows a ship's a lady, not a fierce growling beast, and she ought to have the name o' one.

"Find Mr. Higgs," Captain Scott ordered. "Tell him to assemble the crew. We sail with all speed."

"But sir—" Reggie felt strange making a suggestion to the likes of Captain Scott, but the words popped out of their own accord. "The *Susan Bell* likely isn't rigged for a voyage. She'll need water and victuals and—"

"No, she won't. We aren't going far." The captain raised his spyglass again and trained it on the horizon. "Only far enough to catch that black-sailed bastard."

The ship's bell clanged incessantly for the better part of half an hour and the crew responded to the summons at a run. Even Digory Bock came to stand on the wharf, hoping the captain might relent and let him back on the ship's roll.

"How many pints have you drunk this day, Bock?" Nick bellowed down between issuing orders for the *Susan Bell*'s sails to be unfurled.

"Only four," Digory shouted up to the deck. "Or maybe it were eleven." It was hard to be certain.

"Decide which and come back when you're sober," Scott said as the gangplank was shipped. "I can't use a man who's always three sheets to the wind. You're a decent enough seaman, Bock. See if you can become a decent enough man and we'll talk. Mr. Higgs, slip those cables now!"

"Godspeed, Cap'n," Digory said under his breath as the *Susan B* glided between the inner harbor islets. The captain had as good as given him a berth again. It was only a matter of time before he was sailing with his old mates. Digory was glad he hadn't gone to the magistrate now. He swiped his greasy sleeve across his mouth. "Good news like this calls for a drink!"

Night fell and the *Sea Wolf* was still beyond Nick's reach. But just before the sky darkened to indigo, he managed to take a final bearing on the distant black sail. If Bostock ran true to form, he'd drop some of his canvas for the night watch. Nick had more sail laid on.

"Shall I give the order for the running lamps to be lit?" Higgs asked.

Nick shook his head. "I don't want Bostock to know we're coming. Starlight will do for the old girl." Wind strained the ship's sails, but she glided almost silently through the night. The only sound was the shushing of waves against her hull. "Get some sleep, Pere. I'll stand the first watch."

"I don't know as I can, sir," Peregrine said. "Penny's on that ship."

"And you'll not be worth anything to her unless you're rested. Relieve me at two bells, Mr. Higgs." His tone made it an order.

Nick stood at the helm, letting the ship speak to him

through the wheel while his crew slept. As usual, the *Susan Bell* calmed him. The world was mad, but all was quiet here. There was only the wind and the waves and the mathematical dance of the stars across the black sky.

And then suddenly, he was aware of another presence. The scent of lavender wafted past and he knew immediately who it was.

"I'm sorry, Hannah," he whispered. "I love her. I must have Eve. If he stands in my way tomorrow, oath or no, I'll be sending him to join you."

Or perhaps Nick would be seeing his dead wife again. He and Bostock were evenly matched. It might go either way. A cold finger ran down his spine.

The lavender scent faded so completely, he wondered if between fear for Eve and exhaustion, he'd only imagined it. The soughing in the topsails was probably just the wind, he told himself.

Eve and Penny were taking a turn along the port rail in the pearly dawn. Neither had slept. And neither wanted to remain cooped up in their airless cabin a moment longer.

Penny had cried half the night, but Eve remained dry-eyed. It was as if a shroud had already covered her heart. Nicholas Scott was as good as dead to her.

She couldn't feel a thing.

"A sail! A sail!" one of the crewmen called out from the *Sea Wolf*'s crow's nest.

"Whither away?" Adam Bostock cupped his mouth and shouted up to the seaman.

"A point off the starboard bow and closing fast. It's the *Susan Bell*, sir, flying every stitch of canvas she can bear."

Eve gathered her skirts and ran to the starboard side. She leaned on the gunwale to see the ship bearing down on them for herself. The wind blew her mobcap off, but she didn't care.

Oh, God! He's come.

Her dead heart woke to aching life and the tears she hadn't shed the night before stung her eyes now.

"Captain Bostock, what do you intend to do about this?" Lieutenant Rathbun stormed across the deck. "You can outrun them, can't you?"

Bostock peered through his glass at the advancing vessel. "I could lay on every sail, but the *Susan B* would still catch us. We're fully loaded and she's riding high in the water. Best for us to heave to and see what our old friend Nicholas wants."

"You are obligated to protect your passengers."

"My willing passengers," Bostock agreed with a meaningful glance at Eve and Penny. "Are you willing, ladies?"

Rathbun shot a murderous glare at them. He still held Nick's fate in his verminous hand.

Eve's heart went cold again. "Aye, we're willing." She spat the words out. "Aren't we, Penny?"

Penny nodded miserably.

"There, you see," Rathbun said.

"More than you wish I did," Captain Bostock said stonily. "What's going on here?"

"Nothing that need concern you. Just get us to Charleston and you'll be paid your fare." Rathbun screwed his face into a scowl and reluctantly added, "With a bit more thrown in for this slight aggravation."

Adam Bostock laughed. "You don't know Nicholas Scott a bit if you think he's only a slight aggravation."

Just then a loud boom reverberated over the water and a nine-pound ball whistled past the *Sea Wolf* to splash into the ocean a hundred feet off the prow.

"That madman is firing at your ship!"

"No, he's signaling for us to stop and parley." Bostock glared across the water at the *Susan Bell*. "If Nick was aiming at my ship, he'd have hit it. No, he won't fire. He made a promise to—" The *Sea Wolf*'s captain stopped himself in midsentence and eyed Eve thoughtfully. "He doesn't want to endanger . . . someone he means to take back to Devil Isle with him."

"This is your chance," Rathbun said softly. "You hate the man. I've seen it. Fire on him. Blow the bastard back to Bermuda."

Another cannon ball whistled overhead, dropping harmlessly into the swells in front of the *Sea Wolf*. But the shot was closer this time.

"Blast the man!" Bostock said. "Much as I'm tempted by your suggestion, Rathbun, I made a promise to someone, too."

Adam Bostock bellowed orders to his crew and several seamen began climbing the rigging and reefing the sails. Rathbun stomped and swore, but nothing he could say would dissuade Bostock from slowing his vessel. Eve returned to the rail to gaze across the expanse at Nick's ship.

She could see him, standing at the prow. She couldn't see his face clearly yet. She didn't want to see it when she had to tell him she could not return with him. The heady joy she felt when she first saw he'd come for her disappeared when she realized it changed nothing. Rathbun could still see Nick branded a traitor and Eve couldn't allow that to happen.

The *Susan Bell* pulled to within a boat's length of the *Sea Wolf*.

"Nicholas Scott!" Bostock bellowed. "Why are you firing on my ship?"

"Permission to come aboard and we'll discuss the matter," came the shouted reply.

Permission was granted and the *Sea Wolf*'s crew sprang into action, running a cable through a system of pulleys attached to the main mast. The cable was attached to a line which was affixed to a crossbow bolt. Bostock took aim and shot the bolt squarely into the *Susan Bell*'s main mast.

Nicholas loped back from his position on the prow to yank the bolt from the mast. He pulled the cable taut and climbed onto the gunwale.

Eve's heart constricted. Balanced on the narrow rail, the corded muscles in his forearms rippling, he was magnificent. When he launched himself into the air with a shouted "Now!" her belly turned backflips. But instead of falling into the waves, he rose into the air. Bostock's crew hauled away on the cable and Nick came flying across the distance between the two ships.

Once he was over the *Sea Wolf*, he let go of the cable and landed with a roll on the deck. Eve ran to him and he caught her up in his arms.

He cupped her face and kissed her hard. Then he pulled back and said one word, but it was enough to break her heart.

"Why?"

"I'll tell you why," Rathbun said. "Because she wants to be the wife of an honest man who's loyal to the Crown, that's why. Isn't that right, Miss Upshall?"

A threat simmered beneath his words.

Nick surely heard it, too.

Maybe he wouldn't make her say she didn't want him. Maybe he'd understand she was doing this for him and let it go. Her chest ached so, she could scarcely draw breath. Her mouth wouldn't form the words to tell him good-bye forever.

Surprisingly, Nick smiled at her. " 'Twill be all right, sweetheart. Trust me." Then his face turned to stone when he looked at Rathbun. "Am I to understand you accuse me of being less than loyal?"

"Treasonous is more like it."

Nick drew his blade from its scabbard. "Much as I hate to get blood all over your deck, Adam, I can't let an insult like that pass."

"I'd be disappointed if you did." Bostock folded his arms across his chest.

"So be it. May God have mercy on your traitorous soul," Rathbun said as his sword cleared its sheath with a metallic rasp. "For I shall have none."

Chapter Thirty-four

"I warned you once, Scott. I am a master of the blade." Rathbun took his stance, balancing lightly on the balls of his feet.

Nick had dismissed the man's claim at the time because of Rathbun's foppishness. Now he realized Rathbun was like a scorpion fish, hiding his predatory nature behind a clever disguise.

"No doubt you cut a wide swath through your effeminate cronies in the London coffeehouses," Nick said, trying to unsettle the man's confident glare. "There's no umpire. No rules here."

"Just as I would have it."

Nick saw the strike in the man's eyes before his arm moved, but it still came faster than he expected. He met Rathbun's blade with the edge of his own, but it was a near thing.

Rathbun smiled. It was not a pleasant expression. "No duel, then. No seconds needed."

He flashed his blade to Nick's left side, testing his defenses.

"A bit slow there," the dandy said. "How about this?"

He feinted high and then made a low swipe. Nick leaped back, but the tip of Rathbun's blade caught him across the chest, slicing through his white shirt. A faint red stain oozed through the fabric.

Eve gasped.

"Your wench is concerned for you already, Scott."

Don't look down. Don't look away. You can't even think

about her, he ordered himself. He felt the sticky trickle on his skin, but there was no pain. That would come later. "It's naught but a scratch."

"I can't wait to show you the color of your liver, Captain," Rathbun said with a sneer.

"You're more like to see the color of hell," Nicholas returned and launched a blistering assault.

The world spiraled down to disjointed elements. The clash of blades. A shoulder-jarring blow deflected. The swirl of Rathbun's frockcoat. Nick heard the roar of seamen shouting around them, but it was muffled and indistinct beneath the steady pounding of his own blood in his ears.

"Four to one on the fop!" shouted some enterprising bloke up on the forecastle.

The fight boiled around the main mast. The crowd scuffled to both stay out of the glittering arc of their blades and to secure the best vantage points. Nick crowded his opponent up to the poop deck and was forced to retreat back down.

Nick's sword arm was tiring and he was nicked in a dozen places. Rathbun looked blown, but Nick hadn't even pinked him once.

"Almost finished," Rathbun said with a slight gasp. "It'll be a relief to have it done with, won't it? And you can't deny I'm a better end for you than a traitor deserves."

Nick didn't waste breath with an answer, but the man was right. What he'd done at the magazine was an act of treason. And a clean death was better than hanging, drawing and quartering.

"Nick, don't listen to him!" Eve's voice pierced his ear.

Fresh wind filled Nick's sails. He wasn't ready for death yet, not of any sort.

"No," he growled and married the word to a bone-crunching blow Rathbun was barely able to stop. "No, no, no!"

There was no finesse. No strategy. It was only rage and brute force and the determination to kill, not be killed, that propelled him forward. Nick drove the superior swordsman across the deck toward the gunwale. Then with a lucky glancing thrust, he knocked Rathbun's sword from his hand. It pitched over the rail and turned end over end before slipping into the waves with hardly a splash. Nick planted the tip of his sword in the center of Rathbun's chest. A tiny rosebud of red bloomed around the point of his blade.

A cheer rose from the crew clinging to the rail of the *Susan Bell*, which was keeping steady pace with the *Sea Wolf*.

But Nick didn't look anywhere but into the terrified eyes of the man whose life he held at his blade's end.

"Go ahead," Rathbun said, ripping his shirt's buttons off to bear his chest. "But hear this, one and all. I die a loyal subject of the Crown and this man still lives a traitor."

Damn the man, he was right.

"Bostock," Nicholas shouted. "If I spare this man's life, will you hold him till I return to the *Susan B* with Miss Upshall and Miss Smythe?"

"If that's what you want, Nicholas," Bostock said. "But I had a dog once with that same look in its eye and the damn thing near bit my hand off. I'd advise you to kill him."

"The day I take your advice, Adam, is the day I turn up my toes."

Eve drew a shuddering breath. Her heart was beginning to slow. It was over and Nick was safe.

"I won't kill you, Rathbun. Not so long as I never see you again." Nicholas pulled back his sword's tip and turned to walk away from death and toward life with her.

Then suddenly, Eve watched in horror as Rathbun reached for his boot knife and launched himself at Nick's unprotected back with a snarl.

She screamed his name.

Nick whipped around and plunged his sword into Rathbun's gut till the hilt nearly disappeared. Rathbun's mouth gaped and he blinked several times before his knees crumpled beneath him and he fell to the deck writhing.

Eve ran to Nicholas and threw her arms around him.

"Oh, Nick, I thought he had you."

"A little faith, woman." He kissed her hard. "You're the only one who has me."

"Guess you saw him again rather sooner than you expected, Nick. Take this man below," Bostock ordered, pointing to Rathbun. "The surgeon can't save a man with a belly wound like that, but at least he won't bleed out on my deck."

"We'll be needing the use of your pinnace," Nick said. "I can't ask the ladies to transfer to the *Susan B* the same way I came aboard your vessel."

"No indeed," Bostock said. "Prepare to lower the boat."

"Adam, I'm in your debt," Nick said after he handed Penny and Eve into the small craft to be lowered over the *Sea Wolf*'s side. Eve watched as he extended his hand to his old enemy. "I'm glad I didn't have to kill you today."

"And I you." Bostock signaled for the boat to be lowered. "Next time you raid a magazine, call on me for help. I'm sympathetic to the Americans' cause."

"I didn't do it for the Americans," Nick said as he shook his head. "I did it for Devil Isle."

Once they reached the deck of the *Susan B*, Peregrine Higgs left the wheel to Mr. Tatem and ran to snatch Penny up in his arms.

"Penny, I thought I'd lost you."

"Never," she said.

He whirled her around a couple times before setting her down and covering her mouth with a kiss that had the crew laying odds on which of them would pass out from lack of air first.

Both Penny and Peregrine were still on their feet when Pere released her mouth, but they were listing on each other heavily.

"Captain, will you marry us?" It was as if Higgs feared Penny would disappear if he looked away from her.

"Don't you think you ought to ask the lady first?" Nick asked with a laugh.

"No need, Captain," Penny said. "Peregrine knows my heart already."

"Aye, Higgs, I'll marry the pair of you."

"No, you won't," Eve said. "You won't be marrying anybody until I see to your hurts. You're bleeding from a dozen cuts and you're dripping all over the—"

He silenced her with a kiss. "Aye, lass, I'll be pleased to let you tend me."

She led him back to his cabin amid sounds of rejoicing. The *Susan B* canted sharply and Eve knew she was coming about. Mr. Higgs was pointing her bowsprit toward home.

"Let me help you take that shirt off," she said as soon as Nicholas closed the door behind her.

"Aye, wench, there'll be time for that and you'll get

your way as you always seem to, but not until I've had my say."

Nick lowered himself to one knee.

"I love you, Eve," he said simply.

Her hand shot to her heart.

"I tried hard not to. You deserve so much more."

"No, I—"

"Can you not let me finish? I've planned the whole piece out, you see."

She swallowed her smile. Her heart nearly leaped from her chest with love for this man. "Oh, and when did you have time to do that?"

"Last night, while I was chasing you across the sea," he said. "But just hold a moment till I finish, then you can say what you will."

"All right."

He shot her a cock-browed look. "Where was I?"

"I think you were saying I deserve so much more."

"Oh, right. You deserve so much more. I can't promise I'll always be on the right side of the law. And I can't promise I won't be at sea more than I'm home. And we both know I've no talent at being a husband at all."

"You make it sound so inviting, how can a girl resist?" she said with a roll of her eyes.

"You're not waiting." He pulled her down to sit on his upraised knee and put a finger to her lips. "But I'll always treat you like the lady you are. And I promise I will love you till the day I die. Marry me, Eve Upshall."

She palmed his cheeks and kissed him, long and deep.

"Can I say something now?"

He nodded.

"Yes," she said simply.

Eve kissed him deeply and then pulled back, searching his face.

"That's all you have to say?" he asked.

"Were you hoping for a different answer?"

"No, but—"

She covered his lips with her fingertips. "Then hear me now. I love you, Nicholas Scott. And whatever the future may bring, I'll never know a greater joy than being loved by you. My husband. My life. My Lord of Devil Isle."

Long ago, when the world was dewy fresh and ever so much younger than now, there lived an artist whose sculptures lacked only breath to give them life.
The artist's name was Pygmalion.

Chapter One

Starting from the well-formed foot and ankle, the long line of the man's muscular leg ended in a disappointingly small fig leaf.

How typical, Grace Makepeace thought as she squinted at the illustration. *Psyche must cavort about without a stitch, but Cupid's most bewildering parts are always covered. And since whatever it is fits so neatly behind that tiny leaf . . . really, one wonders what all the fuss is about.*

"For heaven's sake, Grace, you must hurry or he'll leave!"

"Mother, calm yourself."

Grace didn't lift her nose from her new copy of Reverend Waterbury's *Mysteries of Mythology,* but she did flip quickly to the next page. If her mother had the slightest inkling of the number of scantily clad gods and goddesses the good reverend had included in his scholarly tome, she'd have an apoplectic fit on the spot.

"Why should I care if the fellow does leave?" Grace asked.

Minerva Makepeace put an astonished hand to her ample bosom. "Because darling, Crispin Hawke is the best. Simply the best and we dare not settle for less. Why, the man is a bona fide genius with marble. The world is watching, dear, all the time. If we set so much as one foot wrong—"

"We may as well go home to Boston," Grace finished for her for the umpteenth time. She closed the book with a resigned snap.

"Precisely," her mother said. "Oh, I'm so glad you understand how essential this interview is, dearie."

Minerva either didn't hear the sarcasm in Grace's tone, or chose to ignore it. She never scolded or became cross, but when her mother set her heart on something, she wore her family down as surely as a determined drip leaves a dent in stone. Minerva's heart was set on a titled husband for her daughter. And if acceptance by the ton of London hinged on having the fashionable, artist Hawke "do" Grace's hands in marble, then Minerva Makepeace would move heaven and earth to see it done.

Her mother shepherded Grace down the hall from the light-kissed library to the heavily curtained parlor.

"I don't see why we need meet Mr. Hawke's approval. We're paying him, Mother," Grace reminded her. "That means he'll work for us."

Minerva shushed her.

"Which means *I'll* be the one doing the interviewing," Grace finished as they neared the parlor door. But she didn't say it loudly enough for her mother to hear.

Minerva swept into the parlor with a theatrical flourish, bunching the small train of her pale muslin gown in one hand. Grace followed, steeling herself to settle this as quickly as possible so she could return to the library.

"Mr. Hawke, we're delighted, simply delighted that you've come." Minerva swanned across the room with the borrowed elegance of the nouveau riche and extended her bejeweled hand to the man who rose from the settee. His footman, resplendent in mauve livery with silver buttons, stood at attention in the corner.

Now I see what has the ton in a tizzy, Grace mused.

Broad-shouldered and tall, Crispin Hawke certainly didn't seem the sensitive, artistic type. His raw, angular features didn't fit the current vogue for male beauty, which called for a man's eyes, nose and mouth to be smaller and more refined, almost pretty.

No one in their right mind would call Mr. Hawke that. Arresting, certainly. Rough-hewn, yes, but not pretty. Strong jaws, firm, well-shaped lips, unusual pewter gray eyes beneath dark brows—if he didn't redefine the word "male" Grace didn't know who would.

Crispin Hawke was like a total eclipse. Dangerous. The backs of Grace's eyes burned just looking at him.

If his person exuded a feral masculinity, his dress suggested utter civility. Grace would have guessed Mr. Hawke a duke at the least if she'd seen him on the street.

Grace glanced at his skin-hugging buff trousers.

Bet he'd need a much bigger fig leaf.

Grace noticed he leaned more heavily on his walking stick than one would on a mere accessory and his curly dark hair was unstylishly long. Fine lines gathered at the corners of his gray eyes, though she'd bet her best brooch he hadn't seen thirty winters.

Those pale eyes widened in what looked like recognition, but the expression was gone so quickly Grace decided she'd imagined it. Besides, if they'd met before she'd have remembered. No one would forget Crispin

Hawke. His image was already burned in her mind alongside other wonders of the world.

His unhurried gaze traveled over her. The almost imperceptible twitch of his mouth gave her the distinct impression she'd been weighed in the balance. She couldn't tell whether he found her sadly wanting.

"Such a pleasure to finally meet you, sir. Grace, this is Mr. Hawke. Mr. Hawke, may I present," her mother indicated with a wave of her hand, "my dear daughter, Grace?"

Even though the mystery of Crispin Hawke commanded her full attention, Grace would always blame what came next on the upturned corner of her mother's new Oriental rug. As she approached to offer her hand, palm down, as her mother had taught her, Grace caught the toe of her slipper under the carpet and fell headlong onto the Hakkari weave.

"Grace," the footman murmured. "Aptly named."

"Wyckham, I usually appreciate your scathing wit," Mr. Hawke said over his shoulder to the footman as he knelt to help her rise, "but perhaps you might save it for a more deserving subject."

Cheeks aflame, Grace tried to pull away from his grasp, unwilling to meet his gaze. But he didn't let her go.

When she raised her eyes to him, he was looking down at her with such intensity, her belly clenched. A whiff of his scent, a brisk, clean soapy smell with an underlying note of maleness, crowded her senses. His piercing eyes narrowed in scrutiny.

The footman Wyckham cleared his throat and the spell was broken. Mr. Hawke released his grip on Grace's arms.

"I trust you're now capable of remaining upright,

Miss Makepeace." One corner of his mouth curved in a crooked smile.

"Oh, please do sit down, sir." Her mother made a distressed little noise and fluttered over to a chair across from the settee like a wounded sparrow. "Come, dear and mind your feet," she said in a half whisper to Grace as she patted the chair next to her. "I fear we've kept you waiting, Mr. Hawke."

"Nonsense, madam." He lounged on the settee, filling the space with his larger-than-life presence. "If you feared keeping me waiting you wouldn't have done it."

"Oh!" Minerva blinked hard at his bluntness. Grace sank into the chair next to her, wishing she could disappear into the red velvet. Or better yet, back into the books she loved so well. "Well, as I was saying, this is my daughter, Grace, the one whose hands you'll be sculpting—"

"That, Mrs. Makepeace, has yet to be determined."

Grace's head snapped up. What sort of artisan was he, picking and choosing his commissions as if he were doing his patrons a favor by accepting their money?

Her skin tingled under his intrusive gaze. She disliked the sensation. It was almost as if he knew more about her than he ought, as though he'd read her secret journal or sneaked into her dreams some night.

"Mr. Hawke, I'm newly arrived in your country, so perhaps you might clarify something for me." She raised her chin slightly. The ton might be delirious over Crispin Hawke, but that didn't mean she had to be. "Is rudeness what passes for genius in England these days?"

Mr. Hawke made a noise somewhere between a snort and a chuckle. He flicked his gaze toward her mother. "Leave us."

"Oh, I couldn't possibly," Minerva said. "It wouldn't be proper—"

"My man Wyckham will remain with us. The proprieties will be observed at all times, but if you wish me to accept your commission, you *will* allow me to speak to Miss Makepeace without your presence."

"Oh, oh . . ." Minerva was rarely at a loss for words, but the unconventional Mr. Hawke nearly reduced her to incoherence. "But how will I explain to Mr. Makepeace?"

"If you need tell him anything, tell him you succeeded in acquiring my services. At half my usual fee." He raised a cynical brow. "That should suffice."

Grace watched in surprise as her proper mother rose and abandoned her to Mr. Hawke.

"Kindly close the door behind you," he said, his rumbling tone more pleasant now that he was getting his way.

"Mother!"

"I won't be far, dear," Minerva said through the narrow slit in the door before it latched behind her with a loud click.

Crispin Hawke chuckled softly. "Dear me, Miss Makepeace, I do believe your mother thinks I'll throw you to the floor and swive you right here in her very proper parlor."

Grace gaped at him. She wasn't completely sure of all the details involved in *swiving* but she knew a casual obscenity when she heard one. She stood in shock. To cover the fact that she couldn't bear looking at him for longer than a blink—even unpleasant as he was, he was still too striking to contemplate—she began pacing the room.

"Why did you bully my mother like that?"

"Because I could." He propped his arms across the

back of the settee, claiming the space as if by right. "Mind the rug, Grace. If you end up on the floor again, I might be tempted overmuch and I very nearly promised your highly esteemed mother there'd be no swiving today."

"Stop saying that word." She shot him a glare that should have reduced him to cinders, but he only laughed. "You manipulated her for your own amusement."

"You're remarkably astute for a spoiled little rich girl from Boston," he said, managing to compliment and berate her in the same breath. "I bullied your mother because it interests me to learn how much value people assign to my work. As you deduced, it's only a game, but a game with purpose. Money is nothing. But if someone surrenders their principles, that's something. How else can I know my services are sufficiently appreciated for me to extend them?"

"That's despicable. This *game* of yours is thoroughly *un*appreciated." She flounced back onto her chair and crossed her arms over her chest. "Don't expect me to surrender anything for your services."

"Of course not." He leaned forward and reached toward her. "Give me your hands."

"What?" Was this another of his games?

"Your hands, Grace."

She might have found his smile charming if he'd not behaved so abominably, first to her mother and then to her. *Throw me down and swive me in the parlor, indeed, you conceited swine.*

There was a disconcerting flutter beneath her ribs at the thought of sharing the Hakkari carpet with Mr. Hawke.

"I must see your hands, Grace. How shall I sculpt them otherwise?"

She thrust them toward him, but made a great show of looking away, staring with complete absorption at the ormolu clock her mother had recently installed on the mantle.

"Square nails, an ink stain, a bit of a callus on your third finger." He catalogued her hands' attributes as if they were inanimate objects somehow disconnected to the rest of her. "You favor your left hand."

"What of it?"

"I do, too, which makes us a pair of rare birds. I perceive you are either a writer of wicked penny novels or you keep up a lively correspondence with a number of distant friends and relations."

She glowered at him, but couldn't fault his observation skills. When she wasn't reading, Grace was writing.

"You should know that I don't flatter my models."

"How very surprising."

"I only mean to warn you that your hands are not your best feature." Despite his words, he continued to massage her wrists and hands with his rough, thick fingers. When he followed her lifeline to its end at the base of her thumb, pleasure licked her palm. "Would you like to know what is, Grace?"

"You are engaged to sculpt my hands. I care nothing for your opinion on the rest of me," she lied.

He was outrageous and vulgar and totally impertinent. But she burned with curiosity about what he might find most pleasing about her. Asking, however, would only allow him to play yet another game.

"You should call me Miss Makepeace, you know."

"Yes, I really should. And yet, I'll call you Grace," he said pleasantly as he traced between her fingers and turned her palms down to draw his thumbs over her knuckles. A little faerie of pleasure danced up her arm. "And you'll call me . . . Mr. Hawke."

"I certainly will not." She pulled her hands away, her imaginary pleasure faerie disintegrating in a righteous puff of indignation. "If you insist on informality between us, it will go both ways, Crispin. Or should it be Cris?"

His wince was quick, but Grace caught it.

"Crispin will do," he said.

"And yet," she said with an arched brow, "I'll call you Cris."

He rose to his feet, leaning on the ivory-headed walking stick. "Come to my studio tomorrow. Eight of the clock sharp. Keep me waiting again, and it will be the last time."

He pushed the door open, narrowly missing Grace's mother, who crouched at the keyhole.

"Good day, madam. You may rejoice. Your daughter has sufficiently impressed me. And without anything the least earthy having transpired." A wicked grin split his face. "This time."

He turned back to Grace. "Scrub off that ink stain before tomorrow." Then he disappeared around the corner into the foyer.

Minerva's mouth opened and closed like a carp out of water. "What did you do, Grace?"

"I don't know, Mother. He doesn't seem to like me a bit."

"Perhaps not, miss," Wyckham said before he followed his master out. "But you interest him. And not much does."

Pygmalion loved the human form, but hated mankind in general. And mistrusted women on principle.

Chapter Two

Crispin dragged himself from bed and limped toward the window. He pushed open his bedchamber shutters and let silver light bathe his face. He inhaled deeply, taking in the scents of sweet heliotrope and spicy jasmine from the interior courtyard below.

Dawn wasn't far off. There was no sense in going back to bed. If he slept, he'd just dream of her again and he didn't want to puzzle over what that meant.

His thoughts drifted to Miss Makepeace sprawled with her cheek on the Kurdish carpet. The female form held no mysteries for him. He'd seen enough naked women, both in his capacity as artist and lover, to know precisely how she'd look without her maidenish gown.

Her skin is like ivory, pale and smooth. At the base of her spine, she has dimples above her buttocks.

He grinned at the thought that Grace Makepeace might have dimples on both sets of cheeks. He decided he'd pose her in his mind, as if he were doing a study of her.

Perhaps you'd like a pillow under your head. That carpet is deucedly rough and skin as soft as yours should be protected.

Now wasn't that gallant? She'd thank him politely, as if she weren't naked as a hatchling. Then he'd tell her to pull her knees toward her chest, so her bottom would be tipped up to greet him.

Like this? she asks, all innocence.

Exactly.

It wasn't the most orthodox of poses for a nude, but it certainly appealed to him.

Should I tie her? he wondered. He'd heard that virgins especially enjoyed the act more if they could indulge in the female fantasy that ecstasy was forced upon them.

No, he decided. This was *his* fantasy. He preferred a willing partner to pleasure.

Of course, he'd give her pleasure. He'd never take an unwilling woman, so somehow without her saying a word, he'd know she was as hot for the carnal adventure as he. Even in his fantasies, Crispin prided himself on being a considerate and generous lover. His groin stirred to life beneath the silk banyan.

Her bottom pinks with pleasure under my gaze, but I won't start with those lovely round globes.

And of course, they'd be round. This was his fantasy, after all.

Or her glistening cleft, trembling to receive me.

There was no need to rush. She wasn't going anywhere. He'd start at her nape.

I draw my finger along her hairline. She sucks her breath over her teeth. Then my lips follow. Her skin ripples with goose-flesh. Pleasure from my touch.

Then he might strip out of his clothes.

Even though she doesn't move—no artist's model does unless instructed to do so—her amber eyes widen at the size of my cock. Her pink mouth forms an "oh!", but she doesn't say a word.

This was his fantasy. He'd order things to suit him.

I'm tempted to let her take me in, to suckle the tip of me and flick her little tongue around that sensitive spot near the head, but that might be more than a man could expect of a virgin.

He really couldn't say since he'd never had one.

Perhaps later.

His cock tented the dressing gown and he almost reached in to give it a hard stroke. But he was exposed on his balcony to the eyes of any servants who might be working in one of his palazzo's garden-facing rooms.

Then I draw my hands and lips along the indentation of her spine. She mews with pleasure. I reach beneath her to cup a full breast.

Of course, she'd have full breasts, plump and soft, with aching, hard nipples. And she'd make helpless little noises when he circled them with his thumbs. Maybe a satisfying squeak or two, if he gave her pinch.

This was his fantasy, after all.

Then I finally turn my attention to her delicate secrets, all soft and quivering and incredibly wet. I part her like the petals of a lily. Her whole body trembles. The room fills with the sweet musky scent of her arousal. She tastes like heaven, but I put her through torments with my lips and tongue.

She'd pant and squirm and finally she'd beg him to release her from her suffering.

Not until you admit you want me, I say.

I want you.

But a woman might say that to any man. Suddenly, he knew what might send him over the edge without a touch.

My name. Say my name. I want you, Crispin. Say it.

And yet, I'll call you Cris.

Look for Emily Bryan's *Stroke of Genius* next month!
www.emilybryan.com

✂

☐ **YES!**

Sign me up for the Historical Romance Book Club and send my FREE BOOKS! If I choose to stay in the club, I will pay only $8.50* each month, a savings of $6.48!

NAME: _____

ADDRESS: _____

TELEPHONE: _____

EMAIL: _____

☐ I want to pay by credit card.

☐ **VISA**   ☐ **MasterCard**   ☐ **DISCOVER**

ACCOUNT #: _____

EXPIRATION DATE: _____

SIGNATURE: _____

Mail this page along with $2.00 shipping and handling to:
Historical Romance Book Club
PO Box 6640
Wayne, PA 19087
Or fax (must include credit card information) to:
610-995-9274
You can also sign up online at **www.dorchesterpub.com**.
*Plus $2.00 for shipping. Offer open to residents of the U.S. and Canada only.
Canadian residents please call 1-800-481-9191 for pricing information.
If under 18, a parent or guardian must sign. Terms, prices and conditions subject to
change. Subscription subject to acceptance. Dorchester Publishing reserves the right
to reject any order or cancel any subscription.